Gentleman's Agreement

A NOVEL BY

Laura Z. Hobson

Cherokee Publishing Company
Atlanta, Georgia

Library of Congress Cataloging in Publication Data

Hobson, Laura Keane Zametkin.
　　Gentleman's agreement.

　　Reprint of the 1947 ed. published by Simon and Schuster, New York.
　　I. Title
PZ3.H6544Ge　1979　(PS3515.01515)　813'.52　79-27243
ISBN 0-89783-010-5

Copyright, 1946, 1947, by Laura Z. Hobson

Manufactured in the United States of America

ISBN: 978-0-87797-210-5　Hardcover
ISBN: 978-0-87797-325-6　Paper

Cherokee Publishing Company
P O Box 1730, Marietta, GA 30061

For

MIKE and CHRIS

CHAPTER ONE

ABRUPT AS ANGER, depression plunged through him. It was one hell of an assignment.

"You'll find some angle," John Minify said.

"It'll need an angle all right." He squinted his eyes and looked off past Minify's shoulder as if he were taking the measure of some palpable thing there.

"Take your time on it." Minify spoke without urgency. "I think you might turn out a great job."

Philip Green nodded, not in agreement with the comfortable words, but in affirmation of his own estimate of the job ahead. It would be flabby, lifeless, unless he found some special approach to it. Instinct, experience, past failures as well as past successes, all helped him now in his quick appraisal.

"If you want," Minify went on, "we'll borrow the clips on it from some newspaper morgue. There'd be plenty of names of agencies and committees to start on."

"Committees." The certainty of future boredom, of wasted listening, laced his depression with resentment. Minify surely could have found a more manageable subject for his first job as a staff writer. "The clips would help," he said. "Thanks." He half closed his eyes, drew his lower lip in taut over his teeth as if he were shaving his chin, and sat thinking. "I'll start researching it, anyway. There must be plenty of dope around."

"I wouldn't force this series on you," Minify said. "Knock it around awhile and we'll talk again."

"O.K." Phil stood up, without finality. He was in his

1

middle thirties, tall, too thin, with an intelligent, decent face. Eyes and hair were dark; he had begun to go gray. There was a quiet about him, an absence of aggression, yet there was no diffidence in his voice or manner.

"You certainly didn't hand me a pushover for a starter," he said at last. It was matter-of-fact, bare of complaint or chiding. It would take more than a disappointing assignment to topple his admiration for Minify or lessen his confidence in him as an editor. "Would anybody read five articles about antisemitism?" He saw Minify nod. "Three million readers?"

Minify didn't answer. He leaned forward toward his desk, propped his chin on the knuckles of his closed hand. Then he swiveled the hand about so that the thumb stood up vertically across the corner of his mouth. He seemed all at once absorbed in another idea. His thumb tapped lightly against his lips, in a one-two-three, one-two-three rhythm. Phil smiled. Minify was considering three million readers out there somewhere across all the towns and cities of the land.

"No," Minify said at last. "You couldn't print anything in God's world all three million would read. But some of them will."

"Sure. And will it do any good?"

Minify tipped his head back so he could look directly at Phil. "Did your Okie pieces or your mine pieces 'do any good'?"

Phil smiled. "That's nailing me. Fathead question."

"It didn't take that Roper survey to tell me it's getting worse. You feel it. It gets you either mad or uneasy. I mean me."

"Or baffled."

"So you can bet it's hitting plenty of people that same way. If you find some strong way to write it, it'll get read."

2

"If."

Minify offered his half-empty pack of cigarettes as if he counted on a refusal, the way you used to during the cigarette shortage. He lit one himself and then sat examining his lighter. He snapped the flame on and off several times, watching it flare up and snuff out. He gave it a last decisive click and stood up.

"Getting to know people here?"

"Not so many. I'm always slow about that. It's fine, though. My kid likes it, and my mother. She always wanted to live in New York."

"Have you any relatives here? Or are they all in California, too?"

Phil shook his head to both questions. Minify's concern on this personal level pleased him. "One of my sisters is out there, and the other lives in Detroit. Grosse Pointe, rather."

"I've been meaning to introduce you," Minify began vaguely. Then his manner lost its air of improvising. "How about tonight at my place? We're having some people over. Couple of girls and people."

"Thanks. I'd like to."

The editor told him where, and they shook hands with a touch of formality, as if each suddenly remembered he didn't know the other well. With an inexplicable embarrassment, Phil took up his coat and hat and left quickly. He went down the long corridor, past open-doored offices in which people were talking or laughing. The shyness of the outsider came over him. Though the line "By Schuyler Green" was known to every one of them, he himself was a stranger. Working at home was the setup he'd asked for, but it would be wise, now that he was on the staff, to come in every day until he got to know some of these editors and writers. At once the idea disturbed him. On an assignment,

3

he was never shy about meeting and interviewing people, but to make new social contacts was another thing. His mind ran from this self-recognition, with a hurried promise to do something about the office soon.

In the reception room, he stopped to put on his overcoat. The receptionist gave him a neat, exact smile, a precise replica of the one she had bestowed each of the other three times he had come in or gone out through the double glass doors that announced *Smith's Weekly Magazine*. The scene was a replica of the other times, too; in the dark-red armchairs the usual assortment of people waited the signal to go in to their appointments. Could any of these unknowns be some writer whose name and work were perfectly familiar? The notion made him look around once more. With the exception of best-selling authors and syndicated columnists, whose faces looked out of endless book advertisements, reviews, and columns, there was an anonymity about most writers. Perhaps some of these waiting people in the reception room knew his name and work and would yet look blankly at his stranger's face. In his anonymity, he smiled comfortably, and went out to the elevators.

In the street, he turned toward Fifth Avenue. In the two weeks since he'd become a resident of New York, he had passed the stage where he had to watch two successive street signs to see whether he was headed uptown or down. At the corner of Fifty-seventh and Fifth, he turned south and began to walk rapidly in the thin December sunlight. Soon he was striding along as if he were hurrying to a specific place at a specific time. Actually he was walking only so that he could think more rapidly about the new assignment. Already the search for the "angle" completely occupied him. He might take one Jewish family in some particularly antisemitic section and trace its life in the past few years. No, a long string of articles on that would bore

4

readers to death. His mind pushed the notion aside, darted in new directions, hunting possibilities, exploring, rejecting.

Again he was depressed. For days he'd be in for the old familiar sequence—hope as an idea flared bright, then unease and self-mistrust as closer examination snuffed it out. Like Minify's lighter.

It was the rhythm of all living, apparently, and for most people. Happiness, and then pain. Perhaps then happiness again, but now, with it, the awareness of its own mortality. He had made an honest enough search for happiness—in the last year or two, at any rate. All he had found was transience.

The sting of cold air in his throat told him he had sighed deeply. "Cut the philosophy," he told himself testily. He walked on now, thinking of nothing, merely watching, seeing, noting. At Thirty-fifth Street, he turned left, to the remodeled brownstone house just east of Park where he lived. In the vestibule he took out his keys, tapped the bell, and let himself in without waiting. Above, a door opened. His mother's voice said, "That you, Tom?" and he said, "No, it's me." He went up the carpeted steps slowly, suddenly thinking about his mother. Her voice sounded older than her sixty-eight years; all the chivying details of transcontinental moving had been hard on her.

"How was it, Phil?" she greeted him.

"O.K. I've got the hell of a stiff assignment."

She sat down, waiting. He wandered about the wide, tall-ceilinged room in which their own furniture and books looked so different from the way they had in the house in California. When the extra bookshelves were built in and the rest of his books taken out of the stacked cartons, it would be a pleasant room; he would like working in it. This and his mother's room in the rear of the whole-floor apartment were the only good things about it; the kitchen and bathroom had air-suction outlets instead of windows, and the two "hall bedrooms" which were for him and Tom were smaller than their bathroom out in California.

Yet when Minify had told him that he could sublease the apartment from an editor who had been newly assigned to the London office, Minify had said, "Better grab it, whatever it is. The Coast isn't the only place with a desperate housing shortage." He had grabbed it and considered himself lucky.

Actually, the very oddness of living in a rectangular shelf of space rather than in a house set to the earth among bushes and trees had so far stimulated rather than dampened his spirits. He had sought basic change in the patterns of his life. This apartment was physical proof that he had found it, or, at any rate, one facet of it.

He remembered that his mother was waiting for him to go on. "Minify wants me to write a series," he said, "five, six articles, on antisemitism in America."

"That's good." She underlined the "good" with approval.

"If I could find some way to *make* it good."

"I mean, most big magazines—it's nice Mr. Minify wants to do it. You can do such a fine thing on it."

"Minify's a strange guy. I liked him even better today than the first time." He lit a cigarette. "He's all hopped up about the job I could do, just like you."

"And you're not?"

He frowned. "It's a toughie."

"You'll do a wonderful series, dear." She sounded placid. He remembered Minify's comfortable words and was all at once irritated with both of them. It was so easy to say, "This is a great theme and you'll write a great series."

"Christ, I will if I can get some *idea*." His voice flung exasperation at her. "But not just if I spin out the same old

6

drool of statistics and protest." He walked over to the window, looked down on the street. Without turning around, he added a moment later, "Sorry."

"That's all right. How about some coffee?" She started toward the small kitchen.

"Fine. Damn assignment's got me in a sweat already."

A hundred times he vowed never to talk to her in that quick sharpness, yet a moment would come when it sprang out as if he had no power to halt it in his throat. Once he had apologized, too earnestly, and she had said, "It's all right. It's because you're not happy enough." At his silence, she had added, "Being lonely makes people snap. Tension, I suppose."

Now he waited a moment and then followed her to the kitchen. "Where's Tom?" he asked conversationally. "It's nearly four."

"Across the street at Jimmy Kelly's." She looked at him and smiled. "He makes new friends so easily, Phil."

"Yeah." Suddenly he felt obscure pride in himself. Tommy, at eight, without a mother since infancy, was relaxed, outgiving, never "the problem child." Somehow then, he, Phil, had done a sound job of concealing the unevenness of his own moods all these seven years.

"I told him not to be too long," Mrs. Green added. "Belle's in town."

"Again?" His sister had flown in from Detroit to help them get settled the day they'd arrived in the East.

"Just for today—Christmas shopping."

"Aren't Detroit stores good enough for her? That Belle. She's the golden sheep in this family for fair."

"Now, Phil."

"O.K." Suddenly he grinned. "She *is* a little hard to take at times, and you know it."

"So are you, dear, but it's worth it."

7

"Sure, sure. I'd hate to think I'd stodgied up as much as she has in the last few years, though." Mrs. Green made no comment. When the coffee was ready, Phil took his cup, said, "Think I'll start jotting down some notes," and went back to the living room. "I'll quit when she gets here," he added.

But when the downstairs bell rang half an hour later, he left his desk and went to his room. It was too small to serve as a study, taking only a tall chest, one big reading chair, and a narrow bed. He puttered about, dissatisfied, with what he did not know. He drew out a bureau drawer, closed it, and drew out another, as if he were searching for something. At his desk, he had ordered himself to think about the assignment, but like a fractious child, his mind had refused to comply. This was another sign, he thought dismally, that his flash appraisal in Minify's office had been correct. There was in him no itch to get at it, the way there was when instinct told him he had a "natural" by the tail. As he had said, it was going to be the hell of an assignment, and the bitch of a job to bring the stuff alive.

There was a knock at the door. "Hi, Belle," he called, and she opened the door.

"Mamma says you're working." She made it a gentle accusation. "Come out a minute and tell me about the new job."

When he told her, she said, "I should think he'd have assigned it to a Jewish writer."

"Why? I'm not blind, am I?"

Belle went on as if he hadn't spoken. "Anyway, I just wonder. You can't scold people into changing."

"Who said anything about scolding?" Phil asked, and Mrs. Green said, "Now, Belle, you don't mean that. It's not like you."

Belle began to elaborate her point, but Phil scarcely

listened. There was a flat certainty about her statements which irritated him. He had noticed it on her other trip and decided she had changed a good deal during the war years. The difficulties of travel had kept her away from the Coast; for five years they had not seen her. Apparently she regarded New York as a neighboring town of Grosse Pointe.

He sat, dispirited and silent, looking at her and wondering how he could get off by himself again. Belle was handsome, slender, expensively dressed. He looked at her attentively, as if she were someone he would have to describe accurately on paper. There were two horizontal lines grooved in her neck, like necklaces tight to the skin; he had never noticed detail of that sort before. She talked with loud animation as one does in a large room with many voices to combat; her hands moved restlessly in gesture. Now she was describing the large new house she and Dick wanted to buy.

"Did you close the sale on the old place?" Mrs. Green asked.

"Not yet. That cheap Pat Curran keeps trying to Jew us down." She shook her head despairingly, and Phil thought her distress vulgar and ridiculous when millions of people couldn't find a two-room flat. He saw his mother frown at her. He glanced at his watch, offered excuses about a pressing appointment, and left them.

Outside, the city was already dim with the early twilight and sharp with the clean smell of cold, but he still relished New York's positive weather and walked into it as if into sanctuary. He wished it were his sister Mary in California instead of Belle who lived near enough for frequent visits. Belle was seven years older than he, and Mary only four; maybe that accounted for the greater closeness there'd always been between him and Mary. No, it was more than

9

that. Mary lived in a sprawly house near the university and was lazy and easy about things; Belle had a terrific place, smart to the last ash tray. He'd been only sixteen when Belle had married Dick King. Nineteen years ago, Dick had been a college-boy draftsman, and for a long time the Kings had led an ordinary modest life like the rest of the family. Then Dick had designed the new wheel-transmission gadget that did the trick better than the one his company had been using; almost at once he'd become one of the high-priced big shots in the automotive world. That was ten years ago, and as if she'd been tensed and ready to spring, should the chance ever be offered her, Belle instantly changed into one of the "smart set" out there. "Perhaps a long transition period would have made her less of a jackass about being rich," Phil had once remarked to Mary. Now he thought, Oh, well, and forgot her.

He'd been walking along Lexington Avenue. At Forty-second, he stopped and folded his head back on his neck as far as it would go, looking up at the Chrysler Tower. He wondered whether an atomic bomb could really vaporize it out of existence. He knew he looked like any tourist, but it did not disturb him. After two weeks he still was a tourist in his greed to examine all the great city he had only glimpsed in the brief stopovers of the past. But feeling again a tourist brought back the sense of strangeness in this new place; loneliness drifted through his mood. He began to walk again. Christmas decorations livened every shopwindow; though it was only the first day of December, the stores already bustled with shoppers for this first post-war Christmas. In December, seven years ago, Betty had died. Decembers would always be hard months for him.

Perhaps that's why his mind was being so inelastic about the new work; perhaps that's why he'd been so edgy over Belle.

Suddenly he remembered her despair. "That cheap Pat Curran keeps trying to Jew us down."

His mind drew back sharply. All he'd thought then was two-room flats. The verb had glided right by him. His mother, he now realized, had been frowning about that as he was leaving. But he? He hadn't even registered.

Maybe he was the wrong man for this series. Heart in the right place, but tone-deaf. Rot, he argued back at once. It's just the old inertia at the start of a long pull.

At a newsstand he bought the evening papers. On the front page, dwarfed by the headlines about General Motors and the War Guilt Trial, was a story about some Brooklyn hoodlums attacking three Jewish boys. He ought to begin a file of his own clippings if he were going ahead with the series. Maggotlike, the "if" squirmed through his conscience.

Damn it, why couldn't Minify give it to an old-timer and not load it on me for the *first?*

A few blocks later, he passed a newsreel theater, went by it, and then turned back to it. He read the signs about what was showing. Feeling a traitor, he fished a quarter out of his pocket and went through the turnstile. It moved oilily, without a click, and vaguely he felt cheated about everything.

He paid off his taxi and said to the doorman, "Minify, please."

"Eighteenth, sir. To your right."

He went into the small lobby, noted the gleam of the white border on the black linoleum floor, and turned right to a small elevator. Inside, he looked into the square of beveled, unframed mirror and straightened his tie. It was friendly of Minify to ask him, but this sort of setup was somehow jarring. Formality always dispirited him, not be-

11

cause he worried about being gauche, but because what he and Betty used to call "fingerbowl houses" implied alien values and importances. Something had been building between him and Minify since their first meeting two months before. He did not want it destroyed. A husky maid in black and white answered his ring, and he heard Minify calling out, "Never mind, Berta, I'll answer it—oh, you're already there." He stuck out his hand and said, "Hello, Green. I might have thought of this before."

Relief swept up in Phil. It was the same easy Minify. As he followed him into the living room, he felt a whole atmosphere of wealth, beautiful colors and fabrics. A thin middle-aged woman came toward them.

"Jessie, this is Schuyler Green I've been talking about. My wife."

"I've read everything he ever wrote, don't be silly, John. Good evening, Mr. Green. Kathy, this is Mr. Green. My niece, Miss Lacey."

Simultaneously he shook hands with Jessie Minify and smiled at the girl sitting on the sofa just behind her. Mrs. Minify had small curls like gray bubbles all over her head; her voice seemed to bubble too, and he felt that the apartment was cut to her pattern and fitted nothing in Minify at all. He turned and took the hand held up to him by Miss Lacey and knew she was very pretty and that this was going to be a fine evening.

"I haven't read *everything,*" Miss Lacey said, "but what I did read was——" She tipped thumb and forefinger together to form a circle and flicked the circle toward him, braking the gesture in mid-air so suddenly that her hand shook on her wrist. It was the effusive gesture for "done to a turn, monsieur," and it struck him now as absurd and artificial. He smiled and said, "Thanks," but the first flush of approval chilled in him. Her voice had a hint of Jessie

Minify's too-well-bred tone. He felt vaguely resentful to it, as he did to the gesture.

Through the next quick sequence of Minify's "Scotch or rye?" and of Mrs. Minify's "Sit over there, Mr. Green, it's the biggest," and of his own "Thanks, I like big chairs," and "Scotch, please, a light one," he kept on being aware of an uneasy disappointment. From a bar closet at the side of the room, Minify called out, "What do people call a guy whose first name is Schuyler?"

"Phil," he answered, and everybody laughed.

"Thank God, I don't have to say Green all the time," Minify answered. "So hearty, last names."

"It's my mother's name, my middle one. I started signing my stuff 'Schuyler Green' on the college paper at Stanford. Sounded ritzier to me, I guess, than Philip—like Somerset Maugham instead of William, or Sinclair Lewis instead of Harry. My literary heroes then."

"Somerset, Sinclair, Schuyler," Miss Lacey said. "All *S*'s. Maybe that means something."

He wondered if she were laughing at him and felt stiffly young and too explanatory. In that moment also he realized that the maid Berta had held out her arms in a gesture which meant he was to give her his coat and hat and that he had not handed them over but had put them down on a chair himself. Miss Lacey was saying something about noms de plume, but he missed it, feeling embarrassed about Berta and exasperated that he should. Though he hadn't remembered it all day he now recalled his unaccountable awkwardness that morning about shaking hands with Minify. A resigned dismay darted through him, as at the second pang of a toothache. He was in for a tight, watchful evening, after all.

" . . . from California?" Only the end of Miss Lacey's question came clearly to him, but like an aftermemory on his

13

eardrums the first part still registered. The voice was again overbright, but the words were simple and interested. He turned toward her just as Minify came back with his drink, saying, "Here, Phil, light one." She looked natural and friendly, and he suddenly felt he had been too quick to disapprove of her. How furious he would be if somebody made judgments on *him* because of a gesture or tone in the first clumsiness of meeting! For the second time in a few minutes, apprehension fell back. He admonished himself to stop vacillating between tension and ease and enjoy himself.

"Not my first *trip*," he said to Miss Lacey. "But the first time I've ever come here without a steamship ticket for tomorrow or something." She nodded, and he went on more easily with the prefaces of getting acquainted as she or Jessie Minify prodded him. All the while he kept taking an inventory of her, in quick installments, so that it should not be apparent. She was small, with lovely legs, and about twenty-eight or -nine. ("No, I wasn't born there. But when I was seven, we moved out from Minnesota, so we all feel like Californians.") There was a sureness about her manner and clothes which you found in New York or Hollywood or London girls, a self-confidence it was, somehow provocative. ("There was this small private hospital in Santa Barbara, my father was a doctor. I was going to study medicine, too.") She undoubtedly wished she weighed ten pounds less, but no man would. His heart hammered once against his ribs and went back to its ordinary business. ("You *did* read those? I was mad, so I suppose it showed up in the writing. That's when Mr. Minify wrote me to come East about a job.") There was something a little wrong with her looks, but you'd call her beautiful, anyway. She had blue eyes, her hair was dark and smooth, her whole look was somehow very clean and precise and neatly tended. He turned to Mrs. Minify's question about him and the war, but John

Minify was answering it for him, and he glanced again at Katherine Lacey. She was looking up at Minify, and he saw the stretch of her throat from chin down to the dark close dress. Suddenly he knew what was wrong. By itself, in a close-up, say, her face was beautiful, but it was scaled to go with a taller girl and was top-heavy for her. A click of satisfaction accompanied this recognition. She now seemed vulnerable and human, not so perfect that he felt lumpish and nervous.

"So after eleven months of training and a month of transport, he had one vicious week of action with the Marines at Guadalcanal and then out. Isn't that it, Phil?"

He nodded. "Except for the hospital."

"Do you still hate to talk about it?" Mrs. Minify sounded cautious but caught in irrepressible curiosity.

"I never hated to. I *wanted* to tell about my operation the way everybody else always does. Only that wore off, especially after V-J Day. Now it seems a million years back."

The talk veered off to general discussion about the new organizations for veterans. He relaxed further. The first phase of the evening was over. A benevolence went through him; he sipped his drink comfortably. Jessie Minify began some anecdote about a woman he didn't know, and he scarcely listened. She was not the wife he would have imagined for John Minify, but she was amiable and perhaps just the right complement for his high-voltage mind. Some men preferred it that way.

Miss Lacey brought the talk back to him.

"Do you mind telling people what you're writing, Mr. Green?"

"Not at all." He hesitated and glanced at Minify. "Only right now I'm not writing anything—just starting a new thing."

15

"I asked him to try a series on antisemitism," Minify said. "A knockdown and drag-out at every part of it. Here, not Europe."

Phil was watching her. She did an unexpected thing. She grinned.

"Do I get a credit line on it?"

"You, Kathy?" Minify was as astonished as he himself.

"Don't you remember back in, oh, in the spring it was, about that Jewish girl resigning and I asked you——"

"Why, sure." Minify looked pleased with her. "I knew *somebody'd* been at me but I forgot who. I'm always stealing ideas without knowing it."

"Stealing? I gave it to you. I rammed it down your throat." She turned to Phil. "I carried on about how the big magazines and papers and radio chains were helping spread it by staying off it except for bits here and there. And why didn't somebody go after it the way they do taxes or strikes? Yell and scream and take sides and fight?"

Phil was watching her as if she were revealing something immensely important. The affectation in her voice was gone, or lost to his ear already. All he said was, "What I'm afraid of is just stringing those same bits——"

"I fixed it with Bill Johnson at the *Times*," Minify said, reaching for Phil's glass, "about borrowing their clips for a week or so. It's against their rules. Another drink, Phil?"

"Thanks, this'll do it, John."

The first name slipped out on the rush of affection he felt for the honesty and simplicity of the man. He had long respected and admired Minify; it was surprising to like him so much. Minify was sixty, yet each time they had talked together, the quarter century between their ages ripped away and left them contemporaries. Minify looked his sixty. His roundish head was fringed with red hair, wiry and free of gray; it was a remarkable baldness since the scalp was not the glossy pink that usually tops florid complexions, but a dull walnut like tan suède, result of sporadic attempts to keep fit with a sun lamp. Below this oddly hued top, the parallel ellipses of dark eyebrows and the darker crescents of his eye sockets made his gray eyes noticeably light. Unless he stood or sat in determined erectness, his stomach bulged over his belt. But vitality rode every sentence he spoke and played large on every plan he outlined for the years ahead.

That, Phil had decided after their first long talk in October, was what made Minify seem so young. Whenever he talked of the future, he gave forth a confidence about having enough time. There was none of that anxious "I won't be here then" which Phil nearly always found in men of sixty. Nor was there any tacit concession, as they had discussed politics, that there was any basic difference in the older point of view and the younger. In their first interview, Minify had excited in Phil a sharp desire to work with him more intimately than he had been doing as a free-lance special writer for *Smith's*. Coming at a time when his life in California seemed especially flaccid, that one personal meeting with the famous editor had turned the trick.

So far he'd had no qualms or regrets, he thought now, looking from Minify to his wife to Kathy. The bell rang just then, and four other people arrived, exuberant or a little drunk. "Why, Katherine Pawling, where've you been keeping yourself?" one of the girls cried out as she came in. The room filled with voices and noise and movement, and at once the character of the evening changed. He talked around him vaguely for a bit and then moved to the sofa to sit by Kathy.

"What about you?" he started. "You have a pretty complete dossier on me. It's your turn now."

"What should I start on? I heard Aunt Jessie explaining

17

I'd been divorced and was running a nursery school and was called Miss Lacey there." She glanced up at him and then quickly away. The knowledgeable, experienced look that faintly irritated him deserted her for a moment. He was puzzled again; she was always offering some new facet that made it hard to stick to any estimate of what she was or whether he liked her as a person or only responded to her as a pretty girl. The things she said seemed real and good; the manner and clothes and air seemed too, in quotes, upper class. But he was drawn to her, whatever she was.

"Just anything," he said. "And maybe you could finish at a bar or someplace when I take you home."

"Are you?"

"May I?"

She waited a second and then nodded. Sitting side by side with her now, looking down at her, he saw the faintly raised, branching arcs just above the V neck of her dark dress. Again his heart hammered once against his ribs.

CHAPTER TWO

KATHY THOUGHT, He's not very happy. It's more than just being new here and not knowing people. Across the fake-marble table in the restaurant, she leaned forward to the match he struck for her cigarette.

As she drew the flame into the tip, she looked up over it. His face was attentive as it had been all the time she'd been talking, but the puzzled or even critical look that had tightened it at times wasn't there now. She straightened up and inhaled deeply as if this were the first cigarette of the day. A small paroxysm of coughing seized her.

"I smoke too much," she said.

She saw him glance at the ash tray filled with butts, his and hers. It was an indicator of elapsed time as well as corroboration of her comment, but he didn't offer health advice as some men would, nor did he give any sign that he knew it was late or that he cared.

Ever since they'd left Aunt Jessie's, he'd led her on to talk about herself. Apart from one interlude when he'd told her in quick colorless sentences about his wife's death, he'd seemed truly and wholly interested in holding the talk on her. Whenever she'd come to some stopping place and say, "Well, that's enough about me," he'd be ready with some question that sent her on again. He gave her an unfamiliar feeling of being a listener who took an active role in his listening; he wasn't merely neutral but seemed to take sides for or against each segment of her character as he saw it through her recital. When she talked about her childhood, for instance, and the old longing to have a "nice" house like other kids, he nodded with sympathy. But when she was telling him about her marriage to Bill and the way they'd lived, he looked withdrawn. He liked the fact that at Vassar she'd "fallen in with the radical group—we worshiped Roosevelt." He looked bleak when she said she'd been "pretty good at the endless entertaining a banker's life depends on."

It was as if he were voting for or against her on each phase of her story. It could have been annoying, but though her mind marked it, her emotions didn't engage. She saw it only as a trait he was unconsciously revealing, about on a par with the fact that though he needed a haircut, his fingernails were well trimmed and extremely clean.

"Your parents," he prompted. "How'd they take it about Aunt Jessie's house and Vassar and the pretty clothes?"

"They were pleased, mostly," she said. "I guess it ground into my father a little—just highlighting his own failure. But he said he wanted me and my sister Jane to have the things that would make us happy."

"And did they?"

She nodded and thought for a while and then nodded again. "You know, the old idea that privation is good for the character? I don't think it worked that way for me at all. Looking back, now, I don't."

He waited. She could feel him receptive to the mood she'd fallen into.

"I think when I *didn't* have the things my friends did, that *then* I was all full of snobbish misery. But when Aunt Jessie handed Vassar over and let me ask people to their apartment week ends—why, I think I quit being nasty and snobbish right off." She smiled at him. "I just felt easy and right."

"The old business of security."

20

"Maybe. Do you think I'm funny, praising myself this way?"

He shook his head, but remained silent. He looked down at his hand, stretched the five fingers wide, then closed them into a fist, then stretched them wide, as if he were making some important test of their muscular reaction. She watched his fingers. About what could he feel insecure? Not about his talent or his growing reputation. Uncle John said he would be one of the major writers of the country in a few years. But something was empty in his life—she could feel him hungry for staying on here, talking.

Perhaps that was what made her pry into the crevices of her memory for answers to his questions. With other men major landmarks and dates were enough—never the shadowy substance of childhood and adolescence. But this Schuyler Green or Phil Green would not be bought off with her usual quick brush strokes of biography. "Then I got married to Bill Pawling and for a while it was grand and then it didn't work out, so we got divorced in a friendly sort of way, and still see each other every so often at parties and things." That gliding recital would not have satisfied the man across from her. He was still absorbed in whatever he was thinking. His silence made her uncomfortable.

"Would you hit that waiter over the head," she said, "and get me some water?"

"Sure. I forgot." He tapped his spoon against his empty glass and then pointed down into it. He watched her drink. She had been almost arch as she'd asked for the water.

"You're looking all dubious again," she said.

"Am I?"

"Every once in a while, you sort of stare at the words coming out of my mouth, as if you didn't quite understand English and needed help to get the strange sounds."

She was perceptive, Phil thought. His face must show the bewilderment that struck him when she went back every so often, as she just had, to that voice and manner. She'd fallen into it, also, when she'd been talking about her marriage to Pawling and the beautiful apartment and the dinner parties—"I got so I could give a dinner for twelve with my eyes shut." She'd said she had finally found that sort of thing artificial, dull, but the inevitable way the brittle social cloak fell upon her again made him wonder if she really had. "I can't quite make you out," he said.

"Me? I'm pretty easy to understand."

"Parts of you don't seem to go with other parts—Lord knows, *I'm* not all of a piece; nobody ever is." His voice took on anxiety. "Please don't think I'm sitting here approving and disapproving. I'm just damn interested."

"I don't," she said. "Or maybe I do. Anyway, that's enough about me. I feel as if you'd interviewed me." He laughed, and she thought again how nice-looking he was. Not handsome but, what was better, immediately appealing. "I wish I could draw you out the way you do me."

"There's not so much more about me," he said. "You've got the main stuff." He lit another cigarette for her. "Are you engaged to anybody now?" he asked abruptly. She shook her head. "Or in love or anything?"

"Not specially." He was waiting as if he wanted her to amplify that. She said, "Are you?"

"Not anything." He made it unequivocal.

They smiled at each other. She looked at her watch. He saw it and signaled the waiter.

"I have to get up awfully early," she said as if she needed to apologize for thinking of home at one in the morning.

She couldn't get to sleep, anyway. She thought of the

22

whole evening and the pleasantness of beginnings. How wonderful it would be to find somebody who wouldn't matter less each time! So often getting to know a new man was a disheartening business of revising downward from the first impression. She was so ready for something on a more rewarding level than just "dates" and the ever-present will-we or won't-we.

If that question could only lie dormant—but it never did. Even though she was "free" and "a modern girl"—those two handy arguments—love affairs were just not her style. She didn't ponder the why of that. That's the way she was.

She'd never been particularly introspective, not since those college sessions of rooting around in the lumpy soil of everybody's "character." As an adult, she'd fall into self-inquiry only over some specific problem which needed solution. She'd spent many an hour trying to see why her marriage had become so empty, but that was introspection for the sake of decision. When she'd reached the decision, she'd been able to go to Bill with clarity and say they ought to part.

She'd never been cruel enough to say, "I don't love you."

She'd never been rude enough to say, "I can't listen to one more story about debentures and bonds and foreign exchange." She simply knew there was no way to live with Bill and not listen. Unlike many other bankers, Bill was articulate. He enjoyed talking. He enjoyed detail. He enjoyed "sharing his work with her."

She merely said, instead, that they'd developed into people who were incompatible on too many fronts. She merely said, "We seem to disagree automatically about everything." He knew it was true.

"All the unessentials between us, Bill, are right, but all the essentials are wrong."

"You mean about politics."

"Not politics—just, oh, we're just drifting farther apart every year about everything. Even a baby."

"I'll be taken in the next draft," he said angrily. "I'm not going to put that on you all alone. That's a heel's trick."

She could see again his outraged stiffness, the dignity with which he spoke cliché after cliché. If he only knew it, she could have found stimulation in disagreement if there hadn't been the clothy phrases, the awful predictability.

"Darling, wouldn't you just *once* say 'Roosevelt' or 'the President'?"

"What? Damn it, Kathy, that man makes monkeys out of you liberals."

There'd been the way his face would light whenever she talked against Communism or the Soviet scorn for "the imperialistic war."

"At least we're on the same side about the Commies," he'd said once, with a kind of comradely gaiety.

"We're not!"

"But you always——"

"I'm against it as a principle—the slavery to the party line—the killing of freedom—but I'm *not* against it as The Red Menace the way you are."

"It comes down to the same thing."

"It doesn't. It just doesn't. Oh, never mind." It was one of the times when she despised him. He'd never see the difference between her opposition and his Red-baiting.

Everything between them came to differences. Not everything. They both loved their apartment, their week-end cottage in Darien, tennis, dancing, the unessentials. But everything else came to differences. Isolationism for him; intervention for her. A loathing of Hitlerism for her; a loathing of "those Heinies" for him. A disgust with Pegler for her; a "well, he sure gets the goods on those racketeers" for him. McCormick, the *Daily News,* the poll tax, Lindbergh, even books, plays—always he was for and she against or she for and he against.

"Any writer can just put dirty words in a book . . ."

"It's time this country showed those unions . . ."

"I see where Eleanor's on the go again . . ."

"Big deal on foreign exchange. Let me spot in some background . . ."

The boredom, the boredom, the screaming boredom.

It was strange, sad, that a marriage could ratchet apart the way theirs had. There'd never been much overt quarreling. But for their last two or three years, they'd been inching further and further apart from each other, like hostile lovers under the shared and pleasant blanket.

Of all this she'd given Phil no account. She'd seen from his eyes that he'd felt no conviction behind what she did say. But that she couldn't help.

Phil chucked his hat and overcoat at the day bed in the living room and then went over to the fireplace. He had no intention of going to bed. He was keyed up, but not with the old tight restlessness. Meeting Kathy, having her accept his suggestion for dinner tomorrow night as he left her at the door of her apartment house—the whole evening had shot a tingling expectancy into him. He glanced speculatively at the piled logs below him. He felt luxurious; he struck a match and lit the paper under them. Then he stood back and regarded the flames.

In a way, it was Katherine Lacey who had handed him his first assignment on the new job. Obscurely, that pleased him. People who "thought up ideas" for books or articles always felt themselves the ultimate proprietors of them; she would watch for his series as if she, not Minify, were his editor.

25

A drive of aggression uncoiled in him; he would find the way to do this series well if he had to pick at his brains with tweezers. There must be some compelling lead, some dramatic device to humanize it, so it would be read. He went to his desk. The logical start was to make notes of whatever general knowledge he had of anti-Jewish feeling in America. Under separate headings, he began to block out the segments he knew would need research:

Antisemitism in Business
antisemitism in Labor
antisem—social
antisem—housing, hotels, clubs
a.s.—violence, hoodlums, etc.
a.s.—schools, professions
a.s.—growth, counter-efforts like anti-bias bills.
Link up with growth of anti-alien feeling, anti-Negro, anti-Catholic, all minority. (Threat to U. S. most serious, not to Jew.)

He sat back and looked at the list. This was already quite a revelation. That he, before special inquiry, should carry in his mind enough information, fact, rumor, to be able to make so comprehensive a list was proof that antisemitism was seeping into all the arteries of daily life. Right there, jotted down in a few minutes, waiting only for documentation, was a picture of the scope and depth of the thing. If he failed, it would not be for thinness of material. Two or three weeks of research would swamp him.

And swamp the readers of *Smith's Weekly* as well? He was back again at his own barricade. But this time, confidence was in him.

He let his mind wander easily. He might take some anti semitic community and angle everything he wrote to show the

26

damage, not to the Jews in it, but to the community itself —a sort of psychiatric approach about the effects of hatred on the hater. No, that was even worse than the idea he'd had in the afternoon—preachy, hortatory, even surer to bore the reader.

Cheerfully he abandoned the notion and let his mind explore further, as a general on the winning side examines the terrain of a future operation, weighing this point of attack against that, balancing the virtues against the faults, estimating the desire against the probable outcome.

It was two-thirty when he gathered his notes together and gave up. His list made a good start; he'd get the angle soon and show Miss Lacey a thing or two about journalism.

In bed, he lit one last cigarette and thought about her. She was interesting; with other girls he had met, he always sat stiffly through the inevitable anecdotes of family and childhood, but with her he'd really wanted to hear, to visualize everything. He tried now to remember each thing she'd said and to equate his opposed emotions about her.

But soon his thinking moved away from her and became only the unnamable longing which had been the steady accompaniment to his last seven years. It was an unprecise need, to which the specifics of sex and companionship were only tangential. Partly it was hunger for a tightly shared life once more with a woman he trusted and admired; it was also an uneasy sadness that Tom should be an only child without brothers and sisters; in it, too, was sharp distaste for the picture of himself as "a bachelor." A reaching toward the future stirred him. Sometime he might again find the continuing pattern he'd known with Betty. There's always a chance, he thought, and switched off the lamp clamped to the headboard of his bed.

With the dark, long-dulled memories of Betty stood instantly about him, like watchdogs snarling off this new hope, ready to set upon it, tear it, shred it, should it really move forward to claim him.

Phil lay motionless and was again back across the massive distance of seven years and the stretch of a continent. In California, in December of 1938, Betty had died; the whole month had been a time of her dying. The baby was already a year old; all the associative fears of childbirth pain and possible death had long been washed clear of his mind. And then the hemorrhaging had suddenly started, the endless transfusions, the pinker cheeks of one day yielding to the waxy ones of the next. The pendulum of hope and fear had swung deeper and deeper in his heart, grooving it forever in the nameless arc of loss.

"Quit it, quit it." The words gritted in his mind, as they used to grit through his throat when he said them half aloud in those first weeks after her death. His own voice, sounding suddenly in his ears, would shock him, yet there had been a physical need, apparently, to break the unending silence of his bed, where they had lain together, talking, laughing, making love, making long plans. That wide bed had been a focal point of his torment, and, for a long time, each night he would become obsessed with his awareness of the empty half of it. Then he would angrily plan to order a new bed the very next morning, a narrow bed, a single bed. His mother had come to live with him and the baby, and unknowingly she had blocked this simple escape. He could never manage to announce, "I'm ordering a new bed; it'll be delivered in a couple of days; it's for my room."

His mother, his sisters, his friends, praised him for "bearing up so well." The truth had been that he was charged with a grief so raucous that he'd had to silence it complete or yell all of it to the world. He had worked harder than he had ever done, had started a new article the day he turned in a completed one, had traveled, read, told himself a thousand times that "time heals everything." Endlessly time had mocked him. But at last the first savage grief and longing had given way to a pain more patient. In a sense this new pain had been more frightening because of its quieter, more durable characteristic.

The evenings had continued, each of them, to be an assault on his decent courage. That moment when the house had quieted down, Tommy long since asleep and his mother finally through with the clatter of dishes and soft slapping of the refrigerator door—that moment still had remained the signal of the empty time ahead before he could say good night and go off to his room. That necessary empty time to be got through—it seemed a *thing,* tangible, a chunk of time sitting there in the room, an obstacle and an offense. As he forced himself to make talk with his mother, about the baby, about books or politics, the knowledge that it was his mother, and not Betty, who was there to share his house and his evenings would rasp through his nerves until he hated her unruffled gentleness.

Unconsciously perhaps, he had begun frittering away his daytime working hours, so that he should be forced to write at night. It was a good plan. The manuscript in his typewriter became a reliable contrivance, a mechanism down which, each evening, he could cram that offensive chunk of time as into a meat grinder. The thin ribbons of typed words were the end products of that grinding down. As the chunk grew steadily smaller, he would feel less afraid of it, and when his mother would say good night and leave him, he could feel a gratitude that she had been unresentful at being ignored.

"It's harder for people like us, Phil," she had once said, without preamble. "Because there's no loophole."

"I know." He did, exactly and without discussion. The

29

softening of the blow that was for people who believed in some reunion after death was not for him. He never felt that he was an irreligious man, for he had too much sureness that somewhere, still beyond the reach of pondering and searching minds, must lie the great synthesis of life and all its forces. But like his agnostic father and mother, he had always held all organized religions to be wistful evasions from the loneliness and insecurity of that pondering. When the first hours of Betty's death encircled him, he had known she was gone from him finally and forever, with no reprieve.

"Well, quit it, come on, quit it *now*." This time he sat up, switched on the light. He was not in California seven years ago; he was here in this small New York room, in this new narrow bed (bought so many years after the need for it had left him). He gazed about him; he reached out and touched the wall with his elbow. But the old space was in his mind again, the vastness and emptiness and loneliness.

He lit another cigarette and steered his thoughts back to the list he'd made. But the assignment was dead now; he could not force it alive. He put the cigarette out, turned out the light again, and was at once asleep.

Rain was blowing against the tall gray window in the dim room as he woke. For a moment he felt he had only dozed; then he saw that it was morning. Eagerness washed along his nerves, as last night when he had left Kathy. For a moment he could not characterize this unfamiliar mood. He regarded the inner quality of this waking as if it were something in a showcase before him. Good Lord, he thought, imagine waking up feeling *good*.

Ignoring slippers and bathrobe, he went to the bathroom for his shower. The full-bodied rush of city water was still new and pleasing; its battering left him brisk. He was glad to be alive.

While he shaved, Tommy came in, perched on the edge of the bathtub, and began his usual chattering. From time to time Phil glanced down at him. This tall thin boy was such a good-looking kid. He had Betty's cleft chin and small even teeth, but his height, his dark eyes and straight nose were Phil's.

"How old will I have to be, Dad, before I can start shaving?" But before Phil could answer, Tommy was considering how old he'd be before he could fly a plane, then how old before he'd be in the Air Corps. In mixed amusement and surprise Phil listened to the tumble of technical talk about firing power, flying range, rockets, radar. Were all boys like this today, he wondered. In 1917, when he himself was eight, had he had so lethal a vocabulary, been so conscious of the other war? He decided not. There were no radios then, no *Lifes* and *Looks*—no newsreels, no avalanche of comic books about martial daredevils. For him during that war there had been only his parents' talk about it, and the newspaper which came each morning. He'd had none of this war's incessant instruction in the very sounds and colors and sights of killing and dying.

"Couldn't we, Dad?" Tommy's voice was insistent. Phil had missed something and tried to remember what it had been.

"Couldn't we what?"

"Buy a secondhand jeep when they're really demobilized? Jimmy Kelly says his dad's going to."

Phil thought, And the words they use! When I was a kid that age, did I know half the big words he does? Aloud he said, "It's an idea, anyway, Tommy."

"Tom."

"Tom. Sorry."

At breakfast he caught himself just as he was going to remind Tommy not to read the comic strips at the table. It was hopeless. Better to retire with dignity than go on at the boy. His mother's face told him she had watched this change of heart.

"Nice time last night?" she asked, and waited for his nod. "That's good. You really need new people as much as new places. I mean everybody does, not just you."

"It was a good bunch to start on. We talked some about the articles; I moseyed around making some notes when I got in."

He told her about the list he had jotted down. They often talked about his work, and generally he valued their discussions as a good sounding board. He respected her opinions about something he'd written. She never said anything was a failure, but when she remained calm and judicious after finishing a manuscript, he knew that it would leave others cold, too. For when his stuff was really moving, her whole manner told him so before she spoke. He would steal quick looks at her while she was reading, and know. Sometimes she would chuckle and shake her head, sometimes her eyes would fill, sometimes she would wince and say, in a half voice, "It's impossible," or "Imagine!" Then her face would express so much pride in him as a son and so much response to him as a writer that there was no room for doubt about whether he had written well. Now he was not watching her reactions. They were simply talking at the level of preliminaries.

"What's antisemitism?" Tom asked, without looking up from the comics.

"It's——" Phil was taken aback by the size and casualness of the question. Tom finished the last strip and shoved the paper aside.

"Antisemitism," he repeated. "What *is* that, Dad?"

"Well, let's see." He saw Tom's eyes on him, expectant. The boy knew he would get an answer as he always got an answer. There was never any "when you're older, I'll explain" between them. Phil said, "It's when people don't like other people just because they're Jews."

"Oh." Tom considered for a second. "Why? Are they bad?"

"Some are, sure. Some aren't. It's like everybody else."

"What *are* Jews anyhow?"

Phil looked at him thoughtfully. This same unexpected thing had happened on a hundred levels in the last year. A word, a name, a place that Tom had heard over and over without showing the faintest interest would all at once catch at him and become the subject of exhaustive inquiry. Here we go, Phil thought, wondering how to start. If the kid had been given the usual religious training, this would be simpler now.

"Remember last week, you asked about that big church?"

"Sure."

"And I told you there were lots of different kinds of churches?"

"You and Gram think it's prob'ly nature instead, but I can think it's God if I want and go to one."

"That's right. Well, the people that go to that particular church are called Catholics. Then there are people who go to other churches, and they're called Protestants, and there are others that go to still different ones, and they're called Jews. Only they call their kind of church synagogues or temples."

"Oh." He thought it over. "Then why don't some people like those?"

"It's kind of tough to explain." He shrugged. "Some people hate Catholics, some hate Jews——"

"And nobody hates *us* 'cause we're Americans?"

Mrs. Green began to clear the breakfast table. She was going to let him struggle alone.

33

"No, that's something different again. You can be an American and a Catholic, or an American and a Protestant, or an American and a Jew. Or you could be French or German or Spanish or any nationality at the same time you're Catholic or a Protestant or a Jew."

Tom looked perplexed. Phil had an impulse of flight but he repressed it.

"Look, Tom. One thing is your *country,* like America, or France or Germany or Russia—all the countries. The flag is different and the uniform is different, the language is different."

"The airplanes are marked different." This was interesting talk, his tone said.

"Differently. That's right. But the other thing is religion if you have any, or your grandfather's religion, like Jewish or Catholic or Protestant religion. *That* hasn't anything to do with the country or the language or the airplanes. Get it?"

"Yep."

"Don't ever get mixed up on that. Some people are mixed up."

"Why?"

"Oh, they talk about the Jewish race, but never about the Catholic race or the Protestant race. Or about the Jewish people, but never about the Protestant people or——"

"Why don't they?"

Phil searched his mother's face. It was now impassive and definitely not helpful. He glanced at his watch, and a wave of relief rewarded him.

"Hey, it's eight-forty."

Tommy knocked his chair over as he flung himself to his feet. His elbow skittered the newspaper off the table. Tragically he said, "Oh, gosh, I'll be late for school."

"We'll talk some more sometime."

34

Tom raced out, heels hammering on the uncarpeted floor past kitchen and bathroom. Phil stretched back in his chair and looked up at Mrs. Green.

"Whew."

She laughed in wicked enjoyment. Then she said seriously, "It's all right, Phil. You're always good with him."

"He won't remember a word of it."

"If he just gets one little sequence fixed, you've done enough."

"What sequence?"

"Just using the three together every time, as a group. Catholic Protestant Jew, like apples pears peaches. That's a good start."

"I guess it is. I hadn't planned it." He shook his head; his lips pushed out as if he were saying "Whew" again. "That kid'll wreck me yet." He poured more coffee and looked at her as if something had occurred to him for the first time.

"Did *you* and Dad have to go through this sort of stuff with me and the girls?"

"Of course we did. All parents have to if they have definite designs on their children."

"Meaning about their kids' prejudices?"

She nodded. "Out there in California the problem was a little special—remember a boy called Petey?"

"Alamacho? Sure, Dave and I and he were The Gang."

"Well, Dave. Your father and his were such good friends, you boys just would be, too."

"But Petey?"

"You know the Mexican thing there."

"Oh, California." He made a face. "And the Filipino thing and the Chinese and the Nisei and the Negro thing —what a hotbed of a place for kids to grow up in!"

"Every place can be a hotbed. It's only each house that decides it. Belle and Mary and you never heard any prej-

35

udice from Dad or me, even the disguised kind, so you didn't fall for it in school or anywhere."

"Mm, I guess."

"All kids are so decent to start with." She smiled at him and went back to the dishes. He thought uneasily of Belle and wondered whether his mother also had. He picked the newspaper up from the floor. A headline about the Marine Corps caught his eye.

He read it, and went to his desk. He spread out last night's penciled notes and read them. He yawned. Ashy and cold, the stuff lay there before him. The promise of future success it had contained only a few hours ago seemed burned out for good.

The house buzzer sounded. He didn't move. Mail never mattered to him, except when he'd been at camp or overseas. He picked up a pencil. On the sheet headed "Antisemitism in Business," he idly sketched the insigne of the Marine Corps and beneath it scrupulously began to letter "Semper Fidelis." As he drew, he thought of Kathy.

Only after he'd joined the Marine Corps in the spring of 1941 had he begun to go out with girls and remain free of an irrational sense of infidelity to Betty. With some of those girls, the evenings had passed in a vague, tentative unconcern about how they would end; with others, he'd been ridden from the first moment with a kind of sullen plan to get through with whatever preliminaries were needed to get them to bed. There was no beauty in it, but there was reassurance. He was young; he was, after all, not the inert man he thought he had become.

"Package for you," his mother called. She came in with two large Manila envelopes, each one crammed and straining against the red twine twisted around the cardboard button on its flap. Inside were hundreds of clippings from newspapers and magazines.

36

He began at once to read them, making no exceptions and taking them in the order they came. He made careful notes of names, incidents, dates, committees, entering them below major headings that followed his rough breakdown of subjects. On a separate sheet of paper, on which he printed the word ANGLE, he jotted down fragments of ideas as they came to him. Off and on through the next hours he thought back to his breakfast talk with Tom, thumbing through it, as it were, to see if he could spot some clue that might lead to the solution of his problem. Maybe he could slant the whole series from the point of view of parents anxious to keep bigotry from their own children.

Before he finished formulating the idea, he discarded it. Even thinking it embarrassed him. It was real enough when it happened, but it would sound phony, a tear-jerky patriotic kind of phony if he tried to pin a whole series to it. For the first time the conviction that this was an impossible assignment took hold of him. Fine in an editor's head—or a girl's —but journalistically a dud. He should have rejected it; for the first job, anyway.

He was probably pressing too hard, too soon. Minify had told him there was no rush. He'd better spend a week or two reading and thinking and interviewing some of these committee people before even reporting back. As soon as he decided that, he realized he was tired from the eyeballs down. It was long past lunchtime. He made stacks of the clippings he'd been through and on the others he put an oval glass paperweight that had been a gift from Betty. Mrs. Green heard him moving about and came in for the first time since breakfast.

"Lunch is ready, Phil."

"Don't want any."

"It's nearly three."

"I'm not hungry."

She left him. He went to his room and lay down on his bed. He thought of taking flowers to Kathy for their date tonight and veered promptly away from the notion. He was not the man for courtly gestures. Anyway, don't rush things, he thought. This may be important.

CHAPTER THREE

THE DAYLONG RAIN had depleted itself into a thin drizzle, and Phil gratefully saw that the approaching cab was empty. He gave Kathy's address and said, "I'm in luck tonight."

"Sure are, gettin' a cab this far downtown," the driver said amiably. "It's the doormen all along Park, flaggin' us down for them rich Jews." With that, he snapped the butt of his cigarette through the window of the cab and began whistling a tune.

"The taxi shortage hasn't anything to do with Jews," Phil said shortly.

"It's just them fancy doormen," the driver agreed willingly, "doin' it *for* them."

You moron, Phil thought. For the rest of the short trip he searched for some effective thing to say; he found none, and decided that he'd be damned before he'd tip him. But at Kathy's door he paid the driver and found himself helpless to resist the waiting palm. Frustration still clutched at him as he went into the self-service elevator.

Upstairs he rang the bell and heard quick footsteps. She opened the door herself and said, "Hello. You're on the dot."

"Should I be fashionably late?" At once he thought, How cute of me.

She laughed, took his coat and hat, and hung them in a hall closet. She seemed glad to see him. She went ahead into a living room which pleased him before he could look at its

39

details. There were books around and a piano and none of the too-perfect look of the interior decorator.

"Do you want a cocktail?" she asked. "Or Scotch? I have a little, and plenty of Scotch-type blend."

She wrinkled her nose over the last part. He stopped looking about the room and turned to her. She was different from last night, wearing some kind of dress with flowers printed along the bottom and fitting close up under her chin.

"You really look so—never mind." Compliments always sounded false. He went over to the piano. It was a large grand, too big for this room, undoubtedly a hangover from her married life. There were two books of Mozart sonatas open on the rack. One looked clean and new, the other worn. He riffled the pages of the old one and saw pencil marks for loud and soft, for the pedal, for an overlooked sharp or flat.

"Do you play?" he asked.

"Some. The easy ones. Do you?"

"Not any more, but I'm a sucker for music."

"I started taking lessons again this winter." She stood near the piano. He turned the pages further, then closed the volume and looked at her without saying anything, studying her. She stood poised and quiet, letting him, and then moved away. "You still haven't said what drink."

"Whatever you have. Got any ideas about restaurants? I'm lost in this town."

"We'll think that up when we start out." She poured Scotch into an old-fashioned glass and put two lumps of ice into it from an ice bucket. The ice tongs were right on the tray, but she ignored them and used her fingers. He didn't know why, but that pleased him.

He took the glass and waited until she had a drink ready for herself. He raised his in a toast, said, "Here's to——" and stopped. "I'm no good at toasts," he said. "I can never think of anything."

40

"Here's to never thinking of anything," she said quickly. He thought it the most charming, the wittiest—and before he could finish the sentence he thought, Boy, it wasn't *that* good. She was taking a sip of her drink, and he noticed her pursed lips. She started telling a funny thing that had happened at the nursery school that afternoon. She told a story well. The too-social tone was gone. Had he imagined it entirely? One way or the other, it didn't matter any more. She had begun laughing at her own story, and he laughed with her.

"You like kids, don't you?"

"I seem to," she said. "I've got thirty. All stages from training pants to six years. They're more exhausting than the factory ever was."

"What factory?"

"Didn't I—for Pete's sake, did I leave that out?"

"I'm not so much of an interviewer at that, am I? What factory?"

It was her first job after her divorce, the first full-time job she'd ever had. For the first year of the war, she had operated a drill press at Wright Aeronautical in Paterson. After a deep bronchial infection her doctor talked darkly of pneumonia, even tuberculosis, and ordered her to leave.

"I guess I wasn't hard to persuade," she said. "After the first excitement, I hated it."

"I bet."

"Anyway, after a vacation, I got into the school. In those days nobody asked you if you had the proper training. I do like kids."

She asked about Tom, and he guarded himself against sounding boastful. He was a nice kid, fun to talk to and take places. He'd made a good adjustment already to his new school.

"It could be tough on a boy that age," he ended. "Switch-

41

ing from a small country school to a big city one and especially in the middle of a term. He's O.K., I guess."

Suddenly she smiled at him and saw his eyes go uncertain, as if he were unsure of why she had and were asking her not to wound him. She wanted to tell him that she knew more about his inner states than he had told her, that she knew he not only wasn't happy now but hadn't been for a long time, so that possibly he'd forgotten how simple and good it was to feel happy. But she said none of those things. New Yorkers made greatly personal remarks to each other on first or second meetings, but perhaps people from smaller places would get tied up with constraint and embarrassment. He'd be miffed if he knew she thought of him as different from New Yorkers. He'd been abroad three times, he'd traveled a good deal in America, yet there was some of the air of a small-towner about him, indefinable but there.

"You're sort of afraid," she said, "to let on to anybody that you're nuts about Tom, aren't you?" She leaned toward him earnestly. "Don't be, Phil, you don't have to be, with me or anybody."

"It's—well, I just——" He broke it. He was touched, about what he did not know. Ever since Betty he had not found any girl who knew more about him than he chose to put into words. Communication with another human being, communication on the levels where words were needless, was something he had missed so deeply that recognition of it stirred sharply in him. "I guess I cover on lots of things," he said stiffly.

"And when you do, you look—well, all sort of dark and brooding." She suddenly added, "Like *Toledo*. You know, that landscape of El Greco?"

He laughed.

"You mean all dark greens and blacks? Mackerel sky? Storm coming?"

She nodded. "Practically a portrait of you." She waited till he stopped laughing and then asked about the new assignment. He countered by telling her of the taxi driver. She said, "It's sickening, isn't it?" and they fell silent. A moment later, he suggested that she play for him. She went at once to the piano and began a simple Mozart sonata. Several times she struck wrong notes and corrected them without nervousness or embarrassment. She played pleasingly, with no attempts to dazzle by speed or crashing chords. He sat listening to her in a slow suffusion of *Gemütlichkeit*. Toward the end of the short sonata, he went over to stand by the piano, watching her hands. Looking down at her, he saw that her hair was not black as he had thought, but dark brown.

She finished playing, stood up at once, and went back to her unfinished drink. He closed the book of music and set it atop the other volume, squaring the edges precisely with the one beneath. He heard her laugh.

"Sort of old-maidish," he said sheepishly.

"Or bachelorish."

"I like the way you play."

"I'm glad."

Confidence, sureness, the freedom from his own ever-questioning-of-himself—she had that, and he envied her as he envied anybody else who was not forever involved with the weighing, the analyzing, the searching out he went through. She would not know the torment there could be in the fluctuating mood, the shifting decision, the wide swing between clarity and confusion, between cheerfulness and depression. Even though there were things about her that didn't seem to square with other things, she seemed direct, free of complication or self-question.

"Another drink?" she asked. "Or should we start? I'm starved."

When they were finishing dinner, she came back to the articles. This time he did not counter or dodge.

"The thing's got me licked so far, but that's nothing new at the start. I've had a flock of ideas about how to angle it, but they're all lousy." Briefly he told her two of them. She liked them, but he brushed that aside. "They just don't stand up. When you get the right one, a kind of click happens inside you. It hasn't happened yet. Let's skip it."

It was about ten when they left the restaurant. He hoped, expected even, that she would suggest going back to her place, but instead she said there was a movie she'd been watching the neighborhood playhouses for. A displeasure stabbed him, as if she'd said something to offend him, but he agreed that a movie was a fine notion. In the deep loge seats, he felt placated; watching the screen, he was conscious of her nearness, of whether her arm was on the seat rest or not, of her breathing. Each time she fished in her purse, he offered her a cigarette—leaning close to her to light it became a delicate and pleasing thing. The afternoon's unspoken admonition not to hurry this sounded again in his mind. He kept his eyes on the picture, but every time she moved her head, recrossed her legs, shifted about in any way, he knew it.

Was this to be like all the rest? His lips closed hard against each other as though to keep out the bitter taste of the question. He glanced toward her. Her whole attention was on the screen. In the dim light she seemed guileless and very young, and he believed at last in what she had told him about her divorce leaving no residue of bitterness or hatred. She had undoubtedly known pain—what human being could finish nearly three decades and be a stranger to it? But she seemed whole and unchipped in her personality, with none of the braced expectation of further pain.

Across the veil of silence between them, Kathy was thinking, And maybe *I've* forgotten how simple and good it is to feel happy. She hadn't been *un*happy, not even through the first adjustment after divorcing Bill. She hadn't really suffered about anything since those long-ago days back home, in her teens. But it suddenly seemed a long time since she'd known the outrageous delight in life that she'd felt over going to college or getting married. For her, living alone was a stopgap. Three years was a great deal of stopgap indeed.

There were good things about marriage that she'd begun to miss. Small things, apart from the big question of rightness and love. The comfortableness of always having somebody to go to a party with, the normal knowledge that you were a man's wife like everybody else—marriage was a sweet way to live. Or could be.

She glanced over at him. He was concentrating on the movie. He'd be shocked probably if he could see past the thin casing of her skin into her mind.

Mrs. Schuyler Green.

She was amused. That was the adolescent trick; every time she'd met a new boy, she'd instantly thought of what her name would be if she married him. She'd write out his name and then hers beneath it and cross off all the matching letters in each. There was some childish abracadabra for the remaining letters. What was it? "Rich man, poor——" No, that was even younger nonsense, before the dreamy days of thinking about boys. Her mind blanked out—she could think of nothing. Rich man, poor man—her childhood had been spent with that differentiation. The fact that as a small-town lawyer, her father was too poor to do the things he wanted to do for his wife and his two children had embittered him long before she and Janey were old enough to show they wanted things they couldn't have. Probably his own bitterness had helped teach *them* that differentiation.

"Love, friendship, marriage, hate." Suddenly the boy-girl rigmarole tumbled back into her possession—fortunetelling for adolescence. She tried to do the trick in her mind.

Should I take Schuyler Green and Katherine Pawling? Or Philip Green and Katherine Lacey?

In the dark, she grinned. She started to open her bag, but across the arm of the chair, he offered her his pack of cigarettes. She took one, and he flipped his lighter. The sleeve of his coat touched her bare arm, and in the small flare of light she suddenly looked at him and whispered, "This is nice, isn't it?"

As they came out to the street, he said, "And now?"

"Would you mind if we *didn't* go anywhere else? During the week I just never get enough sleep any more."

"Of course I wouldn't mind."

He heard how formal his words sounded. Did they show his disappointment? He felt a fool. In the taxi he sat well away from her. At her house, he loudly told the driver to keep the flag down, took her to the door, and was the first to say good night. Secret and abject, a wish twisted in him that she'd change her mind and ask him up for a nightcap. She said it had all been lovely, and was gone.

A hundred notions discarded, sentences x-ed out, opening paragraphs, phrases for titles.

Attempts at a dry underwriting, at a just logic and reason, attempts at ringing words.

And always the distaste, the dejection, the renewed battering at his mind to yield, to create, to reward him.

Phil reached to the top of the paper in his typewriter and wrenched it out of the machine. The platen whined like line singing out of a steel reel.

"Damn it, I'll go nuts."

For nearly a week he had fought the increasing sense of

failure. Or was it boredom? He had heard nothing from Minify and had neither telephoned nor gone to see him. He had read with minute care all but six or eight of the borrowed clippings; he had made twenty appointments for the following week with head people in each of twenty organizations. He delayed the interviews because experience had taught him that each one would yield him a richer result if he went to it with his own plans already formulated, so he could pin the ready talker down to pertinent material. He had given himself a week's leeway; now he knew it wasn't enough. He still had no plan. The "angle" refused to show itself.

Again and again some clipping would rouse him, and his quickened feelings would carry assurance that he was on the edge of discovery. But an hour later he would know that all he had was one more episode of a store window smashed in Boston, a child kicked and beaten in Washington Heights, a synagogue or cemetery ravaged in Chicago or Minneapolis or Detroit.

"This Christ-bitten stuff won't budge." He considered telling Minify that he'd prefer, after all, to leave this for his second assignment, that he'd surely strain less after he'd rung up one good record in the new job. Something stopped him from doing it. He had a stubborn streak. "It's a mile wide right now," he told himself, and bent glumly toward the typewriter.

Maybe he could make each article a kind of Profile of some Jewish guy who'd been heroic in the war, decorated, all that. Nonsense. Heroes were heroes because they were heroes, not because they were or weren't Jewish. Even offering such a selection—what the hell was different between being brave if you were a Jew and being brave if you weren't a Jew?

My trouble is, he thought, the only difference that rates

47

with me is people's sex. The notion amused him. I *do* care
whether somebody's a woman or a man.

He had not telephoned Kathy all week. Until he felt better about the first stage of this job, he was in no mood for
personal things.

Or was it the other way round?

He shoved back from his desk and stood up. She'd been
on his mind too damn much, that's what it was. Any man,
meeting her after months of nothing—hell, no wonder he
couldn't get on with his work.

He went to the telephone and called her at the school. She
said, "Oh, Phil, hello," as if she were glad.

"You wouldn't be free tonight by any chance?" He admired his offhand tone.

"No, I'm not. I'm sorry."

"Then how about tomorrow?"

"I'd like that. How's the work coming? I've wondered
about it a lot."

"It's not. I'm still rooting around for some special lead-in,
and I just can't hit it." He sounded cheerful. *"You're* re-
sponsible for the hell I'm in. You sold Minify."

"You'll get it, Phil. I *know* it." She made a comforting
sound. "About seven then?"

This time he wasn't irritated that somebody else was sure.
It delighted him. The whole call delighted him. She had
thought about the series; she had thought about him. He
looked triumphantly at the telephone. Tomorrow night he'd
ask *himself* up for a nightcap. Last time, for all he knew,
she'd waited for him to suggest it.

Maybe Minify, too, was waiting for a signal from him.
At any rate, there was no reason to avoid him this way.
Often a suggestion from somebody else, even when you
rejected it, picked you up from the sticky muck you'd been
working in. He went to the telephone once again.

48

An hour later they were deep in discussion. One by one, Phil checked over the ideas he'd had, the reasons for throwing each one aside. There was no surprised look on Minify's face, no careful choice of words to conceal disappointment. Minify knew. Before he turned editor, he'd written too many thousands of newsprint columns himself, too many dozens of special articles for magazines, not to know. His eyes intent, he listened carefully as Phil told him of the material he had already gathered.

"The more you give me, the surer I am I want the articles," he said. "It's getting nasty for fair."

Phil looked briefly at Minify. "One of my sisters was here last week from Detroit. She always gets me on edge, but I used to think she was O.K. underneath. I told her what I was up to, and she went into a routine about 'you can't write or legislate these things out of existence.'"

"Yeah. I get lots of that."

"A few years ago she wouldn't have said that—anyway, not in that pleasant, smug tone. I guess in a place that's running over with the Negro thing and the Jewish thing— I suppose I ought to go out there." He considered Detroit. "But you know something?" Minify waited. "I've a hunch there's a bigger thing to do than just to go after the crackpot story. That's been done plenty. It's the wider spread of it I'd like to get at—the people who'd never go near a Christian Front meeting or send a dime to Gerald L. K. Smith."

"I'm with you on that. But it's harder."

They sat across from each other, smoking, silent. Just in this companionship of searching, Phil found it easier to think. His thorny mood was smoothing out. He let his thoughts drift.

"I wish Dave wasn't in Europe," he finally said, almost to himself.

49

"Who's he?"

"Dave Goldman. We were kids together, in California."
He waved largely. "Undying friendship at eight." He
looked reflective. "I wonder what he feels like when he
runs into it or reads about it. He's in the Engineers. Seems
stuck over there. Captain."

"Still friends?"

"Not especially close any more. We went through everything together up to college. Then I picked Stanford, and
he went to UCLA. We still write every so often. But
letters are no good on this kind of business. I wish——"
He broke off and closed his eyes, leaning a little forward
as if he were trying to hear a sound very far away. Then
he said slowly, "Maybe there's something in that."

"Going to suggest my sending you abroad?"

Undisturbed by the joshing tone, Phil shook his head.
He reached for a cigarette, forgot to make the gesture of
offering one.

"I'm going to start on a new tack," he said slowly. "So
far I've been going after facts, evidence. I've sort of ignored feelings." He shifted his glance to Minify. "How
does it make somebody like Dave feel? The way we feel
only stepped up?" He spoke more quickly. "It's at least a
chance to break the log jam."

"Got any Jewish friends in New York?" Minify asked.

"Who, me? I haven't *any* friends in New York."

"I'll introduce you to Joe Lieberman. He's a physicist
and a good guy to talk anything over with. He was in on
Oak Ridge."

Phil put his hand up, in a "stop" gesture.

"Hold it for now, would you? It's no use till I know
what I want to ask him. I can't just say, 'How do you do,
Professor Lieberman, let's talk about how you react to
antisemitism.' I'd fall on my face first."

John Minify laughed with him. "Joe'd get it," he said. "He's the man you could say it to, once I gave him a line on you."

They agreed to keep the meeting in reserve. Phil rose to go, anxious to explore this new path that had just opened to him. At the door, he turned. Minify looked quizzical, obscurely pleased with life or himself.

"Thanks for letting me barge in," Phil said.

"Any time." He smiled. "You made a hit with Jessie," he said. "And, I gather, with Kathy."

"Thanks." It sounded too abrupt. "They made a hit with me, too."

"She's quite a girl, Kathy. She has a lot on the ball."

Phil wanted to say the urbane, the perfect thing, but he couldn't think for the life of him what that would be. He said, "She's damn attractive," added, "Well, be seeing you," and left.

Even on the way home, the big new question was on him like a seizure. Over and above what any other normal man thinks about it, what must a Jew feel about this thing? That's what he must find out, thinking himself into the very brain of another human being to find his answer. It was a fascinating quest for any speculative guy. It was a human question, it was dramatic. Out of it should come the way to lead readers along.

For the rest of the afternoon and again after his early supper with Tom and his mother, he remained absorbed. Pacing the living room, sitting at his desk, getting up again to wander around and stare vacantly at his books—hour after hour he persisted. Without purposely or consciously limiting his interest, he kept coming back to Dave, trying to think into Dave's mind. It was more valid to think of someone like Dave, the kind of man he himself would be if he were a Jew. He could not "think into" a deeply reli-

51

gious old Jew in a prayer shawl, or into the poor, ignorant Jewish peddler behind a pushcart on the East Side, or into the wealthy tycoon in business. The deeply pious, the truly ignorant, the greatly powerful of any creed or religion were beyond his quick understanding.

Dave was not. Dave was like him in every essential, had the same boyhood patterns, the same freedom from either extreme of poverty or wealth, the same freedom from any creed-bound faith. They had both grown up in a generation when religion did not work itself very deep into life. Whatever Dave felt now—indifference? outrage? fear? or contempt?—would be the feeling of Dave as a man, and not Dave as a Jew. Dave as citizen, as American, and not Dave as a religious being. That, Phil was sure of. And that was good.

He began to glance through his hundreds of notes, pausing over this episode or that to ask himself what would go on in a man like Dave when he read of it in his morning newspaper. Betty's paperweight sat on top of the thin sheaf of clips which he had not yet read. Idly he picked up the heavy chunk of glass and began tossing it from one hand to the other. His eyes were on the top clipping where the oval outline of the paperweight still showed, like the imprint of a doctor's thumb into the puffed flesh of edema. It was the first page of an issue of *Time* magazine, nearly two years old. He began to read it. Congressman John Rankin had stood up in the House to attack the soldier-vote bill; he had referred to Walter Winchell as "the little kike I was telling you about."

His fingers tightened around the cold smooth glass. *Time*'s next words were, "This was a new low in demagoguery, even for John Rankin, but in the entire House no one rose to protest." Shame for the Congress twisted in him. He read on through a column and a half to *Time*'s sentence: "The House rose and gave him prolonged applause."

The House. The Senate. The great Congress of the United States.

He stood up abruptly. "Jesus, what's happening to this country? A country never knows what's *happening* to it." How many of *Time*'s million readers had felt like rushing down there, punching Rankin in the jaw, yelling at the whole House? And if a reader were Jewish—could he be any *more* outraged? What had Dave felt when he'd come on this? The same, exactly the same as he himself did. He'd bet a million on that. He knew that.

The thick glass in his hand was moist. He set it down and wiped his hand against his trousers.

He *thought* he knew. There was that good familiar click of certitude he always felt when his instincts were true. But there was no way to check on himself, no way to prove he was correct.

He would have to write Dave after all, have to get to know this Joe Lieberman, have to do personal research on this as he did on every other problem he had ever worked on.

"How do you do, Professor Lieberman, let's talk about how you react to antisemitism in the good old U. S. A." Damn it, he'd die first. "Dear Dave, Give me the lowdown on your gizzard when you read about Rankin calling people kikes or a Jewish kid getting his face slashed by Jew haters in New York City."

Out. It was out. All of it was out. There was no way he could dig and prod and tear open the secret heart of a human being. This was blind alley, too.

He turned on the radio. In an instant he snapped it off. He picked up the evening papers. The news was stale. He thought of writing letters and abandoned the idea. It was

53

only eleven; if he went to bed, he'd never sleep.

Again he'd felt himself pressing the hard edge of discovery; again he'd slipped right through it. Like the oily turnstile. Flickering across his mind was a wonder about whether he was losing his grip for a while. It happened to writers. Maybe it was his turn.

Grimly he told himself not to start yammering. His gaze traveled slowly over the room as if he were looking for affirmation that other writers had fought and struggled for an idea. Books—the room was full of books. Books told about people's feelings, private reactions. There hadn't been many novels where the main characters were Jewish, but there'd been some.

For half an hour he searched the shelves. He was a hoarder of books—he never could bring himself to throw any book away, so one or two of the ones he remembered owning ought to be somewhere in this conglomeration. Whatever novels he had were old. He'd heard of a couple of new ones in the last year that dealt with "the Jewish problem," but he wasn't much of a novel reader, so he'd missed them. He'd have to ask about them, buy them for whatever he might learn from them.

He finally found one of the books he'd expected to find, and he renewed his search. Then he had two more. He'd known they ought to be there, and they might help him now with his job of "thinking into." As he remembered these books, their central characters had been Jewish. He began to reread, rapidly skimming, suddenly remembering the people, plot, incidents.

For more than an hour he read. And as he read a sickish anger grew in him.

He stood up finally. He placed the three books side by side on a shelf. He stared at them. One, two, three in a row. Exhibits A, B, and C.

In each of these novels the central figure, the Jew, was a heel—dishonest, scheming, or repulsive. A Goebbels, a Rankin might have written these books. But in each case a talented Jew had been the author. It was before the war that each had done it. But he had done it.

Somewhere in the 1930's each had labored long and done it.

What dark unconscious hatreds must have been operating in those very authors that made each of them, with a world of subjects to pick over, finally choose *these* subjects and stay unswerving to their purpose through the long months and loneliness of writing! How neurotic they themselves must have been made by the world of hatred! Did it never occur to one of them to write about a fine guy who was Jewish? Did each one feel some savage necessity to pick a Jew who was a swine in the wholesale business, a Jew who was a swine in the movies, a Jew who was a swine in bed?

He would have to look elsewhere for any valid clue to what a normal Jew would feel about anything—a Jew who was a scientist, say, or a historian, or a businessman, or a housewife. Or a Jew who'd risked maiming or death in the war against the master-race theory.

He sat down and wrote quickly on his typewriter.

Dear Dave:

When the hell you getting back? And will it be a surprise to know we've moved to New York for good, or did I say I was going to, last time I wrote? I've taken a staff job with Minify. I want to talk to you about a series I'm supposed to do, on antisemitism; do you hyphenate the damn word or not, I never can remember. Anyway, what chance your stopping here for a bit before heading for the Coast?

Best, and where's the letter you owe me,

Phil

He put three red stamps on the envelope, wrote, "AIR" beneath them, checked on Dave's APO number, and went down to the street to mail the letter.

Even this much decisiveness feels good, he thought. He could almost taste his own disgust and bile.

He dreamed of Betty. For the first time in months, she was there in his angry sleep, young as she had been, asleep beside him and smiling at something. Somewhere was the sound of an infant's thin wailing, and she wasn't startled, just smiling, calling out, "Yes, darling, I'm coming." There was such readiness in her voice, hurrying to her baby, unruffled, not resentful at being waked.

He turned on his back and knew he had dreamed. "You're afraid to let on to anybody about it, aren't you? Don't be, Phil, you don't have to be, with me or anybody." That was Kathy, his sleep-filled mind told him, and he stirred into a half waking. There had been the overwash of two voices, the second flowing over the first like a new wave rolling in on the outgo of the preceding. Different yet one because each was of the indivisible sea.

Now he sat up, really awake. He turned on the light above his head and reached for a cigarette.

An extraordinary sense of peace ran through him as he remembered the dream and the half dream it had borne with it. He swallowed, and it made a hard, audible sound in the silent room. He heard it and contemplated the tip of his cigarette. He thought, I guess I'm in love with her.

He lay, still warmed with sleep, freed from the incessant striving of the evening, relaxed as a man basking under a summer sun on an unpeopled beach. He heard again her voice on the telephone that afternoon, open, eager. All the complex wariness he'd felt that first time was gone. The doubts were gone. That was good. These seven years had made him too critical of people. Minute analysis of himself was bad enough; minute analysis of others was a preposterous nonsense, an unspoken effrontery. She was on no witness stand under cross-examination, with him the prosecutor; she had nothing to prove, with him the dissenter.

Did she want to marry some other Bill Pawling, but more "liberal" in his ideas? Or could she marry some man who could never give her the beautiful apartment, the expensive vacations? She could, but after a while would she feel cheated?

Oh, quit being a self-appointed bastard of a judge and jury and God. He turned out the light. Illogically, he remembered Belle's visit a week before. Sleep was invading his mind again, like a slow infiltration into resisting terrain. He felt the cold December night in the room, the realm of warmth under the blankets.

A sound came to him, thin, miserable. For one instant he thought he was dreaming again about Betty and the baby. Then he jerked free of his blankets. That had been a real sound.

Swiftly he went through the dark apartment. His mother had called aloud in the night and then there had been a long silence and now she was calling again.

"Mom, what?" The switch clicked under his finger. "You're sick."

She moved her head. Her face rigid with pain, her hand bluish across her breast, the fingers digging into her left arm —fear assaulted him, and the memory of himself as a small boy wondering what he could do to bear it if his mother ever died.

"Heart?" he said. "Does it seem your heart?"

She moved her head again. He stooped over her, his arm cradling her, not knowing whether to raise her or lower her from the propped-up pillows.

"Better," she whispered. "Wait."

He left her as she was. He took the glass of water on the table, held it to her lips, knew enormous relief that she could sip from it. He pressed her shoulder as if to reassure her that this was nothing, hearts were nothing, age and death and pain were nothing.

"Mom, are you all right? Is it easier?"

"It's passing." She looked at him. Regret was in her eyes, apology in her voice.

"I'll get a doctor." Doctor? What doctor? In all this city he didn't know the name of one doctor. "I'll phone Minify or Kathy and ask." He started for the door, stopped, turned. "Can I leave you? Are you really better?"

"Wait another minute." Her right hand fell away from her breast, and her breathing sounded more ordinary. The attack must be over. She had never been really sick in her life and now she was sick, struggling with this first onslaught of deep sickness. He sat on the edge of her bed. He would get a maid for the work; they would move where there was no flight of stairs to strain her.

"Now," she said. She moved, sat forward, and then carefully lay down again. "Angina," she said. "I'd never realized the pain was so sharp." As if it were a startling idea, he remembered his father had been a doctor; she and the girls and he himself knew far more than the usual layman about symptoms and disease.

"I'm going to phone Minify," he said. "He'll know a heart man."

"What time is it?"

"It doesn't matter." He went to the window, closed it, and then went to the fireplace. "Let's have a fire." He struck a match. The wood, dried and ready, crackled.

"It's nice," she said. "You didn't hear the first time I called."

"I thought I dreamed it."

He went out into the hall. Quietly he opened the door to Tom's bedroom. In the dim light from the doorway the slight mound under the blankets seemed motionless. He went to the bed and leaned down. Even and strong, the boy's breathing came up to him. For a moment he remained, listening.

CHAPTER FOUR

"WILL SHE—Dad, will she *die?*"
Phil turned, saw the stricken eyes watching him. He wanted to ease that look away, lie if necessary to replace it with confidence. But always he'd played it the other way, and he would now. Answers had to be answers.

"She'll die sometime, just the way you will or me or Aunt Belle or anybody. But maybe it won't be for a long time."

"Oh, Dad."

He put his hand on Tom's head, ruffling the dark hair.

"The doctor said she might be fine for years if she's careful. She's pretty old, and all the packing and unpacking tired her too much."

Tom moved closer. Phil pushed the lever of the toaster down. The ticking sounded very loud.

"Scram into some clothes, Tom." He gave him a shove toward the door as if they were roughhousing. "Then you can set the table. We can run this place between us, I bet."

"All right." He started to leave, then stopped. "Oh, gosh, Dad."

"It's scary, Tom, I know. I was scared last night, too. But we'll take care of her, and she might be just fine till *you're* grown up and married and have kids."

The shoulders relaxed. Phil heard him tiptoe down the hall. "Nothing to worry about." A dozen times Dr. Craigie's words had come back. With them had come again the four-in-the-morning silence of the sleeping city around the lighted bedroom, the knowledge that between her first calling out and her second, there'd been the time to dream, to wake, to ponder the sense of peace and continuing life, all unknowing that across a dark hall a dying had begun.

"People with hearts outlive everybody else, if they take care," Dr. Craigie had said. The quotation marks around "hearts" had been cheery, a comfortable dismissing. "It may prove to be what we call false angina instead of the true angina. She'll sleep well now, and you keep her in bed for a few days, and then we'll get her to the office and really see. Angina is actually a symptom rather than a disease—some circulatory deficiency, perhaps, or a kind of anemia of the cardiac—well, no use getting too technical this time of the night, Mr. Green, is there?"

No, don't get technical. Be calm, pleasant, willing to be routed out of bed, reassure the patient that the sensation of dissolution was merely part of the clinical picture, like the choking off of air, the sword in the arm.

"I never minimize in a sickroom," his own father had once told him. "I don't frighten, but I don't minimize."

Perhaps Craigie didn't either. John Minify had called him "one of the best in New York." Perhaps the suave voice was only a mannerism, acquired, too.

I must call Kathy, he thought, and break tonight.

The day sped remarkably. There was a curious ease to this kind of work, something like that week on Guad, with the mind nailed to the automatic directions for the next step. Life could be a simple thing of small actions on a string. Cook this, get the tray ready, take it in to her, straighten up this room, that room, phone the market, wash dishes, keep Tom quiet, go in now and talk to Mom, she's awake again, get Tom to bed, wash the dishes. No time for big thinking, no time for foreign policy, losing the peace, badgering your mind. Just do this, then do that. Easy.

It was the first day since he'd got the assignment that he had stayed clear of sifting and seeking. It was a little like

61

desertion, but for cause. At nine in the evening, with Tom gone to bed and no further chores to do, he still avoided the waiting morass. There was no use; he was too tired to think. He had telephoned Kathy to explain why he could not see her. She gave him quick sympathy and offered to find a maid. "At least a temporary one, Phil, what they call an 'accommodator.' "

"Thanks, Kathy, it's—well, thanks. I could phone my sister Belle in Detroit to come for a few days, but she gets me down too much."

He hung up, and began to pace the room. A, B, and C were still side by side as he had left them last night. He looked at the three books listlessly. His fatigue deepened. He had not gone back to sleep after Dr. Craigie had left, nor had he slept all day. It was just as well he'd been forced to desert.

I've got some sort of block on the whole damn thing, he thought. If I *could* dig and pry into some decent Jewish guy, I'd get it. Scalpels of the interviewer. The incision. The probing. You just can't do things to human beings that you do to a Manila envelope full of clips.

Today when Mom had said, "I'm nearly seventy after all, dear," he'd wanted to ask, "Are you afraid? Is it awful to know you might die soon?" There were questions no one could speak. He would know the answers to those two only when he himself was seventy. It was that way about every question that mattered most, about every question whose answer lay in the heart.

Yet he *had* got answers in the past.

"Every article you've done for us, Phil," Minify had said, "has a kind of human stuff in it. The right answers get in it somehow."

Sure. But he hadn't asked for them and pried for them. When he'd wanted to find out about a scared guy in a jalopy with his whole family behind him hoping for a living in California, he hadn't stood on Route 66 and signaled one of them to a stop so he could ask a lot of questions. He'd just bought himself some old clothes and a breaking-up car and taken Route 66 himself. He'd melted into the crowds moving from grove to grove, ranch to ranch, picking till he'd dropped. He lived in their camps, ate what they ate, told nobody what he was. He'd found the answers in his own guts, not somebody else's. He'd *been* an Okie.

And the mine series. What had he done to get research for it? Go and tap some poor grimy guy on the shoulder and begin to talk? No, he'd damn well gone to Scranton, got himself a job, gone down into the dark, slept in a bunk in a shack. He hadn't dug into a man's secret being. He'd *been* a miner.

"Christ!"

He banged his fist on his thigh. His breath seemed to suck back into his lungs. The startled flesh of his leg still felt the impact of the blow.

"Oh, God, I've got it. It's the way. It's the only way. I'll *be* Jewish. I'll just say—nobody knows me—I can just say it. I can live it myself. Six weeks, eight weeks, nine months —however long it takes. Christ, I've got it."

An elation roared through him. He had it, the idea, the lead, the angle. A dozen times he could have settled for some other idea, but each time he'd thrown it away, tossed it, profligate, stubborn. He'd known that there was somewhere, around some unexpected corner, a better idea, stronger, more real, the only. He'd stalked it, beseeched it, spied for it, waited, rushed, fought. And when he'd found it, this burst of recognition shouted out from him.

"I Was Jewish for Six Months." That was the title. It leaped at him. There was no doubt, no editing, no need to wonder. *That* would get read. *That* there was no passing

63

up. Six weeks it might be, ten, four months, nine, but apart from that one change, it was it.

Nobody but another writer could know how goddam good I feel, he thought. This was the reward, the strange compelling excitement of getting an idea. Resistance to the series was a vapor, remembered but gone. Nothing could stop this. It would be simple enough. He didn't look Jewish, sound Jewish, his name wasn't Jewish—well, Phil Green might be anything; he'd skip the "Schuyler" and not have to bother with assumed names. He checked on himself in his mind's eye—tall, lanky; sure, so was Dave, so were a hell of a lot of guys who were Jewish. He had no accent or mannerisms that were Jewish—neither did lots of Jews, and antisemitism was hitting at them just the same. His nose was straight—so was Dave's, so were a lot of other guys'. He had dark eyes, dark hair, a kind of sensitive look—"the *Toledo*," Kathy had said. Brother, it was a cinch.

In California, no, he couldn't get away with it anywhere on the Coast. Too many people knew him there; he'd keep running into them, spoiling things. But here—for once he was delighted with his shyness, with his inability to make friends. He'd meant to hang around the office and meet people, writers, editors, but he hadn't gone in even once. He didn't know a soul in this whole damn city, except Minify and Kathy—they'd see it, they'd be as excited as he, they'd keep his secret.

He couldn't wait for morning to tell her, to tell Minify. He'd phone them right now. No, this was no thing for phoning.

"Phil." From the bedroom, his mother's voice sounded strong, ordinary. He went in. She looked better; her color was good.

"You don't have to stay in," she said. "I feel all right."

64

"Don't crowd things." He looked at her inquiringly. "Feel like talking?"

She sat forward from the bunched pillows. "Of course."

"I've got it. I've got the way to get that series. This isn't like any of the other ideas I told you."

"It must be right," she said. "It always is when you're this sure."

"I'm going to be Jewish, that's all. Just tell people I am and see what happens. See what I feel like. For a while, for however long it takes to feel it."

"Oh, Phil. It's brilliant."

"It won't be the same, sure it won't, but it ought to come damn close." He was almost shouting but he couldn't decrease his voice. "It's worth a try—just put myself into every situation I can think of where being Jewish might mean something. It's so simple. See?"

"Of course. It's wonderful, really."

"*Then* I'll write stuff they'll read." He rubbed his thigh. He looked down at her as if she had done him a favor. She'd got it; he'd known she would.

"If we do have a maid tomorrow," he said, "I'll go tell Minify. And that girl I told you suggested the series, I want to tell her about it."

"Can't you invite them down here now? I'm not going to need anything."

He looked at his watch. It was only nine-twenty. Had all this thing happened to him in less than twenty minutes? After two weeks of sweating it out day and night? Where did ideas come from, anyway? This one had leaped at him when he'd been exhausted, AWOL from his search. Sometime he'd have to try to trace back every step he'd taken. Not now; he had no time now.

"That's an idea." He started for the door. "Will you

65

keep my secret if you meet any new people? It'd have to be without exceptions, you know, to work at all."

"If you're Jewish, I am too, I guess." She waved him out of the room.

He went to the telephone, dialed Kathy's number.

"It's me, Phil. I never thought you'd be in."

"How's your mother? You sound as if she were better."

"She is, lots. Kathy, you haven't a date?"

"I got stood up." She laughed. "I'm just wrapping presents. Why?"

"I can't leave her alone here. I'd be afraid to. But I've *got* it at last, and I thought, I mean, I'd give a lot to tell you about it."

"The angle? What *is* it?"

"You wouldn't—have you any feeling about getting in a cab and coming over for a bit?" It was awkward, saying it. He didn't care. "It's just I'd hate to go into it on a phone and I'm pretty set up."

"I'll be there in half an hour. What's your address again?"

He went to the kitchen for ice cubes. He went to his room, changed his shirt, looked in the mirror, and remembered he hadn't shaved till afternoon, anyway. Then he went into the bathroom and got out the electric razor he almost never used. Once over quickly would do it. He tried to phrase a beginning for her so she'd see what a gold mine of a thing this was. Nothing phrased.

His mind raced. There'd be snags, complications, problems. So all right. Every second made him surer that there'd be validity to what he'd find in himself as time went on. There was no rush. Minify had told him that two or three times. If it did take six weeks or nine months——

Nine months. He didn't usually think in platitudes, yet he kept coming back to this one. He knew he couldn't delay

66

the series for that length of time, rush or no rush. He was using it as a device to get at something arcane and buried. He put the razor down and lit a cigarette. He smoked half an inch of it before he noticed that the razor was still buzzing. He clicked it off and nodded to his image in the mirror.

Yes, that was it. That's what he'd been trying to articulate to himself. There *was* a rationale behind his idea, hesitant, unprovable, but there. Just as the embryo in the womb reproduced in nine months the whole evolutionary process of the race, maybe he could reproduce in himself in a short time the whole history of persecution——

"I wish she'd get here." He finished shaving and went in to his mother's room once more.

"Want anything?"

"No. I'm all right. Don't bring them in to meet me, will you? Some other time."

He shook his head. "I didn't call Minify. Just this Katherine Lacey."

"Is she nice?"

"Fine." Never had he made a confidant of her and he couldn't begin now. "There was some old gag about Michael Arlen," he suddenly said. "Wait a minute. How'd it go?" She saw him screw up his eyes and remembered him at ten or twelve, laboring over homework. "Oh, I've got it—train of thought is a wonderful gadget."

"What was it?"

"Somebody says to him, 'Mr. Arlen, *do* tell me, is it true that you're an Armenian? You sound *so* British.'" He was mimicking the accent of a British dowager. She laughed. "And Arlen answered, 'Would anyone *say* he was Armenian if he wasn't Armenian?'" She laughed again and he with her. "*We* would, wouldn't we?"

"If there was a point to it, and there is."

67

The bell rang.

Behind the closing door, she lay back, her book abandoned. If he could always be the way he is now, she thought. Direct, mobilized, all because he is fired with this idea. He doesn't even stop to think of the difficult parts—there will be many, there would have to be. He could change in five minutes from man of thought to man of action. She had seen him do it when he decided to join the Marine Corps. He signed for OCS and at once he was the officer. The things ahead he ignored, the hardships, the dangers. The inevitable problems of the interrupted career, the separation from Tommy, he had shoved off for future considering. He was that way now—on an island of rock after muddy floundering.

Tom. He hadn't even thought yet whether he'd have to tell Tom about it or not, and that if he did, a child would surely find it impossible to follow or understand. It could start a confusion that might go pretty deep. She sighed. Phil would find the way to handle it, if it came, as he had always found the way for the boy's problems.

"It's nice to have a mommy, isn't it, Daddy?" Three years ago that was, possibly four, with the high voice of a little boy asking, and the solemn eyes looking up at Phil. "Tip and Sky have a mommy."

"Sure it is. It's swell."

"*I* haven't got a mommy. *Why* haven't I got a mommy?"

"She died when you were so little you couldn't even walk or talk. Imagine not even knowing how to walk or talk."

"*Me?*"

"Yep. But anyway, you've got me and Gram, and that's a lot." He had lifted Tom to his lap. "And someday I might marry again and you might have a second mother. Would you like that?" The tone so ordinary, as if he were asking

68

whether he'd like a new train, another picture book. From time to time the small conversation would happen again, taking a new form as Tom got older. Always Phil met it in that same key. Always he used it to enlist Tom's support, long before the event, signing up an ally in plenty of time. If it were to happen, it would hold no shock of surprise for Tom.

Voices came up from the stair well. Phil must have gone down to open the door himself. No words came to her, just the two voices. A woman's voice and Phil's. That was good to hear again. It would be good to see Phil married again before she died.

"Oh, Phil, it's so attractive. All those books."

"It's not done yet. Those packages are pictures." He was startled at how different having her in his house was from his being in hers. She was looking around, taking her coat off, avoiding a direct look at him.

"I wish I had a fireplace that works. Mine's only a fake one."

"I lit it just before you got here."

She sat in the chair close to the fire, and he busied himself with drinks. The moment he had opened the big door downstairs and had seen her waiting there, trying the knob to see if it would turn, physical awareness of her had swooped back into him. The impatience to tell her his idea for the series, to blurt it out and see her interest and approval, seemed not half as big a thing as just finding her beyond the glass-paned door, letting her pass in front of him to go upstairs.

"What is it, Phil? Tell me fast. The drinks'll keep."

"I will in a minute." He put the glass down, looked toward the rear of the house. "I'll just check about——" He motioned with his head and walked out of the room.

"I think I've got the accommodator for you," she called after him.

She could hear his footsteps on bare flooring. Then his voice, "All fixed?" and his mother's answer, "Of course. I'll call if I need anything." He came back and this time he closed the living-room door behind him. Without moving her lips, she felt as if she were smiling. He had gone out just to be able to close the door without making a point of it. She waited for him to say something.

She had thought about him a great deal. She'd even told Jane about him, casually, but she'd done it. She'd never told Jane about anybody else since Bill, at least not after just two evenings. Jane had said at once, "Married?" and she'd answered, "Oh, cut it." But she'd added, "He's a widower with a child and a mother." They'd both made a face at the last word. Then she'd changed the subject.

Now she sat here in this delightful room, alone with him, yet knowing that his mother and his son were in the house too, so that there was none of the raffish air of visiting a man's apartment. She took the drink Phil gave her.

"You're not telling it to me," she said.

"Funny. I thought I'd spit it out the minute you got here."

"You sounded awfully excited."

"I am. There'll be stumbling blocks and holes, and I just don't give a damn. I'll come to them when I get to them."

"That's the only way to do anything worth doing, I guess."

Suddenly from the side of her chair where he'd been standing, he was bending down over her. She was wearing the same dress she'd worn at the Minifys' that first night. Her throat stretched long as she put her head back to look up.

He kissed her hair and then her mouth. He was in the

70

wrong position; it was a half kiss. He twisted her shoulder and kissed her lips as if he had just fought his way to her. She pushed back from him and stood up.

For one second he looked at her. Then he took her into his arms. He heard her breath catch; he felt the first resistance go slack. He kissed her, and this time she kissed him.

"Kathy, this *is* something. It's—for me, it's——"

"I know."

He kissed her again. Everything in the world was gone except this. He couldn't talk, explain, ask, question. Work, ideas, the future, nothing counted.

"Phil, wait now."

He let his arms drop. He looked at her. Then he felt easy again. She was happy. Her eyes shone. Her breasts rose and fell as she breathed hard. She wasn't going to warn him, preach at him, reveal some secret that meant there was nothing possible.

"I have to just wait," she said. "You go away and let me sit here a minute."

He crossed to the chair where he'd set his own drink down. Again, an elation was in him, but not of triumph as the other had been, only of hope. He was shaken by it, tender with it. He wanted to thank her, for he knew not what. He wanted to talk to her, to kiss her again, to tell her of Betty and not of Betty's death alone. He just sat, and coursing through him, like a drug to heal, ran the hoping.

CHAPTER FIVE

MINIFY LOOKED UP, ready to be pleased. On his desk two Christmas packages, stiff with glassy red bows, caught the morning sunlight. A dozen letters, their engraved tops concealed by the addressed envelopes slipped over their edges, lay before him. He shoved them back. On the side of the desk the advance issue of *Smith's*, stamped MAKE-READY, caught his eye. He shoved that aside, too.

"Must be good," he said. "You sounded top of the world on the phone."

"Yeah." Phil's voice was quiet. Minify was no man to "sell" an idea to; you just told him about it. "Remember I said I'd fall on my face before I'd put Professor Lieberman or anybody else through a quiz about this?" He saw Minify nod. "I guess this goes back to that reluctance. And that sense that I'd have to go at it from *inside*."

Minify's whole attention was on him.

"Anyway, I got—hell, let me just give you the title for the series." He waited while Minify clicked up a switch to the interoffice communicator and said, "No calls, Mary." When the switch went down again, Phil said, without emphasis, "I was Jewish for three months."

Minify was reaching for a cigarette. His hand stopped on the way to the package.

"Christ, Phil." He hitched himself forward in his chair.

"Or six weeks or however long, till I get the feel of it." He saw Minify's lips repeating the title, testing it; saw his eyes go to the cover of the make-ready, visualizing it there.

"It's a hell of a stunt, Phil."

"Usually these 'I' titles give me a pain. But there's such a wallop to this one." Minify nodded. "It won't be just the same," Phil added, "but some of it will."

Again Minify nodded. He looked at Phil thoughtfully. "I knew you'd get the series going somehow, in spite of the sticky start. I didn't think—but who'd ever think of *this?* Can you get away with it?"

"If you and Mrs. Minify and Kathy won't give me away. I haven't told Kathy yet, but I bet——"

Minify took over. For unbroken stretches he explored the possibilities, a fever of planning in him. Then he fell silent, to listen to Phil. For half an hour they mapped out a campaign to follow, always allowing for the improvising Phil would have to do as he went along. Clubs, resorts, apartment leases, social life. Interviews for jobs, applications to medical schools. Perhaps some trips to "trouble spots" that came into the news. Getting to know people of all types in New York. "That'll be the toughest part for me," Phil remarked. "I'm not gregarious by nature. But O.K." And when at last both of them were skimmed clean of their top ideas, Phil stretched. He felt good.

"There won't be one bloody thing that'll be news about clubs and jobs and hotels," he said. "I might chuck all that stuff except for the subjective reactions."

"Any way you want. When do you start?"

"What's the matter with now? I told you I wanted to work in the office for a while—I'll get it going right here."

Minify reached toward the buzzer but drew back without touching it. "Remember you said nobody'd read the goddam things?"

"They'll read this."

"Damn right they will."

They grinned at each other, and Phil said, "Well, I'll report progress once in a while."

73

Minify said, "Any time," and tapped the buzzer. Mary Cresson, his middle-aged secretary who had followed him from job to job, came in, her book and pencil ready.

"Mary, Mr. Green's going to work inside a couple of weeks. Maybe more. Get Jordan to fix him up, will you?"

"Mr. Kingland's office is empty."

"Fine."

"I'll go along with you," Phil said.

But outside the door, he heard, "Hey, Phil," and went back again. John had pulled back the sheaf of letters and had his pen ready for signing them.

"Dig up a working title, will you?" he said. "For the file we keep on Futures."

"Right."

"We won't tell the real one to anybody at all; it'd give your show away around here."

"What about just scheduling it as 'Antisemitism in the U. S.'?"

John jotted it down. "And what about help? Secretary for all the letters and phone calls on it?"

"I hadn't thought. I've never had help."

"Might as well have a girl assigned, part-time probably. Somebody good. She'd have to know too, wouldn't she?"

"Why?" They each thought about it. "Can't see why even she should know a damn thing about it. Suppose I were really Jewish and you'd given me this assignment? What difference would it make to her or anybody?"

"Sure. You're right." Again he tapped the buzzer. "Mary, check secretarial, would you, and assign a smart girl to Mr. Green for as much time as he'll need?"

"Yes, Mr. Minify."

"No hurry about it," Phil said. "I always make a lot of notes first."

But when he went to the office that was to be his, he made

74

no effort to get started on his notes. It was a pleasant, two-windowed room, facing south. The austere shaft of the RCA Building in Rockefeller Center was right in front of him, a little to the left. Against the gray of the winter sky, it stood like some monolith, unravageable. He stayed at the window, looking at it, and then sat down at his desk.

From beyond the partition came guffaws of sudden laughter. "Somebody's told a dirty story," he decided, and smiled, too. Next door was the art department, Miss Cresson had told him. That meant loud discussions, many visitors, arguments. He knew. But when he was working well, noise never bothered him.

He tried the typewriter. He called an office boy and sent for stationery, pencils, ink, clips, a jar of rubber cement, and a pair of long shears.

"I'm one of those guys that paste in added paragraphs or rewrites," he explained to the surprised face. "Scotch tape'll do if there's no cement."

But after the supplies had come, he still made no motion to begin work. Lazily he gave himself over to remembering last night. For two hours more he and Kathy had talked of themselves, in the halting half-openness that was all the openness possible during beginnings. No matter how direct and free you wished to make every sentence, and they had each wished it, there were all the blocks that kept standing up, barricades to full revelation. Once, at the fireplace with his back half turned to her, he'd managed to get out one of the things that pressed hardest to be said.

"I'm one of those solemn guys, I guess. You know—always fine to get in the hay, but a wife's what I'm really hoping for sometime."

And from behind him, uncertain, troubled, she'd answered, "Anybody does. A wife, or a husband. If it turns out that way."

75

He'd never heard that note in her voice. She'd always seemed so unruffled and sure, the way she had when she'd hit the wrong keys at the piano. But last night, after she'd said that, he'd wondered whether there weren't sad dark places that she stumbled through in her mind as there were in his.

"Any woman would rather be married," she'd gone on, "but if it's been a mistake once, you're afraid."

He'd taken her into his arms then, just holding her. She said nothing, nor did he. Yet each of them—he had felt it—each, in a secret and separate cave of emotion, was considering the words, married, wife, husband. He had kissed her again, and suddenly, this time, something was promised between them. He had become sure, violently sure, that the moment would come when they'd be in bed together. Not yet. Not for a while. But sometime.

Remembering now, he shoved his chair back from the desk and went back to the window. It had just begun to snow. There was no wind, and these first flakes floated on the tranquil air. Delight stirred in him, memory of the glee he'd always felt with the first snow as a child in Minnesota. The long, impatient wait was at last rewarded—the sled ready on the back porch could at last be used. There was always a kind of victory to it. One had always waited so long.

"I've waited so long."

He was seeing her again tonight. He never *had* got around to telling her what he was going to do. Two or three times she'd tried to bring him back to the series, but he couldn't make the transition to the impersonal world of ideas. That first talking to each other on the level of feeling and not of biography was too engrossing. That first realizing that she wanted him to kiss her, as he wanted her, was too heady. He'd been afraid to shift their mood. "This isn't the time to talk about work," he'd said. "I'll save it for tomorrow."

76

The office door opened. Mary Cresson put her head in.

"Mr. Minify wondered if you'd like to have luncheon with him and Frank Tingler and Bert McAnny?"

"Yes, sure." He glanced at his watch. "Who's Bert McAnny?" Tingler was fiction editor, he knew from the masthead.

"Assistant to Bill Jayson, the art editor. He'd only been here a while before he got drafted, but they gave him his old job back, anyway. About one, then."

This would be the start. This would be the chance to get it across—how, he didn't know. You didn't blurt it out; it had to come up. If it didn't come up, you made it come up. There'd be something that would lead into it. His heart began to pound as if he were going into an unaccustomed place where there was sure to be danger. But his mind felt ready and impatient.

Anne Dettrey was at their table, too. She was woman's editor, though there were no recipe and fashion departments in the magazine. Her province was nonfiction of special interest to women readers, and Phil knew, though he didn't remember how he knew, that she was one of the top editors on the staff. As John had come by with the two men, he'd said, "I've asked Anne Dettrey to come along, Phil," and there'd been a blur of how-do-you-do's all round, as Minify did introductions.

"Phil?" she'd said. "I thought it was Schuyler Green."

"That's my writing name."

Through the shoptalk of the first part of the meal, he'd thought, That's the way you do it. Lie when you have to, but for the most part, it'll be as much what you leave out as what you put in. There was no lie in leaving out the explanation about "Schuyler." Just let them assume he'd made up a pseudonym cold.

She was a woman about his own age, this Anne Dettrey. She talked well, turning the kind of phrases you found in slick fiction and never heard in real speech, yet so effortlessly that she seemed natural always. She had a rather long, clearly boned face, and she was almost as tall as he was. Her reddish hair and brown eyes compelled the attention, though you'd never call her pretty. Because they'd all plunged, even as they were walking over to the restaurant, into some question about the issue going to press next week, he'd had time to orient himself to all of them.

The short, pale man was Tingler. He was middle-aged and ugly, with thick-lensed glasses over protruding eyes that probably meant hyperthyroid. His voice was calm always, almost bored, even when the others were pitched up on some question or other. He was a competent one, clearly. McAnny was a youngster, not out of his twenties. Phil saw the discharge button in his lapel. He'd never worn his own, or the ribbon. But Bert McAnny, with his small features and light voice, would wear his for a long time. There was too much awe in him as he listened to Minify's words. He was flushing now as he asked the editor about "the time you decided to change *Smith's* into a liberal magazine."

"It wasn't that way at all, Bert. I didn't." Minify smiled, but above his genial mouth the gray eyes were thoughtful. "Fact is, when they offered me this job as editor in chief, I said if they were out to run a liberal magazine, quote, quote, I wasn't their man."

"You?"

The sharp inflection from Phil and McAnny pleased Minify. Anne and Frank Tingler showed no surprise. They'd been on the staff since John had taken over. Phil had read about how he'd gone to *Smith's*. Way back, he'd been one of the best reporters on the old *World,* in the days when a by-line was a badge and not just an automatic gadget.

78

After the *World* had folded, he'd knocked about on other papers without finding himself right on any of them. He'd gone abroad, free-lanced foreign stuff for magazines, and returned, surprisingly enough, to become managing editor of one of the folksier women's magazines. But he'd increased its circulation from the first year. When *Smith's*, along with three other magazines, had changed ownership in 1940, Minify had become editor in chief. In a year, *Smith's* circulation jumped thirty per cent; in another, thirty more. The three other magazines had been abandoned, their paper allotments going into this one weekly. By now its circulation was more than double what it had been when he'd taken the reins.

"Sure, I did," Minify went on. "You don't get anywhere with *that* for a platform."

"How do you mean?" McAnny asked.

"Ever hear of anybody calling a bunch of guys together and saying, 'Let's run a reactionary magazine'?" He laughed. "It's never like that—they get together to run a *successful* magazine. If they're mostly reactionary themselves, it turns out reactionary. Same thing the other way around."

"I never thought of it that way," McAnny said.

"I took this job with one idea—to make a go of it. It's been a go because the readers like our stories and serials and pictures and articles. It's true I don't hire reactionary guys—I'd just fight with them all the time if I did. So with the staff we've got, we generally manage to be on the liberal side. But that's all the trick there is to it—not a conscious line you take."

"What about your decision to run a series like the one I'm starting?" Phil said. He did it deliberately. He couldn't let this whole luncheon go by without managing to take his first step.

"What're you doing, Mr. Green?" That was Anne Dettrey, but the others had turned to him also.

"Good case in point," Minify answered for him. "Phil's going to do a series on antisemitism. I didn't assign it because it's the 'liberal thing' to do. I just think it'll get read, start a stink, make talk."

Closer, Phil thought. When the opening did come, how would he say it? How had he put it last night? He couldn't remember. In his mind he rehearsed phrases. "I'm a Jew." Would that be the natural way? "I'm Jewish." That was better. "I'm a Jew. I'm Jewish."

"Got any special slant on it yet?" Tingler asked, turning to him.

"Yeah. But I'm never any good talking about a thing till it's written." Tension stood in his words, in spite of his desire to seem matter-of-fact.

"You sound as if you had something pretty hot," Anne said.

"I *feel* pretty hot over it," he said. He glanced at her. Here it was. "And I don't think the heat has anything to do with my being Jewish."

"Of course it hasn't," she said. "When'll they run?"

"Oh, Phil's just started," Minify put in. "Probably not before summer." He sounded comfortable. "I'm afraid it'll be just as timely then." They all made sounds or gestures of agreement, and the talk went off again to the troublesome next issue.

Phil heard none of it. "It's done; I'm in," he told himself. The odd excitement in him when the moment came had been read as high interest in the series itself; that it had to do with anything more personal than that had been apparent to nobody. Of that he was sure. Of course, this was a special crowd; he'd had no hostility to contend with. Nobody had shown surprise; nobody had changed expression; they didn't give a damn. But it was the first hurdle, anyway, a line of demarcation crossed. He'd said it and he was launched. Like a debutante, he thought, and smiled to himself.

He wasn't due for another half-hour, but Kathy was dressed and ready. She went to the piano, played a few measures, and then stood up. From the small kitchen where Claudia was getting dinner came the teasing smell of roasting beef. He didn't know yet that they would have dinner there. He would be pleased.

The room was too warm. She crossed to the window and threw it wide open. At once snow began to sift over the sill. It had been snowing all day, and the radio said there'd be twelve inches before morning. It felt right to have it snow a week before Christmas. Everything felt right these days.

Last night she'd come home from Phil's and gone straight to bed. She'd propped both pillows behind her as if she were going to read, but she'd never opened a book. She'd lain there, smoking and thinking until past two, just letting the minutes stream by. If ever there was a time, she'd thought lazily, almost cozily, when you're glad you're a woman, it's this first moment of knowing that a man you're drawn to is falling in love with you. That's when you're completely, uncomplicatedly glad you are. None of the vague resentment that "it's a man's world" held its shape against the good solvent of that first knowing. Suddenly it was an unarguable blessed thing to be a woman, and you felt a kind of indebtedness to the man who made you feel so.

All day she'd felt that, and now, waiting for him to get there, she still did. He'd talked of marriage, obliquely, squeezing the words out. She wanted to marry again. She'd never be fully happy without it.

Perhaps "being conventional" had something to do with it. Once Uncle John had teased her because she'd said she'd never go to a theater alone at night—the vision of herself alone in the lobby for a smoke during intermission made her squirm.

"Give up smoking," he'd said, and then, "Vassar and Bill between them didn't have any luck making you conservative, Kathy; they did better about making you conventional."

"Because I won't behave just like a man?" She'd felt resentful. "A man can drop into a bar alone and have a drink and get talking to somebody and go have dinner with him— you think I'm conventional because I can't?"

"Don't get so emphatic. I didn't mean much."

But he'd been partly right. She just didn't feel right on her own, and maybe that was being conventional about "the things a woman can't do." It was trivial, probably a throwback to the nagging envy in childhood about being a boy instead of "just a girl." Trivial or no, it was there.

She wound her watch. It was seven. She was waiting dinner for a man again and found it sweet to be doing it, and if that made her a conventional fool, why, let it. The bell rang.

He was taking off galoshes in the outside hall, and she waited till he straightened up. When he came in, she put her hand out, and he took it in both of his and then released it quickly. "You're on the dot again," she said.

"Should I be fashionably late?" He laughed as he shook snow off his coat. "The other time you said that and I said that and then I was afraid you'd think I was coy or always mugging or something." His voice was easier than she'd ever heard it, his manner surer. She watched him fold his coat and put it on a chair, his hat on top of it. He sniffed at the homely smell of cooking and looked about him. She saw him catch sight of the table, laid and waiting in one corner of the living room. His whole mood seemed suddenly to sparkle.

82

"You don't mean here?" When she nodded, he made a sound of surprise and pleasure.

"So we can talk." She was delighted she'd thought of it. She motioned him to the sofa and went to the bar table. "This time I'm not going to let you get going on anything else. I've tried all day to guess what it could be."

"Have you really?"

"I kept thinking, suppose I were him, and had to find an idea for this, what would *I* do?" She came back with two Martinis, walking gingerly because she'd poured them too full.

He waited, unwilling to say anything. He wanted her to go on, to offer even more testimony that his problems mattered to her. He took the glass and leaned forward to sip it before he brought it closer. She sat on the sofa beside him, in her eyes an eagerness that was all the testimony anybody could want.

"And what *would* you do?"

She wrinkled her nose and shook her head. "I'm just no good at ideas. The ones you told me seemed swell, but you threw them out and kept on hunting."

"You'll see why now." He hitched himself around. He wanted to see her face change as Minify's had. For another moment he said nothing. "I'm going to tell everybody I'm Jewish, that's all."

"Jewish? But you're not, Phil, are you?" Instantly she added, "It wouldn't make any difference, of course."

But something had appeared in her eyes.

"You said, 'I'm going to tell'—as if you hadn't *before* but would now," she went on, "so I just wondered. Not that it'd matter to *me*, one way or the other."

"You said that before." He put his drink down.

"Well, *are* you, Phil?"

He almost said, "You know I'm not," but it choked back.

83

Some veil of a thing *had* shown in her eyes. He'd been watching her face every minute, greedy for the quick approval that would show there. This had been quick, but different. She wanted him not to be Jewish. She knew he was not, knew that if he were, he'd never have concealed it. But she wanted to hear him say so right out.

"Oh, this is nonsense," she said briskly. "I know perfectly well you're not Jewish and I wouldn't care if you were. It's just interesting."

He reached for a cigarette. Of course she wouldn't care, any more than he would. Or would she? If he said now, "I really am Jewish"? He'd be the same guy, the same face, the same voice, manner, tweed suit, same eyes, nose, body, but the word "Jewish" would have been said and he'd be different in her mind. In that very same vessel that contained him there'd be a something to "not-care" about.

"Why, Phil," she said slowly, "you're annoyed." She put her drink down also. "You haven't said anything."

"I'm not annoyed. I'm just thinking."

"Don't be so serious about it—you must know where *I* stand."

"I do, Kathy."

"It's just that it caught me off balance. You know, not knowing much about you because you kept making *me* talk about my childhood. So for a second there——" She laughed and shook her head. "Not very bright on the uptake."

He smiled. He felt heavy, flattened out. With her last sentence, the creamy smooth tone had come back. The laugh was the laugh he'd heard that first night. His hand, listless on the arm of the sofa, dropped over the side. Without knowing that he did it, he felt his thumb and forefinger tip together, out of sight, making a circle.

"But anyway, you don't like my angle," he said. "Do you?"

84

"Oh, I do. It's——" She broke off. Now she reached for a cigarette, and he leaned toward her to light it. Her hair shone. He heard her breathe. Physical knowledge of her moved through him. But there was a sadness to it he couldn't name.

"It's what?"

"Oh, Phil, I just think it'll mix everybody up. People won't know *what* you are."

"After I'm through, they'll——" He couldn't say it. A remarkable thing had happened. Something had seized him that he couldn't argue with. It had started to happen with her first question. Now he knew suddenly what it was. This heavy strange thing in him was what you felt when you'd been insulted. He felt insulted. If he were really a Jew, this is what he'd feel. He was having his first lesson. With Kathy, he'd stumbled into his first lesson at feeling bruised and unwilling to say the placating thing, the reassuring thing. She had reminded him that there was something important about knowing that you were *not* a Jew or were a Jew, no matter what your face or voice or manners or whole being. A slow soreness had been spreading through him. He'd be damned if he'd let her see it. But at last he knew what it was.

"They'll know afterwards that you'd just been assuming a pose?" she finished for him. "Of course they will. And even so, it'll keep cropping up."

"All right. Let it."

His words were calm. No, they were calmly spoken, but the answer was brusque. That much he could not help. Kathy? The Kathy who'd thought up the whole series? She wanted to fight the thing, sure. She wanted *Smith's* to use its three-million circulation to yell and scream and take sides and fight. That's the way she'd put it that night. But she

85

didn't like the idea of anybody misunderstanding anything about *him*.

He saw a perplexity begin in her face. She was frowning. She was thinking, away somewhere from where they were, thinking to herself. Then the moment was over. She made a quick scissoring with both her hands, slashing the last few minutes out of time.

"I'm out of my head," she said firmly. " 'Let it' is right. Who cares? I was just being too practical about things." She smiled directly at him. "It's a *grand* idea. Only, last night you said there'd be pitfalls, and I guess I got looking for those right off."

His spirits rose. This quick change bewildered him, but he felt relieved, at least enough to get by on for now. The mind plays funny tricks—look at his own "slow take" on Belle's Jew-us-down. He told Kathy about it, and she said, "Those nasty propaganda phrases." Again he was reassured. He had been a fool to toss his scheme at her without any windup. You could do things like that with an editor, but with her he'd have done better to explain first, lead her along to make her see the inevitability of it.

"There'll *be* nasty things," he said. "But after all, the whole point is to find out for myself."

"How long will it take, do you think?" He shrugged, and her shoulders imitated his, as if to agree that nobody could ever predict how long anything important would take.

"You and the Minifys will have to promise not to give away my act," he said. She nodded, and he said, "But really. No exceptions for anything. O.K.?"

"O.K." She made a child's cross-my-heart. "What about the people at *Smith's*? Won't they talk?"

"At—but they're not in on it. Only John."

"*They* think you're Jewish?" She sounded unbelieving.

86

"I don't think you understand, Kathy. If this is going to work—maybe it won't—but the only chance is to go whole hog at it." Carefully he explained about having met none of the staff until today, knowing nobody in the East; he gave a brief account of the luncheon and the start he'd made. "It's got to run right through everything," he ended.

"Why, of course. I hadn't really seen it before."

She seemed penitent, and guilt rose obscurely in him. He demanded too much always. He judged too quickly. "I got riled at you before," he said. "I thought for a minute that if I *were* Jewish——" At her quick laugh he broke off. He felt a fool.

"Now, Phil, you're not calling me An Anti Semite?" She made three round words of it.

"Good Lord, no."

There was a pause. They each leaned forward to pick up their neglected glasses. The silence expanded. It's no good analyzing *every* reaction, he thought. Was his feeling a fool the right reaction? Or his being riled? Save it, quit it, he ordered himself. Dope it later, when you can think.

"My trouble is," he said to her, "I'm always too damn apt to weigh and measure and wonder and ponder everything till I don't know where I stand."

"I'm not," she said. Her voice was soft. "Not often. But last night I did that, too. I didn't get to sleep till nearly three."

"Kathy."

He wanted to take her into his arms. We'll work things out, he thought. If there's anything real to work out, we'll work it out. Somewhere behind him a swinging door swished.

"Dinner," she said. "Let's finish these at the table."

The soreness of disappointment wouldn't leave her. The

moment the front door had closed on him, she'd wanted to call him back, find the one more thing to say that would change the feel of the evening.

It wasn't even eleven. She went about the living room, emptying ash trays, tidying up the bar table. Claudia had missed his dinner napkin; it was still on the end table where he'd carried it with him when they'd gone over to the sofa for coffee. She took up the yellow square. "KLP," the monogram said fatly. She tossed it on the coffee tray and carried both into the small kitchen. Claudia was always in such a rush to escape, it had become an unwritten agreement between them that she need not bother with the belated coffee things. Kathy washed the small cups and the slivers of spoons. "KLP" twined on their fiddle-shaped handles. All fancy and twisted, she thought.

She dried the things and put them away. The soreness persisted. The evening had balled up. *She'd* balled it up by that extraordinary reluctance she'd felt about his idea. Remembering that first instant after his announcement, she felt fidgety. What *had* happened to her? She didn't like it.

"It's a brilliant notion, Phil. It'll make a stunning series. You'll be famous." Twice she'd said that, once during dinner and once later on. He'd smiled each time, and each time she'd thought that the snarl was straightening out. But the next moment he'd talked about something else, and the discomfort remained in her.

What *had* hit her? From where had it come?

She sighed. The subterranean paths that twined through human impulses and motives always eluded you if you tried to follow them. At least for her they did. There was no use to will herself to the task. She never had a road map. She always got lost.

It really was a good idea; she knew it in the same blind way she knew when a play had a good plot, or a novel a strong sense of character and movement. She should have said so at once, kept to herself the instant visions of the difficulties he'd get into, praised him wholly. That's what a man needed from a woman. Belief, encouragement, never skepticism, no matter how truly skepticism might be justified. She'd failed him by reacting too quickly.

That's all it was.

Bill wouldn't have minded; he wouldn't even have noticed anything that subtle. Phil was neurotic, she supposed, easily thrown off key, easily let down. But the Bills weren't for her, and Phil was. She needed to learn him a little more to know where lay the craters and bogs of his intricate personality and be quicker about stepping around them. It was so easy to hurt a man like Phil. Yet the sensitive mind was his appeal, and the delight she felt when his eyes went easy and happy was her reward.

She wished he'd not had to leave just then. The accommodator she'd sent him, Emma, was the timetable kind who would march off at eleven, heart patient or no, so he had no choice. But perhaps another hour would have sloughed off their heaviness. He hadn't even tried to kiss her the whole stilted evening. And the quiet look had been on him.

Disconsolate, she turned out the lights and went into her room. As she undressed, dissatisfaction wormed anew through her.

"I'm getting neurotic myself." She'd blundered with him over his idea, so what? She'd said the wrong things, so what? He knew a moment later she was sorry—she'd said perfectly openly she'd been off her head. You blunder, you apologize—that ought to be all there was to it. Instead that good feeling that everything was right had burst like a bubble blown against slate.

CHAPTER SIX

"WE ARE BORN IN INNOCENCE." The phrase was in him, a cluster of words in his mind, a challenge in his blood. A hundred times in the next days it spoke to him. Where it had come from, what it was trying to tell him, he did not know. It was just there, one measure of a stately music.

"We are born in innocence."

Like a phrase written in sleep, laden with an import the dreaming mind strains to hold past the moment of waking, it touched the threshold of his understanding again and again, only to retreat before he could welcome the message he felt it brought. It had the commanding significance of the final spinning sentence he had pursued just before surrender to the anesthetic in the base hospital. And, as then, he felt enormous with its revelation, comforted that he had found for himself some magic litany that explained essence and truth and being.

But though he could this time remember the words, as words, he could not grasp or pin down the implication that hung mistily over them. At Kathy's that night, they had spoken themselves within him, while he looked at her across the table, while he half listened to something she was saying about Central Park under the first good snow. And since then they had sounded their grave cadence through all his changing moods.

Alone now, on Christmas afternoon, he felt them as much in the room with him as the lights on the tree and the blurred voices from the kitchen.

We are born in innocence. In blood and water and pain we are born, but in an unstained purity of heart. Wizened, crushed, our fogged eyes blinded by new light, our outraged skins shocked by a thirty-degree drop in the envelope about us—still we are born a good vessel, innocent of corruption.

Corruption comes later. The first fear is a corruption, the first reaching for something that defies us. The first nuance of difference, the first need to feel better than the different one, more loved, stronger, richer, more blessed— these are corruptions. One by one they pour their drops into the vessel, and the layer forms, seedbed of the future life.

His mother came in, moving slowly as if to test out the returned ease of her body. In her eyes there still was the look of contentment with which she'd watched Tom's bright delight of the Christmas morning.

She said, "You're not staying in because of me, Phil?"

"I haven't a date. I know you're all right. Craigie'll be surprised tomorrow."

She nodded, belligerently, as if she'd indeed show Dr. Craigie and his spying electrocardiograph their proper places. The bell rang, and she moved to the buzzer. Phil went out into the hall.

"Telegram," he said a moment later. "Funny. The girls——" He signed, tore it open. "Dave." He read the brief message. "Got my letter, and he's to start any minute and would like a stopover. Boy, that'll be good, to see Dave."

She was as pleased as he. They discussed the advisability of giving him Tom's room and decided against it. "Dave can have mine, and I'll sleep on the sofa," Phil said. "That way, if we stay up all night chewing the fat, the kid won't be in the way."

The spell was broken. When she left the room, he went

back to the five words. But now they were just words, with no promise of secret meaning.

"Probably had something to do with Christmas coming and the new snow in the park and the new thing I was starting, like getting born again." But why the melancholy that went with them?

"Dad, say, Dad. *Please.*" Tom's shout came as imperious as though the house were on fire. Phil didn't move.

"What's up?"

"It won't *work.* I've got the caps in it, and it just *won't.* Oh, the damn thing's haywire."

"Let's have a look at it." He smiled. Tom's damns and hells were a fine business, traceable to his own liberal use of them. Maybe he was overcasual about the way he ignored them in the kid. He looked up. Tom was standing rigid, just inside the door. From his dejected right hand, the cap pistol dangled. That morning when he'd seen it, he'd gone into a delirium over it. "Iron, Dad," he'd shouted. "Not wooden. *Feel* it; it's cold."

Now he stood waiting for Phil to say something.

"What am I?" he demanded. For the moment the crisis of the gun was forgotten.

Phil looked at him. Across the bridge of his nose, he wore a green scarf, folded into a triangle. Low on his skinny hips hung a studded belt and holster. His corduroy "longies" which the eights and nines wore these days were tucked into his still-new galoshes. Besides the pistol, he had a pearl-handled revolver in the holster and its twin in the belt of his pants. Phil stared at him judiciously.

"You're a—let's see. A sheriff."

"Oh, *Dad.*" (Disgust.)

"A horse rustler."

"No."

"A cowboy in Arizona."

"Dad, you're nuts."

"Well, then." Enough of this game. There never had been the slightest doubt what he was, but the rules of childhood made an immediate guess unthinkable. "Then you're an outlaw, a bandit outlaw."

"Yes, that's it, yessir that's just it." Above the green fold of silk, his eyes gleamed. Slyly he went behind the wing chair, in a movement which brought only the word "skulking" to Phil's mind, and aimed the cap pistol at his father. Then, suddenly, he remembered, and tragedy stood gaunt upon him. "It won't work. The caps stick."

Phil took the pistol and pried apart the two halves of the butt. Kathy had sent it. It had arrived last night, and nothing about the package showed that it was from her. This morning, when Tom had ripped off the bright wrappings, the card had fallen to the floor, ignored by the instantly inflamed child. Mrs. Green had picked it up, glanced at it, and handed it to Phil.

"What a nice thing," she'd said.

"Merry Christmas from Katherine Lacey—just because I've heard a lot about you." He'd read it with a crazy leap of pleasure.

She didn't do it just to please me, he thought again as he worked on the gun. She wants him to like her, too. She needn't have sent any Christmas gift at all to a child she doesn't know, but she did. She went into those shoving crowds in the stores and searched and rejected and kept on and finally found this. She took it home and fussed with the big bow herself and dropped it off here herself.

"Why won't the dingus revolve, Dad?"

"Trying to see."

The creaky, balky misunderstanding which had stood between them before dinner that night had been nothing another man would have noticed. All through dinner he had

93

belabored himself to forget it. When she'd come back to the plan later on, she'd been enthusiastic over it, happy with it.

Twice she had praised it, and twice he had felt only that this was afterthought. He had had the wit to say nothing further of the small doubt which stubbornly nibbled at him. He had excoriated his need for approval as "an infantilism" and ended by feeling clumsy about everything he did. And when he'd *had* to leave he had gone reluctantly, as one does when things still need fixing up.

But the next day at the office, he'd regained all his confidence. About himself, about Kathy, about the series. The girl who'd been assigned to him, Miss Wales, was intelligent, quick, interested. She was going to be a fine help on those parts of the research that could be done by mail and telephone. All day he'd felt integrated and composed. And at four he'd telephoned.

"There, Dad, the little hammer's caught. See? Right *there!*"

"Getting it now, Tom. Wait a minute." He recoiled the spool of caps and inserted it again into the nest cast in the metal. He closed the sliding part and dramatically cocked the pistol. It fired.

"Oh, gee, thanks." Tom grabbed it and was gone. Exit, shooting, thought Phil. As if she had been sitting right beside him, politely waiting for him to finish the repair job, he turned back to Kathy. From his first "hello" on the phone, she'd begun to talk with an earnestness that caressed his fretted spirits. "It was a kind of aberration last night, Phil. I thought about it a lot, after, and didn't like myself much."

He'd blamed himself for having let it matter so much to him. All the while they talked, he admired this ability to say she'd been wrong. They'd seen each other once more before she'd left for the Christmas week end with her sister

94

Jane. The sweetness of reconciliation had been theirs, though there'd been no real quarrel, and he'd had to fight back the words that kept bursting against his orders to them to stay unsaid a while longer.

In his chair, Phil shifted uneasily. He stood up, crossed the room to the tree, disconnected the cord from the wall socket. The tree dimmed as if expression had fled a face. Ornamented, arrayed, it had made the infinitesimal shift from life to death.

He had thought as much of Betty as on other Christmases, had been as subject to all the willful tricks association could play. Specialized tricks at times like Christmas, seasonal tricks, with the help of brightly colored glass balls and flame-shaped bulbs, come forth from forgotten boxes, to set memory going with freshened sharpness.

December had been a month of her dying, and all the Decembers had been echoes of it, each more muted than the last, yet each clamoring in its own way as distance had added the ingredient of lost hope. But this time there was an insulation along his nerves, a buffer to soften the old blows.

And even as he thought, the muscles in his throat knotted, the slow thud of grief took up its interrupted rhythm. Like a devout, stepped briefly into a chapel, he stood again for a moment in the old sorrow.

Dr. Craigie was enthusiastic. "No immediacy." He kept returning to the phrase, and it had its effect on Mrs. Green and Phil. There was enormous calm in his manner, a pleasure at the massed notes and graphs spread on the desk before him. It had been a long visit, an exhaustive inquiry. Waiting now for his mother to come from the dressing room, Phil felt relief mixed with a hurry to leave.

"A good internist, though," Dr. Craigie was saying.

"We'll make an appointment if you wish. Or have you some good man you like?"

"I've been asking at the office," Phil said. "One of the editors there recommended Dr. Abrahams so highly, I made an appointment for Monday."

"Abrahams?"

"J. E., I think she said. Ephraim. Mt. Sinai or Beth Israel or both."

"Yes, yes, of course. You won't need this then." With finality he placed a prescription blank on the desk before him. Phil picked it up. Two names and addresses were written there. Mason Van Dick. James Ayres Kent. "If you, that is, if you *should* decide to have your mother see either——"

The tone was extremely polite. Too polite, raising an issue.

"Why? Isn't this Abrahams any good?"

"No, nothing like that. Good man. Completely reliable. Not given to overcharging and running visits out, the way some do."

"I see." Phil looked at him. "You mean 'the way some doctors' do?" (Do you tell even a doctor that you're Jewish? Was it necessary to produce that fact everywhere? Was it not an affront to a man to offer him the unsolicited fact, when its very uttering carried the implication that it held an importance to *him,* the listener?) "Or did you mean," he went on, " 'the way some Jewish doctors' do?"

Craigie laughed. "I suppose you're right," he said heartily. "I suppose some of *us* do it, too."

Then Phil had not given it the wrong reading. Us, Them; We, They. "If Dr. Abrahams doesn't impress me," he said, "I'll try Van Dick or Kent. I've no special loyalty to Jewish doctors simply because I'm Jewish myself."

Stephen Craigie swallowed. He laughed again. He folded

the electrocardiogram and placed it in the Manila envelope on the desk before him.

"No, of course not," he said. "Good man is a good man. I don't believe in prejudice. And do remember me to John Minify. Haven't seen him in years, since the night his father had a coronary. Fine man, that."

Mrs. Green appeared, and they left.

That's all it was, Phil thought later, stretching back from the littered desk in the office. A flick here, a flick there. Craigie hadn't known he "was Jewish." If he had, he'd have been "more careful." But already in this first week, after he, Phil, had made it a known premise wherever he reasonably could, the same flick had come often enough.

Sometimes it came only from an unconscious train of thought, as with Bill Johnson, of the *Times,* the other day. Returning the borrowed clips himself, he'd worked it in easily, without strain; it had been forgotten before they'd started down the street together for the drink Johnson had suggested at Bleeck's. They'd fallen into talk of the atomic secret, the Pearl Harbor investigation, politics in general.

"You were for Roosevelt?" Johnson began, and then added, "Sure, you would be."

"Why *would* I be?"

Johnson hadn't answered. Phil had let it pass. Flick.

Half a dozen other times, the same thing had happened. That's all these first days had given him. No big things. No yellow armband, no marked park bench, no Gestapo. Just here a flick and there another. Each unimportant. Each to be rejected as unimportant.

But day by day the little thump of insult. Day by day the tapping on the nerves, the delicate assault on the proud stuff of a man's identity. That's how they did it. A week had shown him how they did it.

At Phil's elbow the telephone rang. His mind wiped clear

of every thought. All day yesterday he'd hoped she'd call.

"Phil, this is Belle."

"Oh, you here again?"

"No, home." Her voice was brisk. "Mamma's letter just came. About your wonderful scheme." There was a clacking and whining in the receiver, and he lost her next words. "—and I have no control over what *you* do, but I want you to know *I'm* not having any part of it."

"Keep your shirt on. Nobody's asking you to do a thing."

"You know what Dick's company is like. And no matter how I disapprove of them, I just have to be realistic about it. I can't have people thinking——"

"For God's sake, Belle."

"All right, *be* high and mighty. Just the same, if people are going to think Dick's wife is Jewish!"

He scarcely listened to the swift words, foaming with self-justification. "All children are so decent to start with." His mother's words sounded louder in his mind than Belle's. "So none of you fell for it at school or anywhere." But one wasn't fixed forever in childhood patterns, in spite of what the Catholics believed about the first seven years. Those early patterns *could* be shifted; new values could be superimposed.

"Stop wetting your pants," he said roughly. "I'm not going to drag you into it. Nobody thought you were a miner or an Okie, did they?"

When it was over, he sat glaring at the telephone as if it were Belle herself. There was a knock at the door, and he called out, "Yes?" glad to be distracted from his exasperation. Miss Wales came in, a dozen letters in her hand. "Some answers," she said, and put them on his desk. The envelopes were already slit, and he smiled at her. From the first day she had treated him as if she'd been his secretary for years. She offered him co-operation, friendliness, and no deference. He liked the way she looked, though he supposed it was a little "bold." Her blond hair was an elaboration of curls, her skin pale against the ripe mouth. High cheekbones made her seem Scandinavian, Slavic, something foreign and interesting. She had the curious New York speech that he was not yet used to, plus some extra oddities that intrigued his ear. When she said "bottle" or "settle," she left the double *t*'s out completely, a little the way a Scot did. He had tried, with amusement once when he was alone, to mimic her pronunciation. "Bah-ull." "Seh-ull." No, he couldn't quite do it.

He began on the letters. Just what he'd expected. Nothing new. These were the clichés of the thing, really. Yet as he read on, anger simmered low in him.

"Yes to the Greens and no to the Greenbergs?" Miss Wales asked good-humoredly.

"At least promises to let the Greens know if any reservation gets canceled." He passed the letters over as he read them. This was from the first batch of inquiries to resort hotels in Miami, Palm Beach, Bermuda. They'd gone off in pairs, on blank stationery, and on the same day. Each was signed, "Philip Green," but one of each pair included the phrase, "for myself and my cousin, Capt. Joseph Greenberg," while the other made no mention of this cousin. The ones without bore Phil's own address; the ones with had Minify's address on Park Avenue. He and John had planned this move together, to avoid confusion about the replies. Even the "care of Minify" was unnecessary—"Apt. 18 A" with the street and house number would do it. Jessie Minify, who looked on the whole thing, John had wryly reported, as an exciting kind of secret-service game to which she was eager to lend a hand, had taken on the task of readdressing these letters to the office or seeing them safely into John's brief case.

"Dear old Jess," John had remarked. "She *adores* your idea. Of course she won't give you away. She's dying to give a big party and ask all the antisemites she can think of and introduce you—she didn't say any of this, you know, Phil, but I rather think I'm right—as 'this nice Jewish man, Phil Green, did you hear, *Jewish.*' "

Phil had laughed.

"Anyway, I know she thinks of antisemitism as something sort of naughty, like gambling for too high stakes or not holding your liquor."

Phil finished reading the replies and waited for Miss Wales. She knew the only purpose of these letters was research for the series. She flipped over another letter, smiling and unperturbed. With the best will in the world, Phil told himself, they don't give a damn because it's nothing that'll ever touch them.

"I'll start a file for replies, now," she said cheerfully. "There'll be lots more tomorrow."

"Yes."

"It'll be good material for your pieces." She gave him a look that was part encouragement, part boredom. "If your name was Irving Green or Saul or something, it wouldn't have worked this way." He looked at her quickly.

"We'll have a cross check all right."

"I changed mine," she said casually. "Did you?"

"Wales? No, mine was always Green. What was yours?" His voice had shown no surprise.

"Walovsky, Estelle Walovsky. I couldn't take it. About applications, I mean." She shrugged, matter-of-factly. "So once I wrote the same firm two letters, same as you're doing. I wrote the Elaine Wales one after they'd said there were no openings to my first letter. I got the job all right."

"Damn."

"You know what firm that was?" She waited. She seemed

100

to be enjoying herself. He shook his head. *"Smith's Weekly,"* she said demurely.

"You're kidding!"

"The great liberal magazine," she went on with a kind of impishness, "that fights injustice on all sides. It slays me. I love it."

"Brother! Does Minify——"

"I guess he can't bother thinking about the small fry. That's Jordan's stuff. If anybody snitched, you know there'd be some excuse for throwing them out." She jerked her thumb toward the window, and Phil stared at it till she dropped her hand. "So, anyway, I thought maybe you'd changed yours sometime," she went on. "I mean, when I heard you were."

"You *heard* it? You mean before I told you?"

"Sure. Everybody knew it the next day."

Then his job of "working it in" had been done for him? But how? Who had bothered? And how was it done? Never in all his life did he remember saying to one human about another, "He's Jewish, you know." That must have been spoken about him at once. By Anne Dettrey? By Frank Tingler? By Bert McAnny? Possibly Minify himself, to help launch the thing? No. He could not imagine John Minify saying the words, either. "He's Catholic." "He's a Jew." To talk of another man in the vocabulary of religious distinctions would go against Minify's grain as it would against his own.

He waved to the letters she was gathering together.

"Does that kind of stuff get you sore?"

"Not any more. Yes, sure it does. So what?" She shrugged, and with the same imperturbable look in her eyes she left the room. He looked after her. The Nordic type; the Aryan type. He lit a cigarette. He must search out that article *Life* had run a couple of years ago by Hooton of

Harvard about the balderdash of race and types. Or read Hooton's book. Suddenly he grinned. He'd have a little fun telling Minify about things.

The telephone rang again. Maybe this time.

"Hello—oh, Kathy. You back?"

"It was such a lovely *witty* present, Phil. First I laughed and then I sort of hugged it."

"I'm glad. You'll be getting a grimy note from Tom sometime—he went nuts over the gun. When can I see you?"

"Any time."

"Right now, tonight, tomorrow, I missed you these four days. I wish we were married."

"Phil."

So, he had said it at last. Here, at an office desk, his elbow on a stack of notes and papers, into a perforated black disk he had said the words he'd forced back into his throat all that evening before she'd gone away.

"It's a hell of a way to say it," he said, "isn't it?" There was no answer. "Kathy? You still there?"

"I missed you, too," she said slowly. "Just awfully."

He saw the picture when he came in. The old one that had been over the fireplace lay flat on the piano, and his present hung in its place. Pleasure darted through him, but he said nothing. She knew he had seen it, and remained silent with him. He took her into his arms.

Standing tight to each other, saying nothing, they knew no importance other than the one streaming close about them in this double admission of longing. The tentative was gone. The surprise was gone. Acknowledgment, compulsion, sureness—these they shared.

Later, leaning over her, he looked at her and found tranquillity and an odd return of shyness.

"Darling. My beautiful Kathy."

She smiled and turned away from his asking, knowing that he wanted her to say it, not knowing how to say it.

"You don't look grim and dark now, Phil."

"You don't either."

"Isn't it——" She looked at him and then away. The question hung in the air.

"When it's all mixed with being in love, yes." He waited. "So damn beautiful you can't bear it, I mean me."

"Me, too."

All night they forgot to sleep, except in snatches of drowsy silence which were half sleep. They talked with the candor that could come only in intimacy and confessed love. Already each felt a new loyalty to the other sketching in its first outlines beyond the old loyalty clinging to anything past. She could make him see more now, about her marriage, and he more about his stubborn suffering for Betty. Each had sought, each had hoped and watched for a new beginning, and now together they had found the way to it.

"Should we meet our families first?" Kathy said once. "Or after we're married and surprise them?"

"Which way do you want?"

"Any."

Nothing was settled, no question fully answered, through all the hours until the windows showed graying streaks around the drawn shades. There was no time or need now for decisions. There was all the time.

Only when he was dressed and sitting on the edge of her bed for a last cigarette did they come to specifics. "Darling, I'll tell Mom in the morning. Come and meet her tomorrow? I'll stop by after the office."

"All right. And Tom?"

"Let's have him get to know you first. Then after he likes you we'll tell him. He'll be so happy."

"Sure?"

"Sure. I guess it's better for him to like you first, don't you?"

"Then maybe tomorrow'd be better after he's asleep?"

He nodded. "We'll take him to a movie together for a start. That'll make him all easy with you." He took her into his arms. His clothed body, his sleeved arm around her still bare shoulders, shot a lewdness through him, unwanted, dismaying. He spoke somberly. "You're not sorry, darling, about Tom?"

"Oh, Phil. You know I'm *glad*." She hesitated. "It'll be almost as if my marriage hadn't all been wasted—as if all those years I'd had a boy growing up *for* me."

He suddenly stood up. "I'm a Christ-bitten fool," he said, and heard how thick his voice was. Then he left her.

Behind, alone, hearing him walk through the living room, hearing him click off the lights they'd forgotten, guessing that he looked once more at the framed print of the *Toledo* over the fireplace, Kathy lay in a confusion of fatigue and happiness that banished sleep for another while. He couldn't know, she would tell him sometime after they were married, but now she couldn't utter the words to tell him how right he was with her and for her.

She hadn't expected it. She hadn't guessed that with his moodiness, his complexity, he would have so simple and driving a power to move her. If she *had* speculated, she'd have guessed he'd be a nervous, unsure lover.

It mattered so much—no marriage had half a chance if the two were constantly frustrate or anxious about sex. Phil, she thought. Darling.

I'll make him happy, I can help him, I'm good for being married. All the rest of it about Betty will disappear without his even knowing when it finally slides off into nothingness. I can make Tom feel right; I'm good with children;

why wouldn't I be with *this* one when I want to so much? And we'll have our own.

She reached for a final cigarette, changed her mind, and turned out the light. In the dark she thanked something for having made it happen and did not try to name what it was she thanked.

Lack of sleep didn't matter, Phil thought, when you felt this good. His mother's pleasure over the news that they'd marry in a week or two had only made him indulgent, not uneasy and embarrassed. Whistling, he finished dressing and went back to his desk for the morning's batch of hotel letters. Mrs. Green was still sitting there. Tom was already out.

"The story about Miss Wales made Kathy laugh, too," he said. He didn't want the talk to get back to personal levels. "She was delighted I hadn't told Minify yet—wants to be around when I dish it out."

Kathy had been angry about Dr. Craigie, had sniffed over Bill Johnson of the *Times*. He had forgotten to tell her about Belle's telephone call. One of those shame-caused repressions? Sometime around midnight they'd remembered they'd had no dinner and they'd gone into the small kitchen for scrambled eggs and toast and milk. While they were there, they'd been able again to talk of impersonal things, and she'd wanted to know "everything that's happened so far." Sitting there, while she cooked for him, talking of his work, was like a rehearsal of married life. But he could report only episodes; the nebulous world of his own developing feeling he had to inhabit alone. So far, even for himself it remained uncharted.

"That thing about Miss Wales is the only thing that's *been* amusing," Mrs. Green said. He came to with a start. The letters were still in his hand.

"Funny thing," he said, "the way I felt so man-to-man with Miss Wales when she pitched me that one. Asking her right out how she felt, as if we both were really on the inside. I keep forgetting it's just an act."

She looked at him thoughtfully. "I suppose that's what's called 'Identification.'"

"I didn't think it would come so fast."

"What does Kathy think about it?"

"I *told* you."

"I mean about your doing it at all?"

"Oh. She fretted about it some, pitfalls, stuff like that. She's all for it."

"When's Dave due?" she asked without transition.

"Maybe tomorrow. Maybe next month. You know the army."

He went off, ready for Dave, ready for more letters, ready for work and effort and anything. Never try to dismay a man, he thought in the taxi, about anything in the world the morning after he's made love to his girl. Kathy's face came back, hesitant, a touch surprised. A primitive sense of achievement and self-satisfaction filled him. She'd thought he'd be a goddam intellectual about everything! In the half-dark of the cab he sat back, trying to ready himself for the moment just ahead, the cab pulling up, the flag shoved upright, the making of change and the offer of the tip. The office was there, the series was there, the watching himself and asking himself were all just ahead of him.

"Identification." In a way he was kidding himself. Always he knew that for him it would come to an end when he gave the word. That must make it different. He alone had an escape clause in his contract.

A dart of relief nipped at him.

Jee-sus, he thought then. I'm goddam smug myself.

Of it, yet also apart. The actor on the boards and the

watching audience in the dark beyond. The lumberjack with his ax and the tree awaiting the blow. The invasion barge and the empty beach. The giver and taker at once.

It was fallacy. It could achieve nothing true. He'd embarked on a sort of Dostoevskian insoluble, dark, brooding, ending only in uncertainty. He should never have started it. At best it was an approximation; at worst a fraud.

The taxi stopped. The driver's arm reached out to the white flag on the meter. Phil opened the door. On the street, sunlight blazed; cold air bit at him. Upstairs he went directly to Minify's office. Minify was alone.

"It's no good, John," he began. "The damn idea's a phony from the word go."

John looked up, startled.

"It's glib and trumped up and fake," Phil went on. "I've got an 'out' all the time, and no real Jew has. My unconscious knows about that 'out' even if I forget it."

"Hold on, there——"

"I'm starting over. There'll be some other angle that isn't slick like this one."

Now John cut him short. "For God's sake, stop psychoanalyzing it." His words were brisk with irritation. "It's a good angle—nobody said it was perfect. But it's a new springboard into the thing, and that's good." Phil started to answer, but Minify waved him silent. "You had an 'out' all the time you were a miner, didn't you?"

"Sure. So has a miner."

"Not the usual, run-of-the-mill miner, to mix a phrase." He sat back; the annoyed look left him. "There was nothing slick and fake in that series, Phil. You're just having the usual attack of 'it's lousy—I'm lousy.' "

Phil thought, Maybe that's all it comes to, and wished he'd thought it over longer before coming in. Then he saw Minify smile.

"And if the first couple articles do turn out n.g.," John said calmly, "we've got a good 'out' ourselves." He kicked the wastebasket beside the desk.

Phil looked down at the basket and laughed. "Escape clause," he said. "O.K. I'd overlooked that."

Reassured, he went back to his office and got to work. It was after six before he was ready to leave. Kathy had sounded happy when he phoned, and tired, and had suggested waiting until eight so she could nap. He might do a spot of sleeping himself. All afternoon he'd worked with his usual intensity; he was writing now as well as carrying on the research. The writing was going well; it pleased him. But he was tired, too.

He went through the reception room, dim and emptied of its authors and salesmen and portfolios. Bert McAnny, the assistant art editor, and Anne Dettrey were out in the hall, waiting for the elevator.

"I'm bushed," Anne greeted him. "Getting the book to bed gets worse every issue."

"I thought we weren't to call it 'the book' around here," Bert said. He pushed the DOWN button again.

"True, true," Anne said. "Anyway, what about a getting-to-bed drink? Sound cozy?" They all laughed. "How's about it?"

They decided on the Oak Room and walked to the Plaza. Phil felt at ease with them, as though he'd been on the staff a long time. Shoptalk was what you missed when you worked at home, the lazily given "inside dope" that seemed curiously important: "Say, Luce paid fifty thousand for Churchill's articles"—"When do they start?"—"February. I hear he's fighting with Field for the autobiography"—"Jim told me the bidding was around a million already." As they turned into Fifty-ninth Street, Bert began to talk with relish about a new illustrator he'd discovered. "He's a kind of modern Leyendecker," he said. "Same outfit in the army, and the minute I saw some doodles he did, I knew he had it."

"Leyendecker?" Anne said. "You were in three-cornered pants when Leyendecker——"

"I know them all the way back," Bert said. "This kid's got it. Little Jew boy from the Bronx, but he sure has got it. Signed him for the Dohen serial."

There was a pause.

It's just an expression, Phil told himself. He feels affectionate and proud of this kid. Aloud he said, "What's his name? Anybody ever hear of him?"

"Jacob Her——" Bert stopped then. He's remembering about me, Phil thought, and embarrassment for Bert washed over him. "Jake Hermann," Bert hurried on. "Fine stuff, all right. He'll hit every cover on the stands in two years."

Enthusiasm in the voice, pride, alliance. Don't be bothered by idoms and expressions, Phil counseled himself. Bert feels like a jackass over the thing. But he thought of Belle's Jew-us-down.

Over their drinks they talked about plays and movies and the difference in the holiday mood this year. Bert had missed all the war Christmases, he said, so he couldn't catch the difference. It was Anne who asked about the series.

"I'm still just getting stuff together," Phil said deprecatingly. "God knows there's plenty around."

"Too much," she answered crisply. Nobody said anything. McAnny shifted in his chair.

"You a correspondent during the war?" he asked Phil.

Instantly Phil was hostile. He rescinded the excuses he had made before. He said, "What makes you think I wasn't right in it?"

"I just—hey, don't be oversensitive now."

"I was with the Marines on Guad. First Division,

109

Eleventh Regiment Artillery." Don't be oversensitive. Jews are oversensitive. "Jew boy" is just an expression—let it pass. But how directly Bert had leaped from Anne's "too much antisemitism" to "were you a correspondent?" That fool mind was clearly taping even war correspondents as inferiors, so the train of thought meant, being a Jew, did you choose a cushy berth in the war; were you a slacker?

Idioms, expressions, forgettings, associated ideas. Flick. Tap.

"You don't wear your ribbons, do you, Phil?" Anne put in quietly. "I know you got it pretty badly. Minify told me."

"No." He looked down at his own lapel. "I don't."

He saw her smiling at him, friendly, teamed against Bert. He smiled back. He knew Bert had seen the exchange.

"For God's sake, Phil," he exploded. "I'm no antisemite. Why, some of my best———"

"I know, dear," Anne put in, "and some of your other best friends are Methodists, but you never bother saying it. Skip it. Phil, flag the old boy for another Manhattan, there's a dear."

Bert couldn't stay another round because of an appointment. When they were alone, Anne said, "Little Squirt."

"I suppose Minify doesn't come into contact with him much," Phil said reflectively. "That day at lunch———"

"He was in Tingler's office, so he came along. John doesn't know anybody the way he does the writers and editors. Place is too big." She grinned comfortably and pitched her voice to imitate Bert. " 'For God's sake, Phil, I'm no antisemite.' He believes that. He disapproves of Bilbo and Gerald L. K. Smith and the poll tax and religious prejudice. Really says so. He's just a little snot, let's face it."

He laughed. She was refreshing. And she liked him. He looked at her, more personally attentive than he'd yet been. She was certainly an attractive and colorful girl. Her hat was a silly thing like a man's black Homburg swathed in dark brown veil, but it was becoming.

"Tell you what," she said. "I'm having a flock of people up New Year's Eve. What about pressing out your black tie and coming up?"

"I'd like that," he said. "Can I bring my girl?"

"Of course," she said. Her expression changed for a second, and then she smiled again.

CHAPTER SEVEN

Kathy said, "Won't we have to let Jane in on it?"

He looked quickly at her. "I hadn't thought."

"I hadn't, either, till now." She smiled at him. "She's dying to meet you. I sort of blurted the news on the phone, and she squealed 'Kath-eeee' as if she'd given up all hope." He nodded as a preoccupied parent does when a child prattles. She waited. Then she said, "Phil, my own sister?"

He sat forward in his chair and studied the flames in the fireplace. A minute ago there'd been still the good pleasure of watching her with his mother. Almost a proprietary thing it was, as if he'd not only found Kathy but created her out of his own talents and materials. He'd been impatient for his mother to leave them, but now that she had there'd been this question and the sunny feeling had fogged over.

"*Your* sisters know," she went on.

"My mother wrote them. But they *know* I'm not Jewish. Jane and Harry don't. After all, if you want to keep a secret, the only way——"

"But, Phil. Wouldn't it be sort of exaggerated, with *my* sister, your sister-in-law almost?"

It was so logical. But logic—he stood up, poked the fire, threw on a heavy log. It clattered sparks and chips off the burning wood, and with the side of his shoe he shoved each glowing bit back from the slate hearth.

"Jane was engaged to a boy named Sidney Pearlman," she said at last, "and he died of pneumonia and she nearly went crazy for a long time."

"What's the point?" The harsh tone, the stern pounce

of the disciplinarian—he regretted them even before her quick, "Phil, really!"

"I'm sorry."

"There *is* a point, darling," she went on reasonably, "a kind of pragmatic point. I do think it would be pretty inflexible of you——" Her glance was inviting him to be as reasonable as she. Somewhere there was the neat and simple syllogism that would present no flaw to her, but he was too perplexed to find it. He was on the defensive—how had he got there? She got up and came to him. She put her arm through his. "Don't you see, Phil?"

"I suppose so." It sounded grudging, and he added, "Inside the family."

"That's all I meant." She squeezed his arm. "They'd never breathe it."

"No point running things into the ground, I guess."

Exaggerated. Inflexible. Waiting for sleep, hours later, Phil suddenly remembered Pop and the interest.

"But it *is* unearned increment, Mattie." He could imagine his father as a young man saying it earnestly to his astonished wife. Thirty-two years ago, that had been, and their first savings account. Written in red ink in the small green bankbook was an 0.72, the interest on their fortune. Phil had heard the tale a dozen times. "Of course I can't accept it."

"Are you going to give it back to the bank?"

"Certainly not. But if you believe a thing's evil, you can't give in just because the amount is small." He'd gone off into a lecture which would now be called "Old-Fashioned Socialism."

"Then what *are* you going to do with it?"

"I'll think of something."

All through his life, his father had refused to make personal use of a penny of interest. Each year he would do a meticulous calculation and send off a check to something he believed in. It was never a charity in the accepted sense. Before 1917, he'd sent it to an organization for the defense of political prisoners in Russia; when the Ku Klux Klan was raging in the early twenties, he'd sent it to a group fighting it; when the Civil Liberties Union came into being he'd mailed his little checks there. He never forgot, never relented. It was exaggerated, it was laughable. But it was curiously admirable, too.

Phil rarely thought of his father any more, but when he did he always came on some hard little nubbin like this. It was one of the inevitables in a man like Stephen Slater Green. "If you compromise," he used to say, "you're corrupt." Character, principle, ethic, whatever one called it, was the deciding factor in every life, in every society. Even in the various religions of the world, there was a common extract, the ethic behind the shell of creed. One could reject the shell with no impairment to the essence. But without the essence one was lost.

Phil stretched his arms high above his head and yawned deeply. His wrist struck the bed lamp, and the cigarette still in his fingers shook ashes down over him. Impatiently he brushed them from his face and pajamas. Two o'clock in the morning was a hell of a time to remember Pop and his large-scale talk about ethics. The mind was never a respecter of appropriateness.

In the instant of giving in about Jane and Harry he could see Kathy's mouth and want her; he could write a phrase for the series and wonder what movie they should choose for Tom; he could leave Kathy's side and dredge out of his memory the red handwriting in the interest column.

Unexpectedly, as he was leaving tonight, she'd held her

arms out to him. "Comparisons are awful, darling, but I *never* was so happy before."

They each had comparisons in them; always the later love came equipped with the earlier and with the gray knowledge of what had happened to it and could happen again. Perhaps the knowledge of that mortality added depth as well as fear to the new; else why this passionate resolve in him to let no disaster strike this time?

"Never so happy before." He hadn't consciously measured or compared. Was this the same for him as the round deep joy he'd known with Betty when he'd been a boy of twenty-five? There was in him now the gritty residue of burned-out grief; with Betty long ago he had been an innocent lover in the true sense of the word, guileless toward the future.

He ground out his cigarette in the ash tray and turned out the light. They could take Tommy to see Danny Kaye in *Wonder Man*.

At the office next morning, Miss Wales was upset.

"I don't know *what* I was thinking of. I switched about ten of the applications to colleges and medical schools."

"Oh, well."

"But the answers won't be delivered. The post office will mark them 'Unknown.' " She had just discovered from her carbons that she'd typed in the Minify address on a batch of Greens and his own on the corresponding Greenbergs. Her professional confidence was shaken; two or three times she pointed out that she *never* made mistakes, and this was awful. "If you lived in an apartment house, you could tell the doorman, but not where there are letter boxes downstairs."

"I'll just write in his name on our card down there."

"Oh." Relief smoothed her face. "I never thought of that."

Past the open door Bert McAnny went by with his boss, Bill Jayson, and Sam Goodman, Tingler's assistant on fiction. As they called "Morning," Jayson stopped, looked in, and then came in. McAnny went on with Goodman.

"Photographs, would you guess?" Jayson started. "For your series?"

"I hadn't thought." Miss Wales left. Bill Jayson sat down. He was short and thin, with an odd toed-out gait. In the one brief talk they'd already had, Phil had noticed the pedantic way he enunciated every syllable, but there was an earnestness in him that was attractive. "I thought nonfiction always called for photographic treatment."

"John says you have some special angle that might shift that." Jayson looked troubled. "He says to skip it for now. Then it'll turn out oils, and I'll be in hell rushing them."

"I'll give you plenty of time."

"It's the devil, illustrating a series like that. Why all the mystery? John wouldn't give me a line."

"Well, it's better this way for a bit." He took one of the two cigarettes Jayson held out in his fingers. Friendly little guy.

"McAnny just told me about yesterday," Jayson went on carefully. "He's always doing something. Knows his job, though."

"Sure." He looked at Jayson. "How come he told you?"

Jayson made a sound that could only be described as a titter. "He's scared of Dettrey, I think." Phil laughed. Jayson went on, "Look, could I make a highly personal remark?"

"Go ahead."

Jayson looked unhappy. He scowled. He opened his small mouth and closed it. "Don't keep a—don't wear a chip on your shoulder, Green."

"Do I?"

116

"I used to, about being five foot two," he went on solemnly. "Looking for tactless remarks all day long. Then I just said to myself that everybody's got a low riling point on something."

"That's true enough. Have I? I didn't think——"

"Well, just telling everybody you're a Jew right off. What the hell business is it of anybody?"

"I oughtn't mention it?"

Jayson's scowl returned. He pursed his lips like a pettish child. Then he shook his head.

"I guess that wouldn't go either. Then they'd say you were hiding it. Hell of a note, isn't it?"

They grinned at each other.

Going up the stairs that evening, Phil was in a cheerful mood. The long New Year's week end was coming up. Except for deadline stuff, the office would be closed for four days. Suddenly he remembered his promise to Miss Wales. He went down again to the vestibule and stopped in front of the shining brass plate of bells and letter boxes. He stooped and printed CAPT. J. GREENBERG above the typed name on his box. Behind him the door opened.

"Evening, Mr. Green." It was the superintendent for the three adjoining houses of which this was one.

"Nice night," Phil said, and put his key again in the hall door. Behind him Mr. Olsen made a sound. Phil turned and saw Olsen leaning down to the printed name.

"You could fill out one of them cards at the post office, better," he said. He didn't look at Phil. "Or watch for the mailman and tell him."

"What's the matter with this way?"

"Rule." He reached into his vest pocket and brought out a pencil. Phil saw him turn it upside down. The eraser moved toward the card.

"Just a minute." Phil ripped out the order as he'd done in uniform.

Olsen stopped short. He met Phil's eyes then, his own plaintive. "It's nothin' I can help, Mr. Green. It's the rules. Not in these three houses. The broker should of explained, that is, excuse me, if you *are.*"

"Excuse me, hell. This place is mine for two years, and you don't touch that sign."

"I'll have to repor——"

Phil slammed the door in his face. Queasy rage rode him. Upstairs he went directly to his own room. This sullen moron of a janitor. The rules. He'd seen the owner of these three buildings just once, back in September. Alma Martin was one of those rich widows you saw in movies and never met. At the time he'd merely noted the flash of rings, the beaded eyelashes, the lacy bosom and vulgar voice. Now a hateful snobbery sprang high in him. That cheap tart felt superior to him! The nasty little whore who couldn't get into a cultivated household actually would keep him out of her three citadels! He and Dave and anybody Jewish were to be kept off the premises.

He ought to laugh, but laughter wasn't in him. Every day the thump of insult, the assault on your dignity. The rules of the Alma Martins and Joe Olsens. The flicks of the McAnnys and Craigies, nice intelligent people who scorned the lunatic fringe and wouldn't have Alma Martin in their houses either.

Don't wear a chip on your shoulder. Don't be oversensitive. And don't be clannish. He'd heard that one, too. The trouble with Jews is they're so clannish. If one of them moves into an apartment house, why, pretty soon the whole house is nothing but Jews. Or a hotel or a neighborhood. They just don't want to mix. And the ones that do mix easily

118

and melt right in with everybody, why, they're so quick to take offense at the slightest thing.

Don't be so thin-skinned, Izzy. Don't withdraw from the clever little flick, don't stay off in groups where the tap, tap, tap can't get at you and madden you with drop-of-water persistence. This is America, and there are no torture chambers in Detroit or Boston or St. Paul. Why fret?

Nine months? Two weeks was enough. He'd been doing this for less than two weeks and he'd changed. A mutation had been produced in the bunched nerves, in the eardrums that caught nuance, in the very corneas that gave him sight. Already when he glanced at the over-all gray of a page of the *Times,* if the word "Jew" was printed anywhere on it, that word leaped into his vision. Already when somebody started a story about Izzy Epstein or Mrs. Garfinkel, he felt his teeth on edge. Now the sly little phrases got no obliging deafness or excuses from him. How small a step remained before he might seethe with determination to "show them," to attain some power, of wealth, of fame, that would be impregnable!

Two weeks. Maybe the slow embryo in the patient womb needed nine months to reproduce the sweep from tadpole to man, but no such time was needed to re-create the reaction to prejudice. He'd been a fool that night, a fancy maker of metaphor and simile. Whole history of persecution indeed. He'd forgotten that the inheritance of acquired characteristics was a myth. The baby born in the ghetto was as free of the history of persecution as it was free of its father's skill at making neckties or mathematical formulae. But *these* teachers were soon met, and they taught their devious lessons rapidly and well.

He took the opening pages of his manuscript out of his pocket and threw it at the top of his dresser. It slithered across the mahogany and fell to the floor.

"That you, dear?"

He shook his head sharply as if to snap it free of concussion after big guns had gone off.

"Yeah. No office till Wednesday."

He retrieved the folded pages. He rolled them up and absently beat the brittle tube against the side of his leg. That's where he'd pounded his thigh in that first sweep of elation.

Over the radio, the shouts, toots, whistles notched up in intensity.

"Half a minute to go," somebody in the room called out.

Anne moved through the crowd to the wall switch. Unnoticed before, the two lighted candles on the mantel sprang alive as the other lights went out. At the piano somebody played the opening bars of *Auld Lang Syne*.

"Corny," Kathy whispered, but her eyes glistened. "Happy New Year, darling."

"Happy New Year." They kissed. Around them wives kissed husbands, friends kissed friends. Corny. And curiously, stubbornly moving. The new year, the new hope, the peace, the stumbling effort of man. . . .

"It's a grand party, Phil," Kathy said. "Anne's awfully attractive, isn't she?" They both looked toward Anne in her bright green.

"She looks grand tonight."

"She certainly does," Kathy said. "She likes you a lot."

He looked down at her, and she made a face. She said, smiling, "I'll scratch her eyes out if she makes a play for you."

"You darling." It delighted him that she should show possessiveness. Tonight was the first time, apart from their dinner last evening with the Minifys, that their relationship had become public. "My fiancé," Kathy had said twice when she introduced him to people she knew. The afternoon with Tom and the movies had slid by on silk. In three days they were going for the wedding license. He leaned down so he could whisper to her.

"Let's not stay around too long. You look pretty damn grand yourself." She was in a long black dress held up by shoestrings.

"In this? It's four years old."

"And still sexy as hell."

They both laughed. Then Kathy said quietly, "I wish Bill would get married this year, too."

"Bill?" It sounded stupid. "Oh, yes, Bill."

"Pawling," she said. "My ex-husband. He dropped in today to say Happy New Year, and I told him about us. He was awfully effusive with good wishes. It made me sad for him."

He didn't say anything. When somebody came up to Kathy just then, he was glad to have the subject changed.

It *was* a good party, as Kathy had said, not merely good for lovers. This was what people could find in New York if they were fortunate, the good mixture of talent and interests and ideas. There were Joe Lieberman, the physicist; Jerry Torrence, the novelist, with his beautiful wife; Jascha Rimitov, the violinist, and his gifted wife, who was his accompanist. Lawyers, businessmen, a Congressman up from Washington, one of the younger men in the State Department, a publisher, and a minor actress. The faces in the room were various with many kinds of origin; the speech mingled the accents of Middle West, East, and West, of Europe and America. This, the fluid easy coming together of a dozen worlds, was the bonus life set aside for the luckier ones in the metropolises of the earth. The small city, the town and village, could not offer it. To Phil, grown in small cities and towns, it was as stimulating as the champagne—"Domestic, dears," Anne had said—that he'd been drinking all evening.

Here was a world where a man's name, the shape of his nose, the religion he believed in or the religion he did not believe in—where none of it counted. Here was rugged individualism in its best sense, each man or woman a whole person, the sum of his worth and character left whole, no part subtracted by prejudice.

He'd been pleased to see Lieberman there and went straight to him with, "Minify wanted to get us together. I'm Phil Green."

"He told me he did."

They shook hands. Only yesterday John had told Phil he'd talked to Lieberman about him. "I'm not as easy as you are, Phil, about sliding it into a sentence, but I got it across to him."

Lieberman was plump as well as short, middle-aged, with the face of a Jew in a Nazi cartoon, the beaked nose, the blue jowls, and the curling black hair. Phil saw all of it, and the fine candid eyes.

"I'm writing a series for him on antisemitism."

"Pro or con?"

Phil roared, and Lieberman's eyes twinkled. He seemed pleased with himself, affectionate toward his quick retort, rewarded by Phil's outburst as by a just reward.

"And John thought we might hash over some ideas. I expect you're pretty busy these days."

Lieberman shook his head in denial. "What sort of ideas?"

"Palestine, for instance, Zionism——"

"Which? Palestine as refuge or Zionism as a movement for a Jewish state?"

"The confusion between the two, more than anything."

"Good. If we agree there's confusion, we can talk. I can't really talk to a positive Zionist any more than to a confirmed Communist—there is no language."

They talked on for a bit and agreed to meet soon.

In the taxi uptown, Phil and Kathy discussed the party. She was voluble and gay, with excitement, with champagne. "I thought I'd die at some of the jokes she told," she said, and laughed in reminiscence.

Anne had revealed a gift for mimicry he'd only glimpsed when she'd imitated Bert, and for over an hour she'd regaled one corner of the room with story after story, most of them old ones refurbished with current build-ups and made newly engaging by her uncanny ear for dialect.

"If McAnny told the same ones," he said, "I'd have been puckered as a quince. Why the hell is it so different?"

Kathy shook her head, and they went on in silence. It could be different. With Anne, and in that crowd, you could laugh at a joke about two priests or two Jews or two Negroes and hear no overtone of cruelty. Kathy and he had shouted over the chestnut about Mandy and the colored judge and again at the one about "Lord Chahmly-Chahmly" getting the wrong telephone connection.

"So he gets this little old fellow in the Bronx, you know, long beard, black skullcap, and says, 'I say, is Freddy Breckston theah?'

" 'Who-o-o-? Who you vant?'

" 'Breckston, old chap, Lord Harrowbridge Turnbridge Pethbright, y'know.'

" 'Oi! Hev *you* got the wrung numbair!' "

In the dim cab, Kathy heard him chuckle and said, "Phil?" He took her into his arms.

"I'm just so damn happy," he said, as if it explained anything.

He stood looking down at her as she sat at one end of the sofa. Disbelief, acknowledgment warred through him. His mind strained for understanding, the ache of trying told him it was beyond his reach.

123

"God, Kathy, we're quarreling."

"I *said* we shouldn't talk it out now. It's nearly four, we had stuff to drink, we're just worn out." Her face was pale. Her dejected limpness was an accusation.

"All right. Let's quit it." He stood up and began pacing the room.

"I *know* I promised, Phil. I crossed my heart. No exceptions. And you *were* being reasonable to stretch it to Jane. But it just seems so silly to get her into a *thing* up there when it's not true."

Women always talk in italics, he thought, when they know they're wrong. She must see this is impossible. Aloud he said, "The whole goddam business just depends on my not making loopholes whenever it's convenient, that's all."

"She didn't mean for you to *deny* it. Just *not* to bring it up."

He didn't say anything. They'd been over this five times already since she'd unlocked the front door and said, "Oh, I forgot. Jane wants to throw a big party for us Saturday night." She'd switched on only one lamp in the living room, made a comedy gesture of chucking off her short cape and letting it lie on the rug, and curled up against banked cushions with an unshielded yawn like a child. He'd sat near her, unsuspicious of danger, tired also, and unwilling to admit he ought to be on his way at once.

"What'd she say when you told her?"

"Oh, she thought it was the cleverest way to do research and that you must have a touch of the screwball in you to think it up."

"But she promised?"

"I wouldn't tell her till she did. And Harry, too. Anyway, today when she phoned, she asked if you'd just skip the whole thing for the party and I said——"

"No."

"What?"

"You said, 'No, he won't skip the whole thing for the party.'"

"Why, Phil, I didn't. I said I'd ask you."

He'd stood abruptly then.

"*Ask* me?"

"I'd never say yes without asking you."

"You mean I *should?*"

She looked away. "You know those suburban crowds. Especially Darien and up there. It would just start a whole mess for Jane and Harry for nothing."

"And if it were a mess for something?"

"But, Phil, you're *not*. So—oh, you *can* be solemn about things. It'll just ruin the party for Jane if she has problems at it."

"Why not just tell Jane to skip the party?"

"Oh, Phil, that would look so queer—her only sister." She made an impatient gesture. "If you *were* I'd manage, but——"

"Thanks."

Again the look stood in her eyes. ("But, Phil, you're not really, are you?") The look he'd found excuses for—*the mind plays funny tricks, you're not Minify, I should have led you along*. This time the look wasn't caused by unpreparedness or misunderstanding. This time it was just there.

Over and over, they'd gone at it, round and round. She couldn't see it, and he couldn't make her see it. He couldn't see it, and she couldn't make him see it.

"Nobody's asking you to make loopholes where it counts," she went on now. "At the office, or meeting people right here like at Anne's tonight. But out there's just an occasional visit, and if we use my house for next summer, and anyway, Jane and Harry——"

"I thought you said they were so grand."

"They *are*. But they can't help it if some of their friends —and they'd be saying 'our future brother-in-law' or maybe 'our brother-in-law' by then, and it would make such a——"

"A thing. A mess. An inconvenience."

"Well, it would!"

"Just for Jane and Harry? Or for you, too?"

"Damn it, I'd be so tensed up I wouldn't have any fun either. Heavens, if everything's going to be tensed up and solemn all the time——"

Her voice was hard. Her eyes avoided his. "If." Suddenly he was unbearably tired. "I think I'd better go now," he said.

Outside, a misty cold hung over the still-wet streets. Numbly he walked down Park Avenue. The Christmas lights were dead on the long single line of trees down the center islands of earth. Taxis whooshed by on the puddled road, but he did not try to see whether they were vacant. He walked all the way.

In the dim vestibule of his house the brass plate gleamed softly. He shoved his key into the door.

On his pillow two yellow telegrams were placed where he could not miss them even if he undressed in the dark. He reached to the headboard lamp. They were both addressed to him. He tore one open.

> CONGRATULATIONS ON THE GRAND NEWS ABOUT YOU AND KATHY AND MY BEST TO HER. LET'S HEAR THE EXACT DATE. LOVE FROM ALL. BELLE.

He ripped apart the second envelope. It was unsigned. It had been sent that evening from Brentwood, California.

> YIPPEE.

He sat down on the bed and put his head down on his hands. The telegram from his sister Mary crackled slowly in his tightening fist.

CHAPTER EIGHT

THROUGH HIS SLEEP he heard the telephone ring. He woke sweating and heavy with the familiar weight of depression. For a second he was back in the dragging mornings of California years ago. The radiator spat steam from its leaky valve. It reoriented him; he'd forgotten to turn it off when he'd finally gone to bed. Back of the closed door Tom called, "It's for you, Dad." He sprang up.

"Right there."

The door opened, and Tom said, "He asked for *Lieutenant* Green, not Mister. Gram said to wake you."

"He?" The heaviness hit again. "Who?"

"Gee, I just said to wait. I answered it."

"O.K. Pretty late, isn't it?" He glanced at his watch as he went into the living room. It was past noon. The last time he'd checked, it had been nearly eight. He picked up the receiver and offered it an inert "Hello."

"Phil, it's Dave."

"Dave? Why, damn *you!* Where are you? When'd you get in?" He heard Dave laugh at the burst of pleasure in his own voice. "LaGuardia. Just now. I had a break and got assigned to a plane with my CO."

"Grab a cab. If you're broke, hold him downstairs."

"Hell, I'm not broke. Boy, it's good to be back."

"Well, come on. I haven't even had breakfast yet."

He showered and then carried a cup of black coffee into the bathroom. He sipped and then gulped it while he shaved. His eyes smarted, his eyelids were too small. Hangover. Only it wasn't just hangover. He jerked away from remembering. That wound-up spring inside somewhere— that was depression in the clinical sense of the psychiatrist's office. In the mirror his face looked sullen and dead.

A pan clattered to the floor in the kitchen. He squinted as if sudden light instead of sound offended his nerves. He wished he could be alone in the house, with no noise, no talk, no questions about last night's party.

Dave was a break. Man's talk it would be, of the army, the occupation, terminal leave, the old job or a new one. Good old Dave, thank God for Dave, Dave who didn't know a damn thing about Kathy.

"If things are going to be all tense and solemn all the time."

"Then what?" He should have said it at once. He should have made her finish the sentence, verbalize the threat implicit in the tone she used. "We'd better not get married after all." That's how she'd have ended it. He might as well have heard it, then, not let it hang in the air, a warning to behave, to be lighthearted about things. He had shrunk from hearing it, had gone wise with a soft wisdom and said he'd better leave now. He should have faced her. Told her. "Things *will* be tense and solemn plenty of the time," he should have said. "I'm a guy that gets tense, see? I snarl up and I goddam well can't help myself. I care about a thing and forget about other things. Damn it to hell, that's the way I am. If you don't want my kind of man, O.K., no harm done. Better now than later."

All those things he'd crumpled into a dignified silence while he made a dignified exit. Afraid to slug it out lest he lose her. You love a woman and you lose her—Christ, how do you stand it a second time? You don't—you crawl into a shell and stifle. All the sentences addressed to her later were so fine and right, but they were spoken only in the safe room of his mind. And so this waking with fear, shame, depression—the clinical trio, the three sisters pursuing——

He leaned down over the basin and slogged his face with the stinging cold of winter water as if he were beating himself.

As he sat talking with Dave, a preference for male companionship beat through him, surly, superior. Women talked of parties, of family, of children and summer cottages and love. This with Dave was what a man needed, this bone and muscle for the mind instead of pale plump softness. This men's talk was all in the hard clean outlines of battle, impossible bridges to be built under fire, the split of the atom, the greed of looting armies. Dave had begun in Italy and gone on through the whole business of D Day and the rest. He'd been wounded and mended and thrown back in. Women clawed softly at your manhood. War and work and the things you believed in gave it back to you. *This* gave it back to you, lounging in opposite chairs, taking the good short cuts men could take who'd been through the same things, fiddling through long drinks, arguing, differing or agreeing, but always tight on the tracks of reality.

Separation and time had made him forget how much he liked Dave. He'd told Minify they weren't especially close any more, yet when Dave had dumped his bag down and they'd stood there foolishly thumping each other on the shoulder, Phil had been seized with the old excess of feeling he'd had as a kid for "my best friend." Dave seemed taken by the same kind of upheaval, mixed in his case with the emotions of coming home at last. For him this was a homecoming by proxy, with Tom awestruck at his ribbons, Mrs. Green saying, "Well, Dave, why, Dave," and the house all astir to give him food, make him comfortable.

Phil found himself studying Dave's face as they talked.

129

He looked older, he seemed quieter. Was it just that three years had passed? Was it still the stamp of war and distance and loneliness, which would rub off soon under the caress of ordinary life? Or was Dave the holder of new knowledge which really aged and toughened the whole stuff of which his body and mind and understanding were compounded? He saw the thinning hair, the uneven groove between the eyebrows which showed clear now even when Dave wasn't frowning; he saw, too, the ruddy outdoor skin and knew a fleeting envy for the top fitness that army living clamped hard to a man.

"What's this series?" Dave asked.

"We'll get to it later." Inexplicably he wanted to put off talking of what he was doing. A shyness pervaded him, as if he might seem to Dave like a kid caught playing at a man's game. They went back to their discussion of Dave's plans. He was going to move his family East as Phil had done and was going to stay on now for part of his terminal leave to look over the ground. He'd already had letters from his old boss assuring him that a good job could be arranged with one of several Eastern firms, but the housing shortage might defeat him, if it was as serious as the papers reported. Phil listened and replied. Yet now, submerged but insistent, the series was fingering his mind again. He looked at the expressive face opposite him with new attention while a silent question nuzzled him back to his endless research.

Does Dave *look* Jewish?

Yes, he supposed he did, now that he asked it. He simply could not remember that he had ever thought the thing before in all the years they'd known each other. Where was it, this Jewishness? Dave topped six feet as he did, a little heavier, with no fat but of a bigger bone. His nose was short, stubby even, no hint of hook or curve. Hair and eyes were brown, lighter than his own and, where the unshaved stubble caught the last glint of sunlight from the window behind him, tinged with red blond. Yet if you thought, you'd know this man was Jewish. It was there somewhere. In the indented arcs of the nostrils? In the turn of his lips? In the quiet eyes? It was such a damn strong good face.

"What's eating you, Phil?"

"Me?"

"You've been giving me the once-over for five minutes."

"I got bogged in the series when you asked about it, and I started thinking what makes people look or not look Jewish."

"Come on, let's get down to it. Who's this Minify, anyway?"

Phil started at the beginning, his first jaundiced sureness that "it would be a lousy flop unless I caught hold of some hot idea." Without surprise, he noted that Dave showed as little steam as he himself had, nodding judiciously, trying to visualize it as if he were also a writer, but not aroused. Obscurely it pleased him that Dave should react also on this low-voltage level. He'd been right—they *were* just the same about things like this. He shoved back the tenuous shyness that persisted in him as he got nearer the point.

Once Dave interrupted. "You expecting a call, Phil?"

"A call?"

"You keep looking at the phone every few minutes."

"Hell." A moment later he added, "I had a scrap with my girl. I guess I want her to be the one to phone."

"Suppose I take that shower now?"

Phil shook his head and went on. He'd got to the part about the three books and found himself worked up all over again.

"Why shouldn't they write about swinish Jews?" Dave put in. "Don't Christians write about swinish Christians?"

It brought him up short. He said, "Sure, but——" and

131

then remained silent. Finally he shook his head, rejecting it.

"It's a question of timing, Dave. Fire-in-a-crowded-theater." He walked to the bookcase and took one of the books down, holding it flat on his palm as if he were guessing the weight. "These authors aren't dopes. They know they can add to the panic by this kind of thing."

"Balls. If they wrote only about big beautiful Jewish heroes—you'd get the business of glorifying. Chosen People Department." Idly, Dave tapped his thumbnail against the edges of his lower teeth. In the quiet room the clicking sounded like some new Morse code. "A two-thousand-year start on the master-race business," he said coldly, "by one small bunch of crackpot Jews—and look how many generations haven't paid it out."

"That's a point. I never thought of it." An excited twinge went through Phil.

"I read it somewhere," Dave said. "Doesn't explain the whole thing—too many pat explanations all over the place. The big hole in this one is the world won't be persecuting Germans two thousand years from now because they fell for the same crap."

He went to the Scotch and poured himself another drink. He waved the bottle at Phil and then took it over to the glass he held up.

"But that's not the point right now, Phil. Did you ever get your special angle?"

The odd reluctance arose again. It wasn't the skeptical mistrust that had sent him in to Minify that morning. It was only that Dave seemed cold about the articles. That had been all right at the start, but now it disturbed him. Politely interested he was, nothing more.

"Don't you *want* a good stiff series in a big national magazine, Dave?"

"Me? Sure."

"You sound bored."

"Hell, I'm anything but. In my outfit—no, I'll save that for later. It's just——" Dave smiled, as if in anticipation of his next sentence. "Well, *I'm* on the side lines on anti-semitism." He raised his glass in salute. "It's *your* fight, brother."

Phil thought it over. "O.K., I get it."

"The Jewish part is, anyway. The rest of it's everybody's fight. I bet we're in for a hell of a scrap, what's more."

"I bet. The Jews are always just the first."

"The hell with the Jews, as Jews." Dave hitched forward. He wasn't cold and polite any longer. "It's the whole thing, not the poor, poor Jews." He waved toward the windows, as if he were waving to the whole stretch of country beyond.

Involuntarily, Phil looked outside. The last daylight was still there, wan, impotent against the encroaching dark.

Dave's voice went on, somber now. "The price for anti-semitism is so damn big, Phil. And there's always a price for it."

A current of affection shot through Phil. Dave's face had gone hard; there was neither unease nor concession in it. He was staring into his drink as though there were a speck in it.

"You mean price reckoned in constitutions and preambles, things like that?"

"You know damn well what I mean. Don't force me to make with the big words." Dave shrugged, amiable again. "Anyway, let's hear the rest of it, for Pete's sake. You still hunting for the angle?"

"No, I finally got it." Quickly Phil told him what he'd been up to. "I've been doing it," he ended, "for about two weeks."

Dave didn't say anything. Phil waited. Dave carefully set his glass down and reached into his pocket for a cigarette. Then he remembered they were on the table near him. He got one out and lit it. He inhaled deeply and blew smoke out hard. Then he looked directly at Phil.

"Why, you crazy bastard," Dave said slowly. "You goddam crazy bastard."

Phil suddenly remembered the three of them in the pup tent in the woods near the house. The daylight all but gone, fierce rain battering the canvas. Through the open triangle the streaming pepper trees were as black green as sycamore and eucalyptus. They'd be thoroughly scolded when they got home, they knew, but the chilling excitement of the game held them there. Nine, maybe ten, they'd been. Their wooden rifles were at the ready, their eyes strained into the howling gloom.

"There," Petey had whispered hoarsely, "behind the trees. Lions and the jagers and the big cats. See?"

"Ready, men?" That was Dave.

"Ready, sir." Petey and he together.

Dave's voice went majestic.

"Let them have it. The jungle holds no terrors for Cecil Rhodes and his gallant band."

The delicious feeling of unity, friendship, safety together —whatever it was then, suddenly it stood warm and fresh again in him. He looked across to Dave's chair.

"Crazy bastard yourself."

Would she call him? Was she waiting for him to call her? Off and on all afternoon, the question mark had curled its separate existence in his mind. When Dave finally went for his shave and shower, Phil dialed her number. There was no answer.

Suddenly he knew that through all the hours, using Dave's presence for a screen, he'd been in hiding from his own sense of disaster. If he'd been alone, he'd have watched each hour of silence as a new semaphore of warning. He'd have faced the truth: that she, too, must have been charged with unspoken thoughts, stifled challenges. Dismay must stand thick in her heart, too.

Perhaps he'd dialed the wrong number. Sometimes you got balled up on the simplest mechanical things. He lifted the receiver again. Extreme care went into the operation this time, as if he were Tom adventuring with the delightful fact that if you did thus and so you could really pick Jimmy Kelly's house out of all the houses in New York. Not until the dial clicked hard against the metal stop each time did Phil release it and regard that step as successful. Then he waited. He counted the rings up to seven. There was no answer.

Just before he and Dave left for dinner, he said, "Oh, I'd better call Kathy." Dave waited. Phil whistled a phrase of music while he dialed. "Harder to get tickets for a concert than for the theater," he said, and hung up. "Thought she might join the celebration about your being home," he added heartily. "Guess she's out to a movie or something."

They went to a restaurant in the East Fifties which Kathy liked. As they waited for the Martinis they both ordered, they sat without talk. The tables were all filled; waiters hurried by with platters of charred steaks or creamy mixtures; thick oblongs of butter were forked out to them by a smiling bus boy. When their drinks came Phil swallowed a third of his in the first go.

"Want to talk about it?" Dave asked.

"Just one of those things." Phil put his drink down and lit a cigarette. "I'd probably be wiser staying on my own," he said. "You lose the instinct for marriage after seven years alone."

"Nuts."

"You and Carol get off on tangents much?"

"Who doesn't?"

"I don't mean fights about the kids or money or things. I mean about ideas."

Dave started to ask something but changed his mind. From anybody else it would have been a direct question about Kathy, Phil thought, and was grateful. He stared at the tip of his cigarette. In the amber light of the room it burned greenish white, without redness. Betty and I never— but that was a bad business to start on, even with himself. Betty was Betty and Kathy, Kathy. Nor had he ever set up yardsticks for Betty's thinking; he hadn't himself been moody, susceptible to shift and self-questioning then. Politics and principles hadn't even cut deeply into his existence in those days. All at once he wanted to find Kathy, apologize to her for being ratchety. And go meekly to Jane's party and "just not bring it up"? He ground out his cigarette.

"Those are the toughest fights," Dave said dispassionately, "the ones about ideas. Suppose Carol was a faithful party-line girl—can you imagine our life? Or suppose she'd been an isolationist in the old days or pro-Franco? Families break apart over ideas. In hot times like these, anyway."

"Like the Civil War. Pro-North husband and pro-South wife."

"Like anything that's explosive inside."

The waiter put large menus before them. They ordered. "Damn it," Phil said loudly, "let's cut the gloom." Asperity edged his manner as though it were all Dave's fault.

"Sure. I feel like blowing people to drinks. Know anybody to get?"

"Might try Minify." He laughed. "Not what you had in mind, hey? Trouble is—say, there's Anne, I'd forgotten her. Anne Dettrey, on the magazine, smart as hell. She's always fun."

"Give her a ring, why don't you?"

In the booth, feeling stealthy, he tried Kathy first. Then he called his house. There were no messages. He found Anne's number in the book.

"Nonsense, Phil," she said, "I'm putting my one New Year's resolution to its first test."

"I can imagine."

"To go to bed early—and alone—three times a week."

"You wouldn't want to go into a thing like that too easily?" His spirits rose. This was just anything-for-a-laugh talk, yet it seemed exceptionally important to argue her into coming. He explained about Dave and his first night back.

"By golly, patriotism," she said, and asked where they were.

He watched Dave and Anne as if he were years older, remote forever from the business of flirtation and attraction. Instantly she set in motion a campaign to appeal to Dave; instantly Dave changed, as if he'd peeled off a layer of personality and emerged younger, cleverer, more alive. Phil felt shoved aside. Odd sensations of pride mingled with the thin stridency of jealousy in him. Toward Anne he felt pride that he'd produced Dave; toward Dave it was the reverse. Deftly Dave was managing to inform her that he was a married man with two kids even while he announced that he'd be wanting to catch up on theaters and night clubs while he stayed on in town. She knew he didn't mean to go alone. She immediately accepted the situation and the invitations to come. They'd have a fine lighthearted time together, Phil thought, and again envy squeaked in his heart. High spirits, carefree hours, distance from loneliness and solemnity—perhaps those were the great desiderata of life after all.

He thought of Kathy.

It's *more* than just having fun. All at once he knew

137

she was at no movie. She'd known he would telephone sooner or later; she'd wanted that unanswered ringing to assault him. She'd meant it to bash him, teach him a lesson, bring him to terms. Women knew their weapons well. He glanced across the table. Anne and Dave were laughing about something he'd missed. Two young men in new dark suits, their haircuts still GI, were passing the table, weaving a bit.

"I don't like offishers," one announced and stopped uncertainly. Dave looked up, indulgent. The long-suppressed resentment, he thought, to army brass. The young man raised his voice. "An' shpecially if they're yids."

Dave's arm reached. His hand had the speaker's wrist before he'd shoved up out of his chair. His free hand was a fist, pulling back for leverage. Phil was up too, fury tearing through him. And yet he had time to notice the control in Dave's impassive face.

"Sorry, sir," the other young man cried. "He's terrible when he's tanked up, sir." He pushed angrily at his friend; the loss of balance was too much for the uncertain legs; the buckling body began the slow collapse the expert dancer simulates to get a laugh. Somewhere near, a girl tittered nervously.

Dave's grip was twisting the arm. As the body crumpled floorward it was only his hold which checked the descent. Waiters were hurrying up; heads were turning. Dave let go, brushing his fingers off against each other as if they were fouled. Anne urgently said, "Please, Phil, Dave."

They sat down. Anne muttered, "Horrible little fool," and Phil thought, You're mad, sure, but you're out of it. Then it was as if his whole mind gulped. My God, I forgot again.

Around them talk burst forth while a waiter and the mortified friend struggled to lift the drunk. Heads were averted as if near them on the carpet were a sour pool of vomit. Limp as a hammock the drunk was carried off. Anne asked for another drink.

Phil looked over to Dave; their eyes met. Dave's were hard, but his mouth bore a sardonic twist. "Take it easy, boy," Dave said.

"Let's don't even talk about it," Anne said. "This isn't just antisemitism; it's battle fatigue, too." Dave laughed, and Phil said, "I told you," with a gesture toward her as of the producer of a hit show toward its star.

Like a spitting rain, it was over. The new drinks came; their talk moved on to other things. Secretly, though, a core of rage burned inside Phil. There was that sudden need to crack your fist into bone when it happened; only that sagging, falling body had stopped Dave. You couldn't punch an unconscious man. You had it and you were left brutish when you were balked. He'd read the story about Rankin in Congress; he'd had it; he'd punched no jaws, yelled at no applauding House. Always there were reasons; only rarely was the circumstance so arranged that you could fight back. The rest was this pouring of your adrenalin and this futile dammed-up fury.

He knew. Now he knew. In his own guts and veins and muscles it stood intimate and exact. It wasn't Dave alone who'd been called "yid." Anne was the outsider and onlooker, but not he. Once it would have been he as well as Anne. Not now. Not ever again. Identification. Dear God, yes.

"Don't be grim any more," she said suddenly.

"Who, me?"

He glanced at her and then again at Dave. Composed and indifferent he looked, but his pulse jumped like a nerve at the side of his throat, just above his collar. The antisemite offered the effrontery—and then the world was ready with harsh yardsticks to measure the self-control and dignity with which you met it. You were insensitive or too sensitive; you were too timid or too bellicose; they gave you at once the wound and the burden of proper behavior toward it.

"I was thinking we might go somewhere where there's music," he said to Anne.

"Not for a while," Dave said. "I like it here."

Anne leaned forward so that she addressed both of them impartially. "Tell me why," she said plaintively, "every man who seems attractive these days is either married or"—she looked at Phil—"barred on a technicality?"

Her woebegone look and exaggerated sigh made them all laugh. Dave patted her hand. "Your timing is lousy," he said, "but your instincts are just great."

After an hour they did go on to a night club and later to another. They took turns dancing with Anne; they all laughed a good deal at their own wit. After they'd taken her home, Phil said, "Coffee?" and knew Dave would agree before he could nod. There was something about wanting to stay on together even though they talked of nothing that mattered. In the Third Avenue all-nighter, brilliant with white tile and hundred-watt bulbs, noisy with taxi drivers' talk and dance music from Hollywood, they hardly bothered with each other, but they stayed for a second mug of the hot black chicory-flavored coffee. The night blurred by. Somewhere there was sleep in it, and then Phil was awake and at once in a sharp hurry to get to the office. He would telephone from there. In his bedroom, Dave was sleeping so deeply that Phil dressed without fear of waking him. He would call Kathy without belligerence, without apology. But he wouldn't be able to back down either.

Miss Wales greeted him. "Mr. Minify'd like you in there, Mr. Green. It's some sort of meeting. They've already started."

The personnel manager, Jordan, was there, and Mary Cresson with her dictation book open on her knee. John looked formal, aloof. The round of "Morning's" was without friendliness.

"I've asked Mr. Green in," Minify said to Jordan, "because he might pick up some detail for his series. You know what he's working on?"

"Yes," Jordan said. "But, Mr. Minify, you've really got me wrong. I never think about what a person is."

"It's what's done or what's not done I'm interested in." He gestured toward Phil without looking at him. "Mr. Green would do well to devote a page or so of his series to me for never thinking to check down the line in my own outfit."

"If Mr. Green had come right to me——"

Minify turned so sharply in his swivel chair, Jordan stopped.

"My niece told me about Miss Wales," he said coldly, "so don't imply that Mr. Green did. She brought it up just to twit me. For a minute I didn't even catch—then it hit."

"But *I* told Mr. Minify's niece," Phil said. He stared with hostile eyes at Jordan. "You think that if a bright kid like Wales has to change her name to get a job, nobody should talk up about it?"

Jordan looked back, conciliatory, awkward. But he looked away quickly from Phil's steady examining, and his shoulders rose a fraction of an inch. "Of course *you*'d talk up," the gesture spoke in Phil's mind. Instantly he doubted his reading of it.

He glanced at John Minify and knew he'd caught the same thing. The lightness of Minify's eyes above the dark sockets was startling as he looked directly at Jordan. His face looked older. He sat erect and imperative before them. Then he picked up a pencil and began to write on a memo pad as if he'd forgotten they were there. He wrote several words rapidly, read them, changed them, and then turned the pad face down and went on as if there'd been no span of silence.

"Big talk comes easy, Jordan, and my editorials, too. I've been a fool to assume they'd mean what they say in my own office. Now I'll see they do."

"But really, Mr. Minify, I've never made it a matter of policy just to hire—why, it's just, well, personality." He brightened. "If a girl's personality is the type that fits in, I'd never ask——"

"It's just by chance, you mean, that we haven't one secretary named Finkelstein or Cohen? In the city of New York?" His voice was soft. "Come off it, Jordan."

Phil looked over curiously. Jordan was a man you'd never notice if there were other people about. Medium tall, medium color, neat as to clothes, haircut; even the wrinkles about his eyes seemed neatly rayed out in even, definite lengths. Now his face wore tension and fear. He was expecting to be fired. And he'd hate Jews for it.

"Mary, take a help-wanted ad, will you?" Minify picked up the small pad, read what he'd written, then ignored it. "Upper case, 'EXPERT SECRETARY,' and a couple lines white space. Then, lower case, 'for editorial department, national magazine, exacting work, good pay.' Then single line white space. Then, 'Religion is a matter of indifference in this office. Write full experience to Box ——' Got that, Mary?"

For the first time since he'd met her, Phil saw expression appear in her prim face. She likes this, he thought, and was surprised to find within himself an odd sense of occasion. "Better state the salary, Mr. Minify," Mary said matter-of-factly, "instead of just 'good pay.'"

"O.K. O.K. You fix it. *Times, Trib?*"

142

"Both. And they don't allow white space in want ads—they'll put that special line in caps, though."

"Right." With finality he turned to Jordan. "And in case you have to fire Miss Wales on any ground whatever at any time, please remember that I wish to review the case myself first."

The neat mouth opened, relief shone in the eyes. Minify's nod was as curt as the bang of a gavel. Jordan went out.

"Think I should fire him, Mary?"

"I don't know. I thought you were going to."

"I argued it out with myself for a long time." He looked at Phil. "Confusing, isn't it?" Phil said nothing. He knew Minify wasn't expecting an answer. "But till I do decide, he's not to interview applicants any more, that's sure." He stroked his tan scalp as if he were smoothing down ruffled hair. "Mary, you too busy to take on some personnel management?"

"No, Mr. Minify."

"That's the tone that means you're dead from overwork." They all laughed. "Tell you what. This ad. Get yourself a crack assistant for your regular stuff. Then take over on all new office help. I'll tell Jordan."

She stood up, robust, stolid, but she flushed like a young girl over her first tribute from a man.

"Yes, Mr. Minify."

"In any other ads you run, use that line, please." Vigorously he turned to Phil. "High time heads of firms took public positions on it."

Minify watched her decorous progress across the office and through the door. Then, as if the episode had sped up his metabolism, he embarked at once on a spirited harangue with invisible opponents. Once Phil thought, He isn't as calm and journalistic about it all as he was a few weeks ago, and instantly added, Lord, neither am I. Minify was half shouting at him now. "—the sloppy, slovenly notion that everybody's busy with bigger things. There just isn't anything bigger, as an issue, than beating down the complacence of essentially decent people about prejudice. Not what Stalin's up to, not the bomb or the peace. Because if hatred and bigotry just go on rotting the basis of this damn country"—he glared at Phil—"all the rest is pious hypocrisy."

He lit a cigarette and clamped it into the corner of his mouth as if it were a cigar. "How's your stuff coming now, Phil?" While he listened, the cigarette angled upwards, and above it he squinted one eye against the flaring smoke. It gave him the look of a man persistently winking. When the square box on his desk hoarsely announced a caller, Phil was reluctant to quit this lively office for his own.

In the corridor, his way was blocked by Frank Tingler, the fiction editor, the small neat figure of Bill Jayson, and a tall man with a vaguely familiar face.

"Morning, Phil," Jayson said, and Tingler, "Hi, Green, know Rick Dohen? Mr. Green."

" 'Do." Mr. Dohen said, and offered his hand.

"How do," Phil answered, and disliked him. They shook hands heartily while Tingler explained in his flat voice, "We're running Mr. Dohen's new serial in the first April issue."

"Oh, yes," Phil said. "That new illustrator McAnny found in the army———"

"I must stop by and tell McAnny how delighted I am," Dohen interrupted. "Have you seen the opening spread, Mr. Green? Really a new talent. We were just talking about it. How would you characterize it, Bill?" He looked down at Jayson, and Jayson had to tilt his head back to meet his gaze. Fleetingly Phil hoped Jayson really didn't mind any more being so short.

144

"It's new and it's right," Jayson said dryly. "And you'll have to wait to tell McAnny. He's out in the Middle West on a special strike layout at G. M."

Tingler looked at Phil, but the thickly ground lenses hid whatever comment his glance was designed to convey.

"Sort of a combination of Varga girl and Ingrid Bergman, that first illustration of Gracia," Dohen said, and laughed in his enthusiasm. "That's it. Bitch and saint. Hard enough to catch in writing, but *when* I saw that first oil. Tell that boy Herman I'm—fact, I'd really like to tell him personally." He looked down to Jayson again. "Fix it up, Bill?"

"I'll do that." There was no promise in his voice. "Well, I'll be getting back. So long."

Phil moved off with him. Jayson didn't like Dohen, and Tingler was bored with him. This distinguished-looking Richard Dohen, Phil knew, was one of the highest-paid serial writers in the magazine world. "What's the new one about?" he asked Jayson.

"Well, the gimmick is this gorgeous dame is sitting there exactly ten years from the night her husband walked out to marry the second wife. Sudden impulse. She—— Hell, don't bother me, Phil."

Phil grinned. But they were nearing his office, and all at once nothing mattered but Kathy. Embarrassment plucked at him. The adult thing would have been to telephone her as soon as he'd waked yesterday, gone to her, straightened this out. Dave would have waited for him without resentment.

There was a note propped against his telephone. *Miss Lacey called. E. W.* Underneath it the line, *Again at 11:10. Please call her.*

Without sitting down he dialed the number.

CHAPTER NINE

I'LL TRY AGAIN AT NOON, Kathy was thinking. She moved away from the bedside table so that the phone would not persuade her into a third attempt. He'd ring back the moment he could. This was no crisis to justify asking Miss Wales to put the call through to him in the meeting.

She went firmly into the bathroom and weighed herself as if that had been her intention for many minutes. In a way it *was* a crisis. She'd known it when he left her; she'd known it when she'd fallen asleep; she'd known it all day yesterday when instinct cautioned her from telephoning him and telling him what she was going to do.

She glanced down at the revolving tape of the scale. Two pounds off. Worry it off; toss it off in your chivied sleep; eat it off from the heart. What *made* her go all skewered on this damn business when they talked about it, when they were not apart on it at all, in theory or in fact?

There was something mysterious in the process of quarreling. You said one wrong thing and then tried to justify it and said a further thing. That in turn needed explaining or defense. All the time you helplessly knew that if you could only step off the treadmill of dissension and start anew—but something held you where you were with demoniac persistence. Then it was too late. Emotions came in; his face showed disapproval and surprise; anger spat in you that he should misread your motives. Or pride reared up, and you'd be damned if you'd risk seeming abject and always at fault. The sense of crisis deepened, and your helplessness with it.

146

With Jane and Harry last night she'd been in no snarl at all. She'd been unequivocal, incisive. But he hadn't been there to hear.

"You're saying in effect," she'd said, "that it'd be nice if he just wouldn't embarrass any Jew haters you might have at the party."

It was nice to remember that sentence. Why had she reserved such clarity for Jane and Harry when it was Phil she cared about?

With a start she saw she was still on the scale, staring down at it malevolently as if it were an insect she was steeling herself to squash. She went back to the bedroom. She was tired; her back was tired; her neck was tired. She wished he would get out of the meeting and call her. She glanced at her watch. Less than ten minutes had passed since her second try.

With Bill, when things went wrong, she'd never felt this dull ache or fear or whatever it was. There'd been a kind of remoteness instead. But in those days she'd always felt right on the issue they disagreed on. Twice now with Phil she'd known she was somehow in the wrong. She should resent him for making her feel so; that was supposed to be human nature. But it didn't work that way. She just hurt. This frightened wonder about losing him was what hurt.

The drive to Darien had soothed her. She felt purposeful and clearheaded. But the string of cars parked in front of the snowy stretch of ground before the house warned her that her neat plan would not work. She'd forgotten the usual comings and goings of the suburban world on New Year's afternoon. Inside, she knew there'd be no chance for a serious talk until much later. And as each couple arrived with some variation of hair-of-the-dog remarks, each with the satisfied look of one who coins a bright new witticism, she found herself exasperated and bored.

"Darling, I just heard the news. You're getting married again. Who is he? What's he like? When do we meet him?" Endlessly the questions had come. "What's his name?" "What's he do?"

He's a writer. Phil Green. No, he writes as Schuyler Green. That's right. *Smith's* mostly for the last couple of years. Oh, thank you, I think he's pretty bright myself.

Only when she'd got off alone did she even ask herself whether Phil would have expected her to say anything else. Suddenly she'd flimsily announced that she'd "forgotten to check up on things at the house" and had gone off in desperation to the cottage which needed no checking at all. Unlocking the door, seeing the pleasant rooms as if she were Phil seeing them for the first time, the wide windows that would stream with yellow sunshine on a prettier day, the books and magazines left on end tables as if the place were really lived in—all of it had sent her off into happy planning of spring week ends there with him, and later the whole summer for all of them. And then the question, and with it the doubt, like a checkrein.

Of course he wouldn't have expected her to say anything else. It would be imbecilic to say, "He's a writer, he's Jewish," "His name is Phil Green, he's Jewish," "He writes as Schuyler Green, he's Jewish."

That would be a sort of inverted proof that it did matter to her—or would if it were true. If Phil weren't doing this thing, would it ever occur to her to mention his religion, or his agnosticism, which was much more interesting? "He's a writer, he's Episcopalian," "His name is Phil Green, he's an agnostic." Surely it would be equally clumsy and absurd to say the other. Was that the only reason she hadn't once mentioned it?

And when she'd told Bill Pawling about getting married,

Bill's "What's he like?" had sent her on and on about Phil. But that one thing she hadn't mentioned then, either.

"Oh, God, I get so mixed up."

In the pleasant empty cottage, she said it half aloud. How could she, of all people, get so confused on these things? She'd been so clear always, she and all the other people she knew, like Jane and Uncle John and everybody else. They'd not think about things like antisemitism often, but when it did come up, there wasn't any question that they loathed it and wanted to do something to stop it from growing. And yet now she was in the middle of a different place, where the thing became a personal thing—now everything she did or said was fuzzy.

Twice in so short a time things had gone awry between them. And both times she'd had that dull pull of fear. The checkrein again, tighter.

Now, remembering the cottage, and unconscious of the gesture, Kathy moved her head down and up and around in a swiveling motion. She sighed and reached for something to read. Under her stretching arm the telephone rang. She snatched the arm back as if it had touched hot metal. Then she took up the receiver.

"Kathy?"

"Oh, Phil, I wanted to call you last night, but it was midnight when I got back and——"

"Got back? Where from?"

"Jane's. I went up to have it out with her. Oh, darling, has this been hell for you, too?"

"I haven't exactly liked it." His voice was stiff. "You mean you told her you couldn't *persuade* me?"

"Oh, no. I found myself saying all the things you would have. Jane said, 'Well, goodness, O.K.,' as if she hadn't asked it and started this awful business." She swallowed.

"Darling, don't let's do this any more—we *feel* the same underneath. Couldn't we have lunch and talk?"

There was a pause. In his office, Phil remembered he was standing. He sat down. He hauled back his runaway feelings as if they were lively dogs on a leash. Suddenly he seemed unable to evaluate, even to remember clearly, the nuances that had seemed so tremendous. A hair-splitting nicety endowed them now, nothing more.

"But why the disappearing act?" He couldn't help the tone of resentment. "I phoned you all evening and got pretty beat up about all the silence."

"I just couldn't phone till *after* I'd fixed everything. I drove out the minute I got up, but the place was full of people and I couldn't get them alone till awfully late."

She was hurrying explanations the way Tom sometimes did, so earnest in admission that it became incumbent on him to make it easier, to end it. Damn the inquisitor's role he was always falling into. "Solemn" was a kind way to describe this testy stuffiness of his. He was being a purist, a fool—no girl like Kathy would put up with it forever.

"It *was* hell, darling," he said. "I warned you I could be a solemn ass. If you love somebody, though—— Hold it a second." Miss Wales had opened the door.

"Captain Goldman's on my line, Mr. Green," she said. "Could you lunch with him?"

He raised a forefinger to her and spoke again to Kathy. "Dave's here; he got in yesterday. He's calling in about lunch. Should we—no, we'd better talk this out first."

"Maybe it's good *not* to hash it over any more for a while, Phil." A brighter inflection warmed her voice. "Let's do have Dave. I'm dying to meet him."

He came back to the office in a bouncing energy. He went

straight to the typewriter and began at once to "write forward" as he called it, instead of first rewriting parts of the last page or two—his usual priming device. For nearly two hours there was almost no break in the clack and clatter of the old-timer they'd given him. The needed word leaped forth, the sentences turned and shaped and smoothed on the lathe of his mind so quickly that his speeding middle fingers on the keys were like a secretary struggling to keep up with too-rapid dictation.

He lit a cigarette and stretched back. Then he saw another cigarette, freshly lighted also, tipped against the edge of the loaded ash tray. He smiled. It was another sign. When you wrote in this fierce concentration you didn't know where you were, didn't remember the gesture of a moment before, didn't know what time was elapsing. You felt whole and good and damn lucky to be a writer. You couldn't believe you'd ever again be caught in the sticky, faltering uncertainty, the fretfulness of doubt over progress, the ambivalence about the choice of a word, the point of attack, the transition to the next point. You were master, for the moment, of your element, and no man anywhere could contrive a life you would prefer to your own.

The door opened. He winked at Miss Wales and pointed to the sheets spread on the desk. He knew what she would say and wanted to forestall it.

"Nope, not ready for you yet." He'd explained at the beginning that he would not be turning over each day's rough draft for her professional typing, that indeed she'd not get any of it until the series was virtually complete. For a week she had accepted this odd ukase without remonstrance. Then she began to give daily signs that secretarial protocol was being outraged. Each time she saw new pages of manuscript, her itch to take charge of them became more apparent. She wanted to take those untidy pages and turn them into unmarred manuscript. Phil sympathized. But even if he were to turn over his draft without the title, the first sentences of the first paragraph of the first article would effectively end his role with her.

"I was born, as it happens, of an Episcopal father and an Episcopal mother, whose parents on both sides before them had been Episcopalians. But for the last eight weeks——"

No, she couldn't see even that much for a while. While he was thinking, he automatically gathered the strewn sheets, slapped their edges against the desk, folded them in thirds, and stuck the thin wad into his pocket. He would take this new batch home, to join all the other pages. Not that he wouldn't trust Miss Wales with his life, his cash, or sacred honor. But he would not trust her to enter the office when he was not there and resist even one quick glance at the top page. For in her place, he himself would certainly argue that anything to be published for three million readers need scarcely be treated as a secret.

"I wasn't even going to suggest it, Mr. Green," she said. "If you like to work that way, it's all right."

"Must seem like damn foolishness."

"I just came in to tell you something about Jordan."

He looked up, interested. "Let me just get these notes together. Only take a minute."

Nothing Wales could say about Jordan could disturb this good feeling of satisfaction, of virtue in the old Latin sense. The meeting of Dave and Kathy had added fillip to his own joy at feeling close with her again. Never in any later stage of love could reconciliation seem so pervasive; as if each separate cell of body and brain knew harmony again. They'd had only the taxi ride to the restaurant alone, but that quick time had given her back to him. "Oh, Phil,

I never pretended to be as clearheaded and strong about things as you."

Between her and Dave, there'd been at once an easy, quick affection. She'd offered to help him search for the six-room apartment he'd need, and they'd all laughed when Dave wryly said, "One good thing about the housing shortage, Phil, nothing in it you can pick up for your series." Over their coffee she'd impulsively said, "Come on up on Saturday, Dave, to this party my sister's giving Phil and me."

She'd been perfectly uncomplicated about it. So different, he'd thought, when your own life isn't involved, and chided his mind the next instant.

"Meet-the-family party?" Dave had grinned. "Not me. But thanks, anyway."

A polite cough brought him back to the present. Miss Wales said, "Go right ahead, Mr. Green," and looked at the notes already folded neatly before him.

"Sorry, I got thinking about something. What about Jordan?"

"Well, he's telling everybody about Mr. Minify's ad and he thinks it's a wonderful thing. He's *saying*."

"Quick as that?" He snapped his fingers. Knuckling little hypocrite.

"I'd thought I'd ask you if it's true the ad says right out that——"

"Right straight out. It'll be in the papers tomorrow."

"You mean practically *inviting* any type to apply?"

"Any type? What are you driving at?"

"Oh, Mr. Green, *you* don't want things different around here either, do you? Even though you're an editor and it's different with editors?"

Finally it got through the sheath of his own good spirits that under her usual manner was something new.

153

"Different for editors how?"

She hesitated. She looked away. "Well, I just mean. If they just get one wrong one in, it'll come out of *us*." Her voice edged into stridency. "Don't you hate being the fall guy for the kikey ones?"

Kin to no reaction he'd ever had before, a tiny geyser seemed to shoot upward and spray out within his viscera. An image flashed into his mind of a minuscule Old Faithful. When he spoke, he did so with extreme care.

"We've got to be frank with each other," he said. "You have the right to know right off that words like kike and kikey and yid and coon and nigger just make me kind of sick, no matter who says them."

"Why, *I* just said it for a type. You know the kind of person." She was clearly astonished at being picked up on it.

"We're talking about a word, first."

"But that's nothing. Why, sometimes I even say it to myself—about me, I mean. Like, if I'm about to do something and I know I shouldn't, sort of in my head I'll say, 'Oh, don't be such a kike.'"

The minute geyser rose in stature, crowding his solar plexus. She was not improvising; this was truth she was telling him.

As if the matter were disposed of, she went on, "Just *one* of the objectionable ones in here and——"

He said, "Just a minute." She stopped. It had to be thought through a bit before he could go on. He leaned over his desk, picked up a pencil as though he were about to write. She waited, and this time he felt no compunction about letting her wait.

What made her do it? He had to know something of the answer, guess at it, find it, before he could go on speaking. Did she have so deep a hatred and fear of the word that she needed to fob it off as a light jest to exorcise it? Was it an unconscious need to beat the insulter at his own game by applying the epithet to oneself first? "This is nothing; this isn't a word that can hurt me." The man who cries out to the wife he has betrayed, "I know I'm a weakling, a bounder, a cad, anything you want," in the need to make himself immune from the words she would otherwise hurl—wasn't she doing the same thing? Or did her impulse spring from an unconscious longing, hidden and desperate, to be gentile and have the "right" to call Jews kikes?

He put down the pencil and turned back to her.

"What do you mean by 'objectionable'?" He was proud that no irritation sounded in his words.

"You know, loud, and too much rouge and all."

"They don't hire *any* girls that are loud and vulgar. What makes you think they'll suddenly start?"

"Well, it isn't *only* that." She suddenly turned on him with spirit. "You're just sort of heckling me, Mr. Green. You *know* the kind that just starts trouble in a place like this and the kind that doesn't, like you or me, so what's the sense of pinning me down?"

"You mean because we don't look especially Jewish."

"Well——" She smiled confidently.

That was it, then. They were O.K. Jews; they were "white" Jews; with them about, the issue could lie mousy and quiet.

"Look, Miss Wales," he said slowly, "I hate antisemitism and I guess I'd better tell you I hate it just as much when it comes from you as from anybody else."

"Me? Anti—why, Mr. Green!" She stood up, did nothing whatever for a space of seconds, and then walked with complete dignity from the room.

Bert McAnny was in an expansive mood. He'd been in Detroit for only two days, and already his assignment was

155

well wound up. The press photographer Jayson frequently used on free-lance assignments in the Middle West had proved responsive to his direction and ideas, and there'd be enough good shots for ten articles instead of one. The second batch of enlargements should be done by evening, and he could start East at once. Everybody had been friendly and helpful, whatever side they took on the strike. That was because *Smith's* was so big. This man across the luncheon table had made himself an old friend in two days.

Jefferson Brown was public-relations counsel for one of the smaller automotive companies, and not involved with the strike, but he'd given Bert McAnny much time and help with collateral pictures for background and fill-ins. Bert liked him.

"Want to see some shots, Jeff?" he asked. "All I've got are Leica-size glossies, though." He reached into his pocket.

"I'm no good with them while they're just postage stamps." But Jeff Brown took the envelope and went through the pictures.

"You sure slant the whole damn thing for the strikers," he grumbled when he returned them. "Orders?"

"I told you I was pro-labor." McAnny shrugged. "You go after stuff you feel sympathetic to."

"You going to print those nigger ones?"

"If they fit the story that's turned in. Why not?"

"Stir up—God, you people that don't have to live with it the way we do!" McAnny sat there looking superior. Jeff Brown thought, Righteous little bastard. Pro-labor, sure. Pro-underdog. Pro-the FEPC. They were all Jew lovers, coon lovers, Roosevelt lovers. Communists.

"It's plenty stirred up without any help from *Smith's*," McAnny said.

"You guys in New York ought to wake up. Why, out

156

here, between the Jews and the coons, we're——" He stopped at the look McAnny gave him. "Skip it."

"You'll be telling me next that Bilbo and Rankin are great fellows," Bert said. A combative look came into Jeff Brown's face, and Bert abandoned sarcasm for persuasion. "There's no sense us fighting, Jeff. We've had a swell time for two days, and it's a free country."

"Until they take over the rest of it." Brown raised a fork for emphasis. "You know something? Guy over at Ford told me. There's a boycott on the radio against Christians."

"Go on, you're kidding."

"Fact. All the networks and their Jew owners have ganged up—last two weeks all they've carried is *White Christmas* just so they wouldn't have to play *Silent Night* and *Adeste Fidelis* and things like that."

Bert guffawed, and Jeff protested, "It's no joke—it's true."

"Come on, Jeff, you're falling for a lot of antisemitic stuff. It gives me the creeps, hearing cockeyed talk like that. That's nothing but witch-hunt stuff."

"They've taken you into camp, too, hey?"

"I just don't go for antisemitism and all that business," McAnny said. He took a sedate sip of coffee. "At the office about four of the editors are Jews, but you couldn't ask for better guys. There's this fellow, calls himself Schuyler Green—you must have read some of his stuff. Well, except he's too touchy, you'd——"

"Schuyler Green?"

"Know him?"

"No. I just—name rings a bell somewhere."

"Probably seen some of his things. Take him now." Bert's manner was judicious; he would not indulge in panegyric. "Oh, sure, he's pushy the way they all are, gets himself

157

asked to lunch with the boss, won't give Jayson a line on a series he's doing just to make us dance around waiting. But he's really O.K." He saw that Jeff Brown wasn't listening.

"I knew it," Jeff said suddenly. "That name. Vice-President over at Naismith Motors is married to his sister. My wife plays bridge with her, and she brags about her famous brother, Schuyler Green. King, Belle King, probably Bella to start with—well, will you just imagine that!"

"Imagine what?"

"The hot shot's wife, Dick King's wife, being a yid." He roared. "Is that something!"

"You mean you didn't know it?"

"Christ, a thing like that? She's never let on, or King either. Belong to the Grosse Pointe smart set, clubs, all that."

"Passing, hey?" McAnny said. He wrinkled his nose as at a sudden stink. "I'd have the guts to admit it, wouldn't you?"

Brown shook his head, the amiable expert. "Yellow underneath, all of them. They'll do it every time if they can get away with it." He paused. "Bella doesn't look Jewish. Does he?"

"Well——" He thought back to Phil's face. "There's that Jewish something when he smiles, around the mouth."

Suddenly Jeff Brown slapped the table and began to laugh. "Wait'll Helen hears this. Oh, brother."

It had been a successful party any way you looked at it. As Phil drove off with Kathy from the music and talk and laughter behind them, he felt that an invisible imp perched on the dashboard and pointed a derisive finger at him.

"Was fun, wasn't it, darling?" Kathy said. She had wanted to go up in her car and had insisted on his taking the wheel.

"Except for meeting everybody. But that's me all over. A goddam violet."

"Nobody'd ever guess it. They all think you're wonderful."

They drove on in easy silence. It was midnight; they were going to join Anne and Dave for a nightcap at Anne's place. Beside him Kathy hummed the tune they had danced to in the cleared dining room. "You old smoothie," she'd said after their first steps together. "Why didn't you tell me you dance like this?" His dancing was dated, and he knew it perfectly, but her praise made him feel young and smug. He'd promptly tried a fancy rhythm break and muffed it. They had laughed over it, and the whole evening had gone just that way.

Pleasant people, good talk, faintly lascivious remarks about the wedding license and waiting for their marriage next week—spurts of discussion about price control and draft extension and taxes, disagreement, agreement, no tension about anything. He had "brought it up" when they asked what he was writing, and nothing had happened. No look, no lull in the talk, no quick glance. The talk and jokes and laughter drifted on, and the pride in Kathy's eyes exhilarated him as much as the sense of being liked and even lionized a little as "a real live author."

He took his eyes briefly away from the road and looked at Kathy.

"Who's that Mrs. Manning?" he asked. "The one said she was hipped on education?"

"Ellen? She's got three boys and she's been up to her ears starting a sort of Springfield Plan in the schools here. Her husband Tom is hipped on skiing—drags her off to Placid every other week end."

"She told me, at least about the schools. I got on fine with her. I guess I understand people that get hipped on things."

"Darling." She looked up at him. In the bluish light from the instrument panel he looked tired. But he was happy. His moods never needed to be guessed at; he was transparent because he was without a touch of the devious. In the first minutes after they'd arrived for dinner alone with Jane and Harry, she'd known that everything was going to go smoothly and she was proud of him, pleased with herself for belonging to so pleasant a world as Jane's delightful house indicated. They'd talked about his series. Harry called it "a smart stunt" in his booming way, but she'd warned Phil on the way up that Harry Caulton was the hearty extrovert about everything. "He was against Dewey, though," she'd said, and Phil had chuckled at the recommendation. "For a big corporation lawyer that *is* sort of bright, Phil." Jane had praised *Smith's* for "going after this awful thing," and by the first ring of the doorbell they were all four in a party mood. And now it was over and without mishap. Confidence and anticipation surged in her. By next Saturday they'd be man and wife, and whatever other problems arose would be vanquished, too.

"He can have my apartment," she said suddenly. "Dave."

"Yours?"

"Oh, no, I guess they just couldn't squeeze in, with two children."

"It's sweet of you, to worry so about him, darling." She'd gone to every broker in town with Dave for the past three days, bought the papers at midnight, and marked the addresses that were not in "impossible neighborhoods." He was as grateful as Dave himself. "Maybe the kids could sleep in cots in the living room for a while, anyway. We'll ask him."

His mother's room was to be theirs. Just yesterday, she and Kathy had discussed it with a serene practicality that left him fidgeting. About some things women were tougher than men. He doubted whether Kathy would be as ill at ease as he himself if their first nights were to be spent right in the apartment with Tom and his mother. Not that they would be. They were going off for five days to the White Mountains.

"Why'd we ever say we'd meet them after the theater?" Kathy asked. "It'll be way past one when we hit town."

"Should we phone them no soap?" Under the casual words, the secret hammering. They'd been out with Dave or with Dave and Anne every night for a week.

"Let's, darling." He could scarcely hear the words. Automatically, his foot inched the accelerator nearer the floorboard. They drove on in silence. It had been a strange week; they had never been alone enough even to "talk out" the quarrel they'd had.

"I felt pretty damn much of a fool at Jane's," he said. "For all the fuss I'd kicked up beforehand."

She made a little sound. She was touched by his apology. It felt good to offer it, so simple, so casual, the daisy impulsively picked from a meadow and handed over in a moment of love.

"Can't think why she even bothered to ask," he went on lazily, "if I'd lay off for tonight."

She shrugged. And all at once he knew why and clamped the reason back into his throat. It had nothing to do with Kathy. It was no fault of Kathy's. But all at once he knew what had gone on in Jane after Kathy's straight talk on New Year's Day.

" 'Well, goodness, O.K.' " She had said it and accepted the fact that "it" would come up. She hadn't even considered breaking her word. She hadn't given his secret away to a soul.

She had merely weeded out the list of guests she'd originally meant to ask. She'd left out some of the friends who normally were part of "the crowd." Or if she'd asked some of them anyway, she'd "cleared it" first with them to be sure there'd be nothing awkward.

That was for tonight and its special circumstance. But at her next party and the next and next, at all her parties, those very guests she'd banished tonight would be there again, welcome in that charming house, comfortable with all those pleasant people, many of whom, like Jane, had praised him and *Smith's Weekly* for "going after this awful thing."

"Say, Dad," Tom said in a conversational tone, "are we Jewish?" Phil looked up from the morning newspaper. "Jimmy Kelly said we are."

"What'd you tell him?"

"Gee, I just said I didn't know and I'd ask you."

Phil folded the paper, creasing it lengthwise and then across as if he were wedged in by a subway mob. But it was time he needed, not space. He might have known this would happen and thought out in advance what to do. It would be simple to say "yes" for now, but lies weren't the way out with other things. With this intangible one, a temporary yes would sow deep confusions for later on.

He glanced once at his mother. She was waiting with the same offhand interested look the kid had.

"Well, Tom, let's go back a bit." He needed to decide, but his mind busied itself with other matters. The superintendent, Olsen? Had to be. Olsen to Alma Martin to somebody else on the street until it reached Jimmy Kelly's house across the way. Three weeks ago Phil would have been unbelieving and dumfounded. Now he felt only recognition. He looked at Tom. "Remember when you said you were a bandit outlaw?" But a better idea suddenly struck him. "Remember the Danny Kaye movie?"

"Sure."

"And how you asked if a dead brother's ghost could really get into his twin's body and make him dance and sing and talk like him?"

"Kathy said it was just pretending." His eyes brightened in memory, and he began to laugh.

"Well, I'm pretending I'm Jewish for the stuff I'm writing now."

"You mean it's like a movie or a game?"

"Sort of a grown-up game."

"You mean you're not Jewish but just as if you had a twin brother's ghost in *you*, like the movie, and *that* one is Jewish?"

"Something like that." He grinned at Tom and in a singular flare of pleasure leaned toward him and gave him a shadow-box punch to the shoulder. The kid had caught something up into a phrase for him. Tom punched back and giggled. He often took recourse in this silly giggle when something was happening which was pleasant but beyond him. Now he immediately masked his face with severity, plunged both hands deep into his pockets, and looked at his father in man-to-man deliberation.

"D'you suppose I could let Jimmy in on the game, too?"

"Too? You mean you want to get in on it yourself?"

"Can I, Dad? What do you have to do?"

Phil didn't answer. His mind darted ahead, skimmed the possibilities that might be there for a boy of eight. He remembered the navy's searchlights, picking over dark, ominous shores and beaches.

"Look, Tom, this isn't a game a little boy would know how to play right," he said finally. "I'd like it if you'd just promise not even to tell anybody it's a game. Would you promise that?"

Tom turned serious, to match his father's new look. He placed the backs of his hands hard against each other, lacing

163

his fingers stiffly. "That's our special G2 sign for the pledge of honor."

"O.K."

For the first time, Mrs. Green spoke. "What'll you tell Jimmy?" Tom looked quickly from her to his father. A sly look came into his face. "White fibs aren't wrong for G2," he said, "even if they stick needles in you." He shuddered deliciously. "I'll tell him I haven't any information."

It didn't satisfy Phil, but he let it go. Tom rushed away from the table to get his books and the new stamps he'd collected for trading at school. Mrs. Green sat very still. She looked tired again these last two or three days. He asked when she was to have her second check-up at Dr. Craigie's and at Dr. Abrahams', but as she answered he was suddenly hearing Bill Jayson's rueful "Hell of a note, isn't it? Then they'd think you were hiding it."

Tom clattered back on his way out.

"Wait a minute," Phil said. "I'm not so sure that's a good idea." Tom stopped. "To tell him you haven't any information."

"Oh." He looked crestfallen.

"Maybe you'd better say you asked me and I said I was partly Jewish."

"O.K. But not say it's the ghost part!" His face brightened again, and he banged out of the house.

"That's better, I think," his mother said, but Phil didn't answer. From his room came sounds which said Dave was getting up. In a way, he thought, it's always going to be true, at that.

CHAPTER TEN

"SORT OF TRIPLE PLAY," Anne was saying, "till he finds an apartment big enough." She glanced at Kathy, then across to Phil, ignoring Dave as if they were three doctors in consultation and he the patient who could listen but not object.

"It's awfully bright," Kathy said.

"Certainly better than giving up this grand job he's hooked," Anne said, "and going back to California."

"Nuts. I wouldn't consider it." The patient refused to be relegated to the passive role any longer. "I'll widen my field of operations, that's all. Brooklyn, the Bronx, the suburbs."

Dave's firmness put, if not a period to the discussion, at least a semicolon, and it came to a temporary halt while they all shifted positions in their chairs, sipped their brandy or coffee, and looked appraisingly at him and each other. Behind them, ignored by common consent, was the cluttered table they had just left. They were at Kathy's; it was Claudia's day off, and the girls had got dinner together. Anne had been efficient and gay, offering some joking comment every time she came in from the kitchen. Kathy had been quiet and so clearly happy that she sent forth to Phil an indescribable assurance that being a wife, a mother, a provider of food and comfort was her natural role. In two days they'd be married and alone together and their life truly launched.

"You won't find a thing anywhere," Anne began again to Dave, "and anyway"—she gestured to the whole room—

"*this* would be a promotion from my dump. By summer you'll find a sublease at least."

"Your place is lovely, Anne," Kathy protested, "even with all that glamorous mob hiding the color scheme."

Lazily Phil wondered whether there really was an undercurrent of antagonism between the two or whether he imagined it. It didn't matter. In this exchange, Kathy's voice again wore its silken envelope as it had once or twice at Jane's party. That no longer mattered either. For now he knew it for a clue that she was straining a bit for that air of suavity which so many people in and around New York seemed to regard as desirable. It was silly and a little insecure, but no longer did it antagonize him; rather he felt it a touching recourse for her to have to take.

Dave was again resisting Anne's plan and he let them argue. He'd been as astonished as Dave when she'd come out with it. It was fantastic, some ten days after she'd met him, but no more so than that the housing shortage might force him to turn down the Quirich-Jones offer. In his own concern for Dave—the last two long-distance calls to Carol and the kids were tempered with discouragement—he had kept himself mute in this discussion for fear he'd weight it to Anne's disadvantage. Even a temporary move would be a good deal of nuisance for her. Why had she offered it? Was she falling in love with Dave, married though he was? "It's you she's really interested in," Dave had said casually one night. "I mean if you weren't engaged." No, her motive in this offer was surely free of anything personal. Lonely people were often the generous ones, as if they unconsciously sought ways to prove themselves needed and important. Anne was looking at Dave directly, on her face only a matter-of-factness, undecorated by sympathy or generosity.

"So it's a cinch," she summed up. "Kathy moves in with

166

Phil; I move here; you and your wife and kids move into my place. No cots in the living room."

"We'll see." Dave took her empty glass without asking her and said, "May I?" to Kathy.

"Let me," Kathy said. "How's yours?" He raised a half-amber glass, and she turned to Phil, repeating the question. She looked not at his drink but at him. Her face still wore the smile she'd just given Dave, friendly, wanting to fetch things for welcomed guests, but this private glance was a question for Phil alone. "Did they?"

His eyebrows moved up as if in a shrug, but a dart of unwillingness pricked at him again. "We're practically arranging an affair for them," Kathy had said last night, "deserting them in her apartment in the middle of the night." Her words came back, casual and even gay. There was no reproof in them, no prying for a counterremark that might consolidate her assumptions into fact. She was willing for them to be in bed together; she would not turn to the moralist's vocabulary for terms like "adultery" any more than he.

Yet the very notion had nicked reluctance into life like a touched nerve. He had pulled back sharply last night from speculation and now again he did the same thing. He gave Kathy a bland smile, waved to the piano, and said, "You wouldn't play that sonata for us, would you?"

Instead, she opened the phonograph and clicked a switch. A record must have been lying on the turntable, for at once the room filled with the lilting cadence of music which Phil did not know. He listened, trying to identify it, and knew the record was from some middle movement; the first measures were a continuation, not an opening. He said, "Mozart?" and Kathy nodded, and came to sit near him. He looked at her and heard the music spill forth in a rippling, simple beauty. All at once he hungered to be free of all

167

angers and resentments and confusions always, to know only this contentment trickling into the secret layers—so vulnerable—inside him.

For perhaps a quarter hour there was no talk from anyone. When a record wound down to its eccentric grooves, Kathy would rise to turn it over or change it, and during the silence each of them seemed unwilling to break the serene emptiness and waiting in the room.

Suddenly Anne leaned forward. She stamped her cigarette out with an energy that was decisive, even ill-tempered.

"Let's go somewhere and dance," she said. "All you happy people give me the willies."

Kathy's eyelids hooded her eyes. They don't really like each other, Phil decided. "Wait'll we hear this thing out?" he asked Anne. "Then we'll discuss." Anne leaned back in her chair again.

But now the music was only a pleasant backdrop to his thinking. No longer was he listening to it directly, separate note after separate note, as one reads a compelling book, word after word, but in a vagueness, as to the sounds of summer wind and rain through the open window of a comradely room. Curiosity bubbled in him; he needed to know more about Dave and Anne, about Anne and Kathy. He told himself that he would always need to know about people, that's what made him a writer instead of an engineer or a businessman; instantly he derided this as a pious attempt at promoting a gossip's eagerness into something more respectable. He grinned. Kathy touched his hand and smiled also. The record was stopping again. "This is the last of it," she said, and turned it over.

"Whereabouts in the White Mountains?" Anne asked.

"Franconia Notch," he answered. Simultaneously, Kathy said, "Flume Inn." He was looking at Anne, stirred to a quick, sad knowledge by the revealing question she'd asked,

168

the offhand question that documented and implemented her jibe at "all you happy people."

Anne sat forward and said, "Flume Inn?" Her face blanked of expression, then took on a look he'd never seen there. Disapproval? Disbelief? "Oh, you wouldn't," she said vigorously.

"Why not?" he and Kathy said together.

"Why, Phil, *because.*" She wasn't looking at him. She was looking at Kathy, asking, estimating. "Phil doesn't know anything about resort places here in the East, Kathy." She said it gently, without chiding. Kathy looked back at her, then to Phil. Her single quick breath could be heard against the pianissimo measures from the phonograph.

"Restricted, hey?" Dave underlined the word with mockery. Faintly his eyes gleamed as if this were a pallid joke, not really execrable, not really funny, just familiar and worth some notice.

"God damn it," Phil said. He stood up.

"Oh, no!" Kathy cried. "I never—oh, Phil, I'm sorry, darling, when I sent the wire I never——" She looked at him with candor, with a shocked misery that she had— what? Forgotten that he "was Jewish"?

"Of course you didn't think of it," he said. "Civilized people don't go around forever thinking, This man is Jewish, that one isn't."

She had done only what he'd have done himself—been unable to translate the bald facts in his researching mail into a close and live reality. Joseph Greenberg, the researcher's fiction, had read, from dozens of hotels and resorts, the little phrase, "indefinitely booked up," and had dismissed each with impassive dignity, with scorn for the evasiveness of it. "Just the clichés of the thing; people can live without these places."

But that was for a man who did not exist. Now a resort,

one resort, was barring Phil Green—or would if they knew he was Jewish.

"This isn't your fault, darling," he said to Kathy. Nor her failure any more than his own. Neither of them could transform the individual they knew him to be into a man an innkeeper in the White Mountains would refuse to admit.

"Are you sure?" Kathy said to Anne. "Have you been there recently?"

"No. But I'm sure."

"I can't believe——" Kathy turned to Phil. "They wouldn't——" But she thought of her golf club and beach club at Darien and broke off.

Phil glanced at his watch. "Only nine." He went into the bedroom to the telephone. She heard the three short dial swings. 2-1-1 for Long Distance. The music from the phonograph suddenly was an offense—she snapped the metal button viciously. Dave leaned back and lit a cigarette. Anne reached for one. Kathy thought, She's the only one here who doesn't know Phil isn't Jewish.

From the bedroom, his voice came clear and efficient.

"—check on reservations for five days starting Sunday, for Mr. and Mrs. Philip Green of New York." There was a pause for the flattened voice in the receiver. "One more thing," Phil said. "Is your inn restricted?" Kathy went into the bedroom and sat beside him on the bed. Now the metallic sounds became words she could hear.

"Is this Mr. Green himself?" There was caution in it.

"Yes."

"Well, could I ask you why you—I mean, Mr. Green——" The voice waited, the sentence hung along the wire unfinished.

"Is it or isn't it?" Phil said.

"Well, I wouldn't say it was 'restricted.'" The voice sounded plaintive.

170

"Then it is *not* restricted?"

"Ah—may I inquire, Mr. Green, are you—that is, do you yourself follow the Hebrew religion, or do you just wish to make sure that——"

Phil had a desire to shout, "You goddam little coward," but he forced his voice into calmness.

"I've asked a simple question; I'd like a simple answer."

"You see, we do have a very high-class clientele and naturally——"

At his side, Kathy stirred. She put her hand on his arm. "Don't, darling," she whispered. "Cancel it."

"You mean you *do* restrict your guests to gentiles?"

"Why, I wouldn't say that, Mr. Green. But—just a moment, please." There was the muffled thud of a receiver being laid on a table. Phil put his own hand over Kathy's on his left arm. They sat in silence. From the other room, Dave's voice and Anne's came to them in indistinguishable sounds. "Hello, Mr. Green?"

"Yes?"

"There seems to be an error somewhere, Mr. Green. We have no rooms open for Sunday or the following days."

"I beg your pardon." Phil stripped all inflection from his words. "I have a wire accepting the entire reservation."

"These new clerks—I mean to say, well, suppose I wire you after I can straighten out this mistake with Mr. Calkins?"

"Just a minute." The dubious voice, the hedging, the counting on proud withdrawal. Some legalism prodded Phil's mind. "I'm not canceling from this end," he said. "Good night."

Immobile and silent, he sat staring at his own hand holding the receiver hard against its prongs. Obviously they would not go there, ravaging the first hours of their honeymoon. But there was something he must do besides accepting this. He could not think what it might be. Not yet.

People could live without smart clubs and resorts. Indeed they could. In a world where only yesterday human bones powdered to ash in blazing furnaces, the barred register of a chic hotel could scarcely be called disaster.

But this maddening arrogance, this automatic decision that you were not quite the equal——

"We'll open the cottage, darling," Kathy said in soft agitation. "It's so lovely. We won't even tell Jane we're there."

"We'll go somewhere." He turned toward her. "Go in to them for a minute, Kathy?" He looked an apology. "I've got to think."

She stood up. "The nasty little snobs aren't worth fretting over—*don't* be so upset, Phil."

He nodded; he wanted to respond. Her distress for him was real; it came warm and strong. But the right answer eluded him. From the doorway, Anne spoke, and they both turned around as she came in.

"If Disraeli and Irving Berlin and Danny Kaye and Einstein got up a happy skiing party, Phil," she said harshly, "that place would send for the Northwest Nazi Police and keep them out. And all such places, too."

There was no distress in her voice. Anne didn't give one good damn about his lacerated feelings or outraged pride. She had used that one word, "Nazi"—it was the *meaning* of the thing that angered her. While Kathy only—— Cut it, Phil ordered himself. Dave had come after Anne, and all four stood there in a cluster, as if in meeting.

"The thing is you can't fight them back," Dave said coldly. "You can never pin them down. I heard you try to."

"Anti-bias laws," Anne said. "Possible lawsuits. They never say it or write it."

172

"It's horrible," Kathy said. "It's——"

Behind them the telephone rang. Phil started to it and then knew it could not be Flume Inn calling back. Kathy answered.

"Is my father there, Kathy?" Tommy's voice, tense, shrill, sounded through the room.

"Yes, Tom, right here."

Phil took the receiver while she was still speaking.

"What's up, kid? This is me."

"Oh, Dad, I—oh, it kept mixing up on the dial."

"Is Gram sick, Tom?"

"She—oh, Dad, her mouth is twisted sort of queer, and she said to look in the little red book and then I couldn't get the dial to——"

Calm. The voice calm. The kid's badly frightened.

"Tom, listen. I'll be there right away. O.K.?"

"Yes, Dad. And she talks sort of thick."

"I'm on my way this minute. Give her that bottle of medicine——"

"She took some."

"Good. Five minutes and I'll be there." He hung up. "Stroke," he said. "Facial paralysis, sounds like."

They were all at the front door with him. "Dave, find Dr. Craigie in the book. Stephen Craigie. Park in the Seventies. Get him down there right off, will you? And Abrahams, Dr. J. Ephraim Abrahams, call him too, would you?"

Kathy said, "I'm coming with you." The elevator clanged open its metal door, and she stepped in before him, her coat and hat in her hands.

It was Sunday morning.

Phil leaned his head flat against the small panel of glass so that he could see more. On the rolled clouds below, the shadow of the plane was a moving finger of gray. He followed it as if it were his only orientation in this indescribable arc of space and brilliance. Since they'd flown him back from Guadalcanal in the hospital ship, this was the first time he'd been up. In the seconds just before they'd swept off the runway some whisper of the excitement and fear he'd known at eighteen in the first moment of feeling himself airborne had come back; then the superstructure of years of uneventful flying had erected itself once more. But now again, gazing down and out and around him, the loneliness and conquest of flight tingled along his nerves.

Yet he could not shake off the sense of omen.

It was Kathy who'd suggested the postponement of their wedding, quietly, without weighing it or hesitating. Across nearly three turbulent days and nights her words came back to him. "It isn't only that missing it would break her heart," she'd said. "But we'd feel just heavyhearted while we were gone, and wrong about—being happy."

Of course she was right. It wasn't merely the five-day absence, particularly with Dave living there. A business trip would not have needed to be canceled.

"Just a week, Phil, two at thè longest, Abrahams said. Postponing a wedding isn't so awful."

"No, I suppose it isn't." They both felt that it was. "It's Tom more than anything," he'd suddenly said. "Funny, you don't fuss around much with your kid until something hits into him hard. But *then* nothing else seems to count for a while."

She'd nodded and said she understood. Now he wondered whether it had hurt her. It had leaped out. Any parent would know how he meant it, any parent whose child had clutched his arm in the stiffness of fear.

Both Craigie and Abrahams had returned the next morning and corroborated their first opinions. A minute lesion in the motor-control system on the left side. She would undoubtedly regain normal speech, almost free of the characteristic thickening and word confusion. It was not related to the heart attack. Not directly related. It is true that at her age, the degenerative——

The memory of the phrases again irritated him. The point, the only point, was that it was the first break in the vessel that held reason and co-ordination. If you could choose, you'd choose death in one abrupt instant instead of this inchmeal dying; a cell here, a nerve there, a valve, a steady emptying of the veins as with Betty.

He turned his mind back to Kathy. Yesterday and the day before, she'd been at the house whenever she could, easy with Tom, fine with his mother. But four o'clock on Saturday hadn't been exactly good for either of them. It was right, it was necessary, and if she hadn't suggested the postponement it would have been for him to do and he would have done it.

Again the persistent feeling of something ominous weighted his spirits. He looked out once more. He had been flying for more than three hours; in another twenty minutes it would be over. He would be in the hired car the air line had promised, speeding along dry-packed roads, rehearsing at last what he should do and say.

The decision to turn in only one plane ticket had made itself for him on Friday. He'd just arranged the change of date with Judge Mayhew and normally he'd have followed through with a call to the air-line office and a wire to Flume Inn. Maybe seeing Craigie with Abrahams the second time, so affable, so agreeable—maybe that had signaled his mind back. Suddenly the phone call was blasting him apart again as if it had just happened.

He'd be goddamned if he'd play their game for them. Wiring now, even for cause, would hand them the easy way out they counted on. He'd pulled their wire out of his pocket

—he'd told the squirt he wasn't canceling. He'd taken the airplane tickets out and fingered them as if he were blind and they in Braille. And the idea had apparently jumped into him from the finger tips upward.

He'd looked over to Dave, still doing KP. The house was quiet. Mom was asleep again, and Tom at school.

"I'm going up there for a couple hours on Sunday, Dave. I'll be back the same evening."

"You're wasting your time."

They'd argued, but in the end Dave had said, "Sure you have to face them once. I did it once at Monterey."

Apart from the research need to test it all the way himself as he was doing with everything else, there was this inability to acquiesce by default. He'd make them look him in the eye and then do it; force them out of the generalized evasion into a boxed refusal to him, one specific individual. Flume Inn must be all the inns and hotels and clubs and landlords anywhere across all the innocent horizons below him where antisemitism was part of the "rules."

"They're more than nasty little snobs, Kathy." In his mind he addressed her as if he were leaning forward in urgency. "They're the enemy. Call them snobs, and you can dismiss them. See them as persistent little traitors to everything this country stands for and stands on, and you have to fight them. Not for 'the poor, poor Jews,' but for the whole damn thing the country is——"

Weariness overcame him; he slumped back and closed his eyes. His own phrase, "the first break in the vessel," came back to him and, as he so often had in the last three days, he found himself at once thinking of death. Not of that final moment toward which his mother had just taken her second tentative step, not of Betty's death, but simply of death and dying, of irreparable loss and desolation. A desperate longing for Kathy seized him. He wanted her near him; he must never lose her. As if from nightmare, he jerked his eyes open and sat upright in his chair.

The plane swept through a layer of cloud. He hadn't realized they'd been losing altitude. At once the golden brilliance of the light dimmed to gray. The oblong signal at the pilot's door went on, and Phil fastened his seat belt and put away his cigarette. In another few minutes they were on the ground at Montpelier, Vermont, and the mountains lay serene and white under a lowering winter sky.

As the Ford sedan moved along the miles, he sat almost in silence. He had chucked his suitcase in the back and got in with the tall blond boy in corduroy slacks, woolen cap, and heavy navy jacket. The boy's face had the sallow look of farm folk during the winter absence of outdoor work. Did he hate Jews and Negroes and Catholics and foreigners? Or only summer folk and rich people and city slickers? Or nobody who hadn't angered or injured him?

"I'm taking the four-o'clock back," Phil said. "Will you kill half an hour over a beer and come back for me?"

"You up from Boston?"

"New York."

"Just for half an hour?"

"Business trip."

"Sure, I'll just wait outside."

"No, that won't be right. I want you to drive off as if I—well, just drop me and then come back. Better skip the beer, at that; just drive around and be back in ten minutes, will you?"

"Whatever you say."

They were nearing the inn. Laconically, the boy played guide, but Phil scarcely listened. The Flume, the Great Stone Face, the Notch. But he saw the grand rise of the mountains—here all about him were beauty and serenity and the peculiar American story of New England, the new

177

version of the old England, the town meetings, the small groups of protesting men, the freedom of conscience, the freedom of worship. And here now amid all this stately calmness, the corruption.

The car swerved as it turned into a long crescent that was the approach to the inn. In couples or groups, ski-suited men and women made vigorous splashes of color on the whited landscape. Phil looked at them with special curiosity. Some looked charming and well mannered and intelligent; two couples were already drunk, uproarious and vulgar. They can make it, and I can't, he thought. Dry and amused bitterness invaded him.

The tires squeaked against the snow. As the car stopped, a smiling page boy in green opened the door for him, spotted the suitcase, and lugged it out, asking, "Skis, sir?" Phil shook his head and nodded to the driver. The car drove off. Behind, a door opened heavily, and Phil turned. His peripheral vision told him a man was waiting in the open door, but he stood still and looked about him with interest. Sprawling, faced with half logs, smoke rising bluely at half a dozen massive stone chimneys, the inn sent off its instant message of being expensive, comfortable, and what was meant by the word "smart," which blanketed a thousand variables. At one side, along its shallow depth, was a porch studded with more of the bright raw colors of mittens and scarves and caps, restless with movement as skis were scraped and rubbed and waxed. Everywhere was the smell of new snow, the stretching whiteness, the crunch of boots through the glazed top surface to the hardness below. It would have been a calm and happy place for him to bring Kathy in their first living together.

Abruptly, he turned toward the front door. The man waiting there gave a pleasant half salute and called out, "How do?" in the rising, puzzled tone of somebody excepting nobody, but not perturbed by the unexpected. His face was pale, his hair thick and gray; he was as tall as Phil, middle-yeared, not homely, not handsome. He wore grayish tweeds, with a plaid wool shirt, an island of color and impudence in his general indefiniteness.

"How do," Phil said. "The desk right ahead?"

"Just inside. Driving through?"

"No, I came by air." He went past him, into a large lounge. The registration desk was at his left, and he turned to it, but his snapshot picture of the place had already given him the blazing fireplace, the deep chairs, the beams overhead. Behind the counter the tall man was gently pushing forward a leather-cornered pad with a registration card slotted into it, saying affably, "I hope it won't be for *too* many days, but with one bag and no skis———"

"I have reservations," Phil said, and took the pen angled toward him from its plastic base. "For a double room and bath, today through Thursday."

He wrote, "Philip———"

"Reservations? In what name?" There was a stiffening all over him, mouth, voice, the arms on the counter.

Phil wrote, "S. Green" and his address. Then he said, "Green. My wife will get here tomorrow."

"The Mr. Green who———"

"Yes," Phil said. "You're Mr. Calkins, the owner?" He didn't wait for the nod. He pulled out his wallet, opened it without haste, took out the telegram, laid it on the desk, and set the wallet on top of it. Absurdly, a shakiness began in his knees, but the slow-seeping juice that caused it merely deepened his steady voice.

"But there's some error, Mr. Green. There isn't one free room in the entire inn." His eyes sent the page boy an almost imperceptible look, but Phil saw it. It signaled "no" or "hold it" or something which the boy understood well

enough to make him shift from his rigid attention to an "at
ease." And with the signal, a curious thing had happened to
Mr. Calkins' face. It had drawn all mobility into itself,
absorbing it, blotterlike; it presented now only the even,
dead stain of on-guardedness.

"You were about to give me a room—apart from the
reservation. What's changed your mind?"

"Why, not a thing. It's unfortunate, but there isn't——"
He reached toward the telegram. Quietly Phil shoved the
wallet aside so that the message and the signature, "J. Calkins," became visible. But he let his hand rest on the lower
part of it. Mr. Calkins said, "Perhaps the Brewster Hotel
near the station?" and reached toward the telephone.

"I'm not staying at the Brewster," Phil said. He looked
directly into Calkins' eyes. Calkins raised his shoulders,
drew his hand back from the telephone, and said nothing at
all. "I am Jewish, and you don't take Jews—that's it, isn't
it?"

"Why, I wouldn't put it like that. It's just——"

"This place is what they call 'restricted'—is *that* it?"

"I never said that."

It was like fighting fog, slapping at mist. A man and
woman came up, saying "Air-mail for these," left two letters, and began to go off.

"If you don't accept Jews, say so," Phil said. The pair
stopped. Calkins picked up the letters.

"I am very busy just now, Mr. Green. If you'd like me to
phone up a cab or the Brewster——" He reached into a
drawer, took out a strip of air-mail stamps, and folded two
back on the perforated hinge. The couple moved on. From
behind him, the woman's voice came clearly back to Phil.
"Always pushing in, that's the Jew of it." Calkins turned
aside to a rustic box with a slit top and dropped the letters
into it. There was something so placid, so undisturbed about

the gesture that all the backed-up violence Phil had been grinding down exploded. His hand suddenly had plaid wool and buttons in it; he had leaned across the counter and seized Calkins under the throat, twisting him forward so that they faced each other once more.

"You coward," he said and dropped his hand. He turned to the page, signaled for his bag, and said, "My cab's waiting; I've got tickets on the four-o'clock plane."

The page grinned widely. "So it *is* just books in it. Clothes aren't ever this heavy, sir."

Calkins made a sound. Comprehension was in it, and nervousness. A cold shaft of triumph shot through the heat and poison boiling in Phil. Mr. Calkins had caught on to the fact that something was going on besides the hiring of a room. Mr. Calkins was frightened.

CHAPTER ELEVEN

G LUEY AND INESCAPABLE, the extraordinary melancholy clung to him. For more than a week he was never fully free of it. The fast-thickening pile of manuscript in his desk at home, usually the rising barometer of his spirits, offered no permanent release. His mother was definitely improving, the spastic pull at her lips easing; Tom was himself again; Kathy had greeted his account of Flume Inn with disgust for Calkins and praise for him; their new plans were already in order. They were going to Nassau for the first week of February. "I came right out with it at the travel agent's, Phil—there'll be no nonsense in *this* place."

But still there persisted in him the odd sense of omen, heavy-heavy-hanging over. Almost constantly he was strung on an unhappy tension, a man racing for a train and uncertain of the watch that said he still had a minute to go. Impatiently, Phil tried to locate the source of this new infection of moodiness—the inn, his mother's stroke, the hostility of Miss Wales, the continued fruitlessness of Dave's search for a place to live, the postponement of the wedding—but not any one of them, nor the sum of them all, convinced him that he had isolated the cause of the sticky sadness in him.

He had accepted the fact that in a few weeks he'd undergone a swift and deep transfusion into his own blood of a million corpuscles of experience and emotion. He pointed that out one night to Dave, during one of their "sessions" at one in the morning, and Dave had given him a knowing and compassionate smile.

"You're not insulated yet, Phil. It's new every time, so the impact must be quite a business."

"You mean you get indifferent to it in time?"

"No—unless you're a pachyderm. But you aren't as quick and raw. *You're* concentrating a lifetime thing into a few weeks; you're *making* the thing happen every day, writing letters, asking questions, going to meet it. The facts are no different, but it does telescope it."

"Christ, it must be worse on the organism, though, to have it drag out year after year."

"It's not too good." Dave shrugged. "Know something, Phil? Remember I said the other night I've never felt that 'proud to be a Jew' stuff? Any more than you're proud or not proud to be a Christian?" Phil nodded. "Well, there's one thing about Jews that does make me feel sort of set up." He seemed to be thinking it out, and Phil said nothing. "You go talk to a psychiatrist, Phil; tell him about some guy that got his first feel of insult and contempt as a little boy, went on right through life being taunted or held apart, knew that people like him were being beaten and butchered and killed. The psychiatrist would expect a screaming psychopath as a result, wouldn't he?"

"I never thought of it that way," Phil said. "And the wonder is, you're going to say, not that some Jews are aggressive or thirsty for money or power, but that most of them are so ordinary and patient and able to lead regular lives."

Dave smiled. "Kind of remarkable, isn't it? Even happy lives, with love and work and kids and plans. Takes guts, especially the last ten years or so."

They fell silent. Phil wondered if he'd have the guts himself. A dozen times since he'd started this, he'd been called "sensitive," as if it were a failing. But who wouldn't be sensitive or oversensitive, with this sort of daily raw-rubbing

183

technique? Only the gross, the truly vulgar, could remain untouched and unchanged, in an idiot slumber of indifference. Since when was it a flaw of character to be sensitive, anyway?

"Minify said something the other day, Dave. One of those office arguments about how you fight off Communism or Fascism in this country."

"The old malarky?" Dave winked. "Let me guess. True democracy!"

"Not from John. Jobs and economic security, sure—even the Fascists and Communists promise that. No, he said it had got down to a matter of equal self-respect, pride, ego, whatever. Take Communism. It's got one good thing, anyway—equality among white and black, all minorities—only the price there is so big, too. If we did it, without the price of free speech, free opposition, free everything—then we'd really be fighting the Communists where it counts."

"Smart cookie."

"So he feels beating antisemitism and antinegroism is a political must now, not just sweet decency."

"What the hell chance have we of getting decent with thirteen million Negroes if we can't lick the much easier business of antisemitism?"

"What indeed?" Phil said. "That's why *Smith's* is going after it so hard. My stuff will be just the first—he's planning an endless amount to come."

For a long time they sat on, talking, and when he went to bed Phil felt more cheerful. *Smith's* wasn't alone; plans were afoot in many places, more than forty cities were trying their own Springfield Plans, legislatures everywhere were considering and passing anti-bias and civic-rights laws, town meetings were discussing subjects that didn't seem hot a decade ago. As the bigots got more active they inadvertently mobilized the anti-bigots. There were millions of honestly democratic people in the country; they were the great majority, and when they really knew what was in the balance, they'd throw the full weight of their convictions into the scale.

The next morning at the office, he began the fourth article of the series and knew they were holding up, perhaps even building up beyond the level of the first one. Minify had just read the first three in rough draft and asked him in and suggested arranging for book publication later. Might be; might be. He'd never had a book published, and the suggestion excited him. He considered phoning Kathy at the school just to tell her about John's notion, but decided against it. He was calling for her and taking her home with him at four-thirty; she'd been insistent on getting the dinner there every night, with him and Tom to help and Dave doing the dirty work afterward.

But when he saw her he said nothing about the book.

"Dave's going tomorrow," he greeted her. "He just phoned me."

"Going? Where?"

"California."

"No! And give up that Quirich——"

"He can't abandon his wife and kids forever. Or find a house or apartment. The housing shortage isn't going to end overnight. You *know* he'd never let Anne give him her place for months at a time."

A knobbed something was inside his ribs. For longer than he wanted to admit he'd waited for Kathy to say one thing. All along, stubbornly, he'd kept on believing in the flat Dave would find, the small house, the shack, the cottage. And all the time, along one fine thread of his mind, he'd listened for the thing she would finally say.

The taxi stopped, and he paid the driver. Upstairs Dave greeted them cheerily, "Hi, you two. I'm off on a date.

Should I wind up here with Anne? Your mother's fine, Phil."

His bag was already packed, lying open to receive tomorrow morning's last-minute things. After he'd gone, they spent half an hour with Mrs. Green and then went into the living room. Phil told himself he was just tired. The depression was upon him once again, mucilaginous and cold.

And then Kathy said, "I suppose you're thinking of the cottage, Phil."

"I had thought of it."

"So have I. I thought of it when Anne offered to move."

She fell silent. She had brought it up herself; she'd only been waiting to see if there was not some other solution for Dave. She'd confided that she meant to work on the cottage during the spring months, changing curtains and slip covers, altering its "personality" so there'd be no associative thing with past summers when she and Bill were there. But now Dave was going back to California, driven to reject a job with twice the future of the one he'd go back to. Now a matter of redecorating would no longer hold back the words that could alone keep Dave here. She was looking at him.

"It just would be so uncomfortable for Dave, *knowing* he'd moved into one of those damn neighborhoods that won't take Jews."

"Kathy."

"I loathe it, but that's the way it is up there. New Canaan's worse—nobody can sell or rent to a Jew there. But even Darien is—well, it's a sort of gentleman's agreement when you buy, especially in the section where Jane's place and mine are."

"Gentleman—oh, my God, you don't *really*—you *can't* actually——"

He was standing. He did not remember getting up. I mustn't fight with her; she's my girl, my wife, almost; I mustn't yell. I've been bunched up in a tangle these last days; I've got to hang on.

"You won't buck it, Kathy? Just going to give in, play along, let their idiotic rules stand?"

"I don't play along—but what could one person do?"

"Tell them to go to hell. What could *they* do?"

"Ostracize him. Even some of the markets. Not deliver food. Not wait on them promptly. And I couldn't give him guest cards to the clubs and——" She saw his eyes, and added, "But, *Phil,* you'll be all done with the series before we get there."

He made a gesture so sharp that she stopped as if she'd been struck. His face was new. Rigid in self-control, half sick. She was frightened.

"Do you expect *us* to live in the cottage," he said, "once I know all this?"

"Oh, Phil, don't! We can't make the whole world over."

"Or go happily to the clubs?"

"You know I'm on Dave's side."

"I'm not on Dave's side or any side except against *their* side. My God, Kathy, do you or don't you believe in this? And if you do, then how——"

The door opened. It was Tom. Phil wanted to order him at once to his room; interruption now was intolerable. Tom said "Hi" in a lifeless voice and looked at neither of them. Had he heard their angry voices on his way upstairs?

Tom had closed the door. He was standing still, just inside it. He made no move to get out of his overcoat or throw off his cap. Phil glanced at him.

"Anything wrong?"

Tom didn't answer. Kathy took a step toward him.

"Tom," Phil said. "What's up? You look funny."

Tom shook his head. He opened his lips; they worked

at something, but no sound came. He stood there, taut with effort, staring, only his jaws moving. Suddenly Phil knew he was trying not to cry.

"Fight, hey?" His voice was hearty, parental. "An argument with one of the guys?"

"Dad." The word was tight. He was ignoring Kathy, looking only at Phil.

I've never seen him like this, Phil thought, state of shock—— and he went to him, everything else forgotten. "Tell me what happened, Tom."

Bewilderment showed in Tom's eyes, and then, suddenly, he put the back of one hand up to his mouth and was sobbing.

"They called me," he said at last, " 'dirty Jew' and 'stinky kike' and——" The next was too broken to make out. "—and they ran off and I——" His bitter crying claimed the rest of it.

Explosion in the mind—they have hurt my child. Roar of hatred different from any fury when it's only yourself they hurt. Murder for what they've done to my kid——

He put a hand on Tom's head. Kathy was down on her knees, her arms around him.

"But it's just a mistake; it's not *true*, Tom," she cried out to him. "You're not any more Jewish than I am."

Savagery toward her now, blinding, for these words rushing . . . offering the Benison, the Great Assurance that he was all right, as all right as she, with white Protestant all-rightness, unquestioned, unassailable.

Phil couldn't speak. Kathy looked up. There was no sound in the room except Tom's clutching sobs.

Slowly, she stood up, and Tom turned toward his father. "Let's get your coat off, Tom," Phil said quietly. "We'll talk about it in a minute."

Without a word to her, he led Tom from the room. In

the bathroom, he took off Tom's cap and washed the streaked face as if this were years ago and Tom still a baby. Calm him first with ordinary things.

"Suppose you start over," he said then. "Was it at school? Was Jimmy in it?"

Tom shook his head to both questions. He was no longer crying, but the indrawn breathing was effort enough. Phil dried his face, using his own bath towel in some impulse for closeness out of the ordinary. Then he sat on the edge of the bathtub and asked, "Anybody sock anybody?"

"No. They just yelled it. It was at our corner—I sort of walked over to Lexington before I came up. You said I could."

"Sure."

"And then this bunch."

Phil saw the small face go red and contorted again and the dazed look of shock come back. He wanted to take him into his arms, hold him, but boys of eight have the right to give some signal before they are babied. Tom gave none.

"One was a kid from school, about eleven. I don't know the other two and they were playing hop and I asked——"

Phil waited. "You said could you play, too?"

"And the school one said no dirty little Jew could ever get in their games and they all yelled those other things. *Why*, Dad? Why *did* they?" He didn't wait for an answer. "And I started for the school one and he said my father had a long curly beard and they all ran away."

"Here's a glass of water, Tom. Drink some." He got the glass, filled it, offered it. Only while he was drinking did Phil notice he was still in his overcoat. "Give me your coat; it's hot in here." Tom started automatically at the buttons, and Phil said, "You didn't want to tell them you weren't really Jewish?"

Tom gave him a glance that was not only startled but

189

critical. His hands backed each other, fingers laced, reminding Phil of the G2 pledge.

"Good boy. I like that." Phil nodded judiciously. "Lots of kids just like you are Jewish, and if you said it, it'd be sort of admitting there *was* something bad in being Jewish and something swell in not."

Tom nodded, too. Then his eyes hardened; his lower jaw pushed out. For the first time anger replaced hurt. "They wouldn't fight. They just ran."

"Damn cowards," Phil said. "There are grownups like that too, Tom. They do it with wisecracks instead of yelling." They looked at each other. Tom was getting calm again. A moment later, Phil said, "O.K. now?" Tom picked up his cap and overcoat from the wicker hamper. "Then will you go read or something? Gram's sleeping, and I have to talk to Kathy awhile."

He put his hand on Tom's shoulder and squeezed down on it. "Let's keep it to ourselves till Gram's well." Tom hunched against the pressure and smiled uncertainly at him. Then he left.

For a moment Phil stayed on, his thoughts rocketing back to Kathy. "When something hits into your kid." Just names? Just exclusion? Or equally the sly corruption, the comforting poison of superiority? "Any place can be a hotbed, Phil; each house decides it." His house would decide it for Tom—by a phrase, a nuance, an attitude. Each day it would go on being decided, through the rest of his childhood, through adolescence. A passion tore through Phil, to protect this one boy from that slow sure poison.

He went in to Kathy and could think of nothing to say at all. She sat in the chair she'd been in that night he'd first kissed her, when he'd felt the vast hope, like a drug to heal the long misery. Now she looked withdrawn, unwilling; she offered him only silence.

Idiotically, he thought of Miss Wales these last days, the punctilious politeness, the unspeaking docility with which she sat there, taking down every letter he dictated, never looking up inquiringly as he paused, never mentioning the talk they'd had, and never forgiving it. Punishing him was so much easier than questioning herself.

Kathy's silence was as unforgiving. "It was an aberration, Phil——" She would not say it now, candid, eager. He could not, simply could not, say words now to minimize and condone. The inflection in her cry to Tom betrayed her more than any action. The doctor comforting the patient, "You're as healthy as I am"; the psychiatrist saying heartily, "You're no more insane than me." He wanted to explain what he felt, but knew they would quarrel again. "Those are the toughest fights, Phil, the ones about ideas. Families split apart——" Suddenly he saw himself facing Kathy over and over with some such fight between them, next month, next summer, next year. Again and again there would be the distance, the coldness. In this one moment were all the unborn moments.

This was recognition at last. This was the underlying heaviness, the tenacious melancholy, stemming from the unwilling knowledge that they stood miles apart—once the top words were said, the easy words, the usual words. A dozen times he had overlooked, explained, blamed his own solemnity. A dozen times some new evidence had come. Each time, his yearning for her, his love and passion, had conspired to help him skirt the truth that lay, bulky and impassable, in the road before them.

"I'm pretty tired of feeling in the wrong," Kathy said slowly. "Everything I do or say is wrong, about anything Jewish."

He said nothing. He had never heard this ring in her voice.

191

"All I did just now was to face the facts about Dave in Darien. And then tell Tom just what you told him when he asked that day if he was one."

"Not 'just what.'"

"You really do think I'm an antisemite! And Jane and Harry and everybody who simply recognizes things."

"No, Kathy. I've just come to see more clearly that——"

"You *do* think it. You've thought it secretly a long time."

"It's just that I've come to see that lots of nice people who aren't *are* their unknowing helpers and connivers. People who'd never beat up a Jew or yell kike at a child. They think antisemitism is something way off there, in a dark crackpot place with low-class morons. That's the biggest thing I've discovered about the whole business."

He put his hand up to span his eyes. His stretched fingers and thumb rotated the flesh at the corners of his closed eyes as if his temples throbbed there. . . . That *is* what I've come to see. She isn't consciously antisemitic, nor is Jane or all the pleasant, intelligent people at the party or the inns and clubs. They despise it; it's an "awful thing." But all of them, and the Craigies and Wales and Jordans and McAnnys, who also deplore it and protest their own innocence—they help it along and then wonder why it grows. Millions like them back up the lunatic vanguard in its war for this country—forming the rear echelons, the home front in the factories, manufacturing the silence and acquiescence. . . .

"You mean we're *not* going to Darien for the summer or to the club, even though you're through by then?"

He dropped his hand. "Let's save that for another time."

She stood up abruptly. And suddenly she was saying, "Oh, damn everything about this horrible thing. They always make trouble for everybody, even their friends. They force everybody to take sides with them——"

"Quit it." He was on his feet, facing her. "Quit that."

192

He heard the rasping voice and was powerless to control it. " 'They' didn't suggest the series—'they' didn't give me my idea—'they' haven't one single goddam thing to do with what's happened between you and me."

"I won't have you shout at me. I know what you're thinking about marrying me—I saw it in your face when I said that to Tom."

"My God, you charge me with thinking you're an anti-semite—I answer that and you switch to Darien and the club! You blame everything on the Jews, and I lose my temper, and you switch to my face and our marriage!"

"Or swear at me or treat me to sarcasm and implication, either. I'm *not* going to marry into hothead shouting and nerves, and you might as well know it now. Let's just call it off for good."

She walked to the table where her purse and hat and gloves lay. She took up her coat and put it on.

"Kathy." The word was only half spoken. "I'm sorry I shouted. I hate it when I do it."

"It isn't the shouting. It's just everything. You've changed so since the first night at Uncle John's. I just know there's no use."

She went to the door. Phil watched her. Then she was gone.

CHAPTER TWELVE

THE CITY WAS ASLEEP. New York, the nervous, keyed-up city, was almost at rest two hours past midnight. Watching the sleeping stone under the quiet sky, the mind might know that there were still people laughing in night clubs, trucks and taxis still speeding through streets and avenues, swift subways underground still thundering into lighted stations.

But to the eye itself, the city was dark, sleeping, motionless. Here an oblong of shaded yellow cut its way out of the surrounding block of stone, and there a strip of continuing light showed a whole floor of a skyscraper café, a shelf of life and animation bracketed high above the city. But apart from the single window, from the single strip, there stretched from river to river, from street to sky, a city's surrender to oblivion or dreaming.

Watching the night from her own lighted window, Kathy wondered about the other yellow oblongs. Who were the people behind their bland faces? Why were they awake now? Could there be delight and love behind those unwinking surfaces, or only this sleepless despair? In her childhood she had known this plunging of misery, but never before as an adult. Yet it was right to break with Phil now; it would be worse to have it come afterwards and bring a second divorce, a second failure. Nobody could live with a man who'd turned crusader. At the beginning he'd been the way she was about the dreadful thing, the way any civilized person was. It was a problem, a danger to be fought, but he'd been sane and objective about it. Twice he'd shown

a perfectly human resentment at being saddled with so difficult a subject for his first stab as a staff editor. He'd ad-
mitted frankly once that all those interviews with various
committees wore him down as committee talks always did.
He'd been simply the journalist doing an important job and
perfectly normal about everything—the way she was or
Jane or anybody.

Then he got "the angle" and began to change.

That night when he told her his plan, she'd drawn back,
and at last she knew why: she'd known it instinctively for
an impossible thing. You were what you were, for the one
life you had. You couldn't help it if you were born Christian
instead of Jewish, white instead of black. It didn't mean you
were *glad* you were——

"But I am glad. God, it would be awful."

The words spoke out in her mind. She drew into herself
as if she could shrink away from them. Then combativeness
reared—this was abject readiness to feel in the wrong, and
she'd had enough of it.

"It's just that in this world, with the way things are,
I *am* glad." That was it; it was purely a practical recognition, not a judgment of superior status. Here was another
case in point. If Phil had been there and she had said that
very same thing aloud, he'd have worn the quick look. Try
as she might, she'd have been unable to make him see how
innocently she meant it, how devoid of prejudice it was. It's
just a fact, like being glad you were good-looking instead of
ugly, or comfortably fixed instead of poor, healthy instead
of crippled, young instead of old. But Phil, this Phil, the
Phil he'd become, would twist it into something horrible, a
conniving, a helping, an aiding and abetting the thing she
loathed as much as he. They'd quarrel—their life would
be the sudden chill between them, the words, the quarrel to
be made up, and then finally to be left unmade up.

That time after he'd gone to see Professor Lieberman and she'd said something perfectly casual about "the Jewish race." Phil had explained once or twice that the phrase was based on old misconceptions which were completely disproved by modern anthropologists. But she'd said it— it was just habit. She wasn't fighting the scientists when they said there was no such thing. She knew perfectly well that the three great divisions of mankind were the Caucasian Race, the Mongoloid, the Negroid. She remembered his finger pointing out a phrase in a pamphlet written by leading anthropologists. "There is no Jewish 'Race.'"

"Kathy, sweet, every time you say it, you carry on the myth that Jews are a race apart instead of just a religious group, or just a ghetto group or a persecution-conscious group."

"I forgot, Phil. It's just an expression."

"That's what half this thing thrives on—just an expression, here, there, and everywhere. What you yourself called nasty propaganda phrases when I told you about Belle and McAnny."

He hadn't been irritated then. True. She'd been the one to lose her temper—at the analogy. She was different from Belle or McAnny, and whatever Hooton and Boas and Benedict and Mead and all the great anthropologists said, people would just keep on saying "the Jewish race."

That time the quarrel had been her fault; other times it had been his. Blame placing wasn't the point; the only point was the frazzling nerves, the ratcheting apart each time.

Especially if he thought Tom was concerned.

No. It was better to end it now. Get it over with; endure this jagged grief, but get it over with now. Time would pass, she might go away for a change of scene, she might meet some other man.

At the window, she suddenly shivered and remembered

she'd been standing there a long time. She went back to the untidy bed and lay down. The cold, wet place in the pillow struck her cheek, and without sitting up she raised her head so she could turn it over. All at once hatred seized her— hatred for Phil for making this happen. They had been so in love; they could have been so happy, had so much to share, so much to enjoy together. And he had snatched it away from both of them because he'd become a man possessed. It was she who'd broken their engagement, but he who'd made the break inevitable. She wanted to hit him, beat at him with her hands, spit names into his face.

As quickly as it had come, the spasm quitted her, and in a listless note taking she observed that the hair bunched under her neck was getting damp once more.

Hour followed hour, and Phil sat on alone, without reading, without working, without even thinking in the sense of orderly pursuit of any idea. After she'd gone there'd been the small, definite things to do, and he had done them, the automaton still performing accurately while the inner mechanism inched toward collapse. At supper, neither his mother nor Tom had suspected anything about Kathy's departure. Tom needed extra time and attention tonight, and Phil had given him both; in private they had reopened their discussion about "the cowards" and then gone off into a thorough exchange of opinions about winter training for baseball players.

But then came the evening alone and, with it, the stupor of silence in the room. Then it had hit, a paralysis that kept him sitting in one position in one chair, a torpid drunkenness remarkable only because he had had nothing to drink.

This time there was no watching the telephone, no wondering if she might call, no impulsive decision to dial her number. This time there was only the shock of amputation.

At midnight, he undressed and went to bed, not for the sleep he did not expect, but to avoid Dave and Anne when they came in as Dave had said they would. That much clarity he did have—he could not talk and laugh; better to fool them into a tiptoed retreat down the stairs in search of whatever *bon voyage* doings they would be in the mood for.

Ten minutes later he heard Dave's key and then his "What do you know?" The door closed. "He's asleep."

"On your last night?" said Anne. "Nonsense. We'll have to wake him up."

"Let the guy alone."

"It's against my deepest principles." She laughed, and the next minute she was sitting on the edge of the day bed, saying, "Phil, wake up, it's us." The smell of cold fur, of perfume, of leather and winter air assailed his nostrils, and for the first time he disliked her. His massive unwillingness kept him motionless.

"Let the poor lug alone," Dave whispered, but she said, "I told you I never let any man alone," and laughed again. They'd been to the theater, but they also had been drinking. She touched his shoulder, and Phil stirred.

"What the hell?"

"Where's Kathy?" she said. "I thought we were expected?" Dave clicked the switch, and Phil sat up.

"You look *nice* in pajamas," she said, and Dave hooted.

"She went early," Phil said. They'd ascribe the gruffness to the weighting of sleep. He was not trying to act out his deception; the tone came honestly enough.

"Get a dressing gown on," she said. "I'll close my eyes."

"Come help with ice cubes," Dave ordered, "and he can dress. He wouldn't let any dame see his ratty bathrobe."

On his way to the bedroom, Phil remembered the dirty dishes in the kitchen; he had forgotten them and the opened cans on the sink tray. She'd know that Kathy had left before dinner and begin to speculate, just as Kathy had done about her. But at once their laughter came to him, a vigorous duet of good spirits, and as in the restaurant the night he'd introduced them, envy for all lightheartedness hooked into him.

When he went back, Anne gave him half a glassful of what looked like straight whisky except that it bubbled. "Here's a mean one, to catch you up, Phil." She surveyed him. "Men oughtn't wear ties and coats ever. Much more attractive in shirts and pants."

She was flirting with him while Dave watched, and laughing and talking intimately with Dave a moment later. What was all this?

"Dave's going to ask Quirich-Jones to hold the offer open for one more month," she said. "And while he's out home, I'm going to find some place for them to live if it kills me. You help?"

"Sure." He looked at Dave. "Think they'll do it?"

"They've heard of the housing shortage."

"Dave says his wife isn't one of those that just die if they don't live in the sma-a-artest places and know the sma-a-artest people, so——"

Phil lost the rest of the sentence. She meant Kathy. She was using her gift of mimicry to catch that suave-stretching vowel. The venom of the imitation he could forgive, but the content of the words was an uglier attack. And unjust. Kathy liked pleasant apartments and houses and clothes and parties as any other person did, but Anne was imputing an excess of importance that wasn't true.

"Your own apartment is pretty smart, Anne." He sounded lightly conversational, nothing more. "Don't all girls like nice places and yet not die if they haven't them?"

"Jumpy, my man," she said. "You're jumpy. Now why?"

"Being dragged out of bed," Dave said, "would explain it." To Phil, as if she weren't there, he said, "That Anne Dettrey is one of the nicest and one of the bitchiest people I've ever met. I'm warning you."

They all laughed. His laughter astonished him. The laugh, the bland face, the polite badinage—he'd worn them all seven years before, and six and five. Here they were again, preserved all along in some indestructible camphor, ready to be donned and worn in this new season of secrecy and loss.

Anne looked about her. "Where's the bathroom, Phil? Don't you hate people who say 'little girls' room' or 'little boys' room' or must-wash-my-hands?"

As she disappeared, Dave at once changed. He studied Phil. Concern made him look forbidding.

"What's wrong, Phil?"

"Skip it." To speak of Kathy was impossible. He added at once, "Tom got called dirty Jew and kike. He came home bewildered and stunned, and I had pure murder all through me."

Dave's teeth made a grinding sound. "Now you know it all," he said harshly to Phil. "There's the place they really get at you—your kids. Now you even know about that. You can quit being Jewish tomorrow. There's nothing else."

Bitterness, hate. Dave had never before revealed either. Often enough Phil had speculated at Dave's ability to joke, flirt with Anne, go about all the business of jobs and house hunting and long-distance telephone calls. In every discussion they'd had, he'd admired his tough, muscular attitude toward whatever aspect of antisemitism they were talking over, free from fear or self-pity, unshackled even by self-consciousness. This was a new Dave.

"My own kids got it without the names—just setting their hearts on a camp their bunch were going to and being kept out. It wrecked them for a while." He looked briefly at Phil and then down at his own fists. "The only other thing that makes murder snap in you is——" He stood up. "There was a boy in our outfit, Abe Schlussman, good soldier, good engineer. One night we got bombed, and he caught it. I was ten yards off; this is straight. Somebody growled, 'Give me a hand with the goddam sheeny——' Before I got to him he was dead. Those were the last words he ever heard."

"Christ."

Anne came back, smiling, ready for fun. They ignored her. "I——" She looked at both of them, sat down silently, and picked up her drink.

"Remember when I said it was *your* fight, Phil?" Dave saw Phil's warning gesture and nodded as if to say, "I haven't forgotten; I can phrase this so as not to give anything away." He went on, "That was, of course, just for the sound effect. I'm in it up to my neck every way I can find."

"I always knew that." Phil's throat ached. There was silence. Then Dave said to Anne, "Well, my girl, you look beautiful with the new lipstick. How's the drink?"

Phil let them talk on. Anne's gaiety was muted now, and for no reason his affection and respect for her came back— she went off on strange detours from her natural paths, like everybody else. An odd conviction took him: if Kathy could hear Dave's story, everything confused in her would straighten out for all time. Maybe even this full break would yet prove mendable between them. Only death was the unbridgeable difference between two people who loved each other. Maybe instead of shouting in exasperation, he would yet find the wisdom to reason, explain, reach her inner sweetness.

When Dave at last took Anne home, Phil again got into bed, slugged through with fatigue as during the first days of basic so long ago. One sentence formed, with which he would try to reach her, another, another. Then he was sleeping.

Sometime during the night he turned over. Have to work at home a few days, with Dave gone, he thought, and then get hold of a maid again. His sleeping mind had stripped clean of illusion. It had faced the loneliness ahead and was arranging for it. Certainty tore through him. This was no temporary quarrel. He had lost her, and it was not for the flash of temper and shouting.

He reached for a cigarette and turned on the light.

Hour followed hour, day followed day, and finality hardened into an almost palpable knot against which his heart seemed to do its heavy beating. Yes, he could endure this. And as it had been seven years ago and six and five, so would it be now—through work he could help himself most.

Day after day he wrote. Night after night, he wrote. There was nothing to turn to but the driving concentration of more and more work.

After Betty, at least there had been a finis that was unarguable. Now it was not true, as it had then been, that there was not one thing to do, to say, to write, to undo. Now there was the scurrying of the mind, the frenzied excursions into the if's and but's and perhaps-after-all's. And always the dead end to bring you up short.

You could take most solemn oaths never again to quarrel, shout, even argue. But to keep them would necessitate a pliability on the issue involved—docile willingness to live in the house, go to the club, play at affability with the mores of the group which was her acceptable world. And soon you'd fall into the tacit concessions that would be necessary —if the Goldmans visited you for a month, you'd not be crude enough to ask for guest cards for them at the golf club or beach club.

You'd become the victim of your oath—or the betrayer of it.

No, it wouldn't go down. You have to stick by some guns or be lost. If you feel lost, you drag everything down with you in your guilt and self-disgust. No love could stand against that sullen drag.

He worked. Within a week he was beginning the fifth and last article. It had become so simple a thing to write. It was only a matter of disguising a name, a face, the background, but for the rest it was recording instead of contriving. Each thing as it had happened was put down; he was only the biographer of a Phil Green who was Jewish. The power of the inventing novelist or the devising playwright was as nothing to this simple strength of the biographer; here was truth, not fantasy, here in these paragraphs unrolling were only fact and record. A delicate thread of scorn for the so-called creative writers stitched itself on the fabric of his comparison. In the next instant he spotted it and tore it loose as if he were a tailor and it a gross basting cotton in a smooth lapel.

All nonfiction writers—he remembered the long-ago days of his newspaper work and the discussions with other reporters—always tried to feel superior to all fiction writers. And fiction writers reversed the process and felt superior because they could create people and events which had never happened except in that world which sat between their foreheads and their top vertebra. The childish need to feel oneself bigger than, smarter than, stronger than——

Among writers there was no danger in it. But when masses of people did it, when whole nations did it, then it became the corruption that could attack the very tissue, the very tree. Tree? Why the tree? Why had he thought of corruption and tree? It was an odd juxtaposition.

He got up and walked about the living room. He was still working at home. The accommodator had a steady job, and he had been unable, or too inefficient, to find another maid. Now that his mother was almost well again, he had finally written Belle and Mary of her attack, underlining the sharp improvement, and, to Belle, the fine way he was managing alone. He had even left her alone this afternoon for an hour, for the meeting Minify had arranged with *Smith's* lawyer, Stuart Weldon. The Flume Inn story had fired John with desire to bring suit, establish a precedent which could be publicized widely. But for all the "presumptive evidence" which Weldon spoke of so learnedly, there was no action which could be brought. "We couldn't prove our charge."

"They play it so safe, damn the slimy bastards," Minify had said, and banged his fist on the desk.

John was free of the corruption. Anne was free, his mother, Jayson, Mary, Dave, Tingler—there were plenty of people who truly were whole and sound. They were the roots and trunk of the—there it was again, the juxtaposition.

He took down his Bartlett. From "corrupt" and "corruption" he found no clue. He turned to "tree." As he searched, diagnosis of his own actions rocked his busy mind. He was manufacturing devices to keep him from acknowledging the longing in his blood, the memory in his flesh. For the first days he'd been enslaved by thought—barred from images of passion and physical love. Treacherously they had come back, to engulf him. Could anything matter more than *this* rightness between them?

Finger moving down six-point type, steering one's eyes rigidly, perhaps one's mind—it was the device for this moment. A dozen times already he'd forged other devices and used them even as he mocked them.

"Is known by his fruit, 1115." That might be part of it. The Bible, as he had half expected. He'd always been deeply moved by certain parts of the Bible, by their grave intonations, their humanity and beauty. He found the quotation on page 1115 and knew it was not the one. But it was from Saint Matthew; he crossed to the bookshelves, took down the worn leather volume and began to read the Gospel According to Saint Matthew. Something about a tree. Something about corrupt. He read on, certain now that he would be rewarded.

"Either make the tree good, and his fruit good; or else make the tree corrupt, and his fruit corrupt: for the tree is known by his fruit." There it was, uncompromising, noble— Jesus addressing the Pharisees. It was the everlasting choice for wholeness and soundness in a man or in a nation.

They had known it, the patient, stubborn men who for years had argued and written and rephrased and fought over the Constitution and the Bill of Rights. They had known that injustice could corrupt the tree. They had known that its fruit could pale and sicken and fall at last to the dark ground of history where other dreams of equality and freedom had rotted.

That was the choice, and most men knew it as their hearts knew how to beat and their lungs to draw in air.

A comfort pervaded him. The slippery danger would be fought back and conquered. Freedom was men's sturdiest hope; it would stand off the new onslaughts against it in this nation and others.

"This is the century for it."

The words spoke themselves as, a long time ago—was it only on Christmas morning?—another phrase had sounded itself in his mind. As with that other one, this was charged with import. "Maybe this is the century for it."

Other centuries had had their driving forces. Perhaps

the twentieth would have its own singular characteristic as men looked far back to it one day. It might not be The American Century after all, or The Russian Century, or The Atomic Century. Perhaps it would be the century that broadened and implemented the idea of freedom, all the freedoms. Of all men.

Phil walked back and forth, back and forth. His old patterns were re-establishing themselves quickly. A few brief weeks of shared love, fulfillment—and then they had come back. You live in loneliness; you ache and work and think, and sometimes the work or the thinking lifts you for a moment out of the embrace of agony.

After the week at home, going back to the office was like an escape to safety. At last the inevitable question had come from his mother. "What's wrong, dear? You're not seeing Kathy." He'd been unable to look up from his manuscript. "No, we've put things off awhile." Sometime later he would have to tell her. And write to Dave to head off any wire of congratulations on the second of February. He had let Dave go off that next day with no mention of anything.

He went into Minify's office, with an offhand "Here's the fourth—won't be long now." He studied Minify's face. The other time, Weldon had been there and personal talk impossible. Had she told him? And Jessie and Jane and Harry? Formalizing it? He was relieved when Minify spoke only about the series. It was now scheduled to begin with the first issue in May. Jayson ought to get started on illustrations in a week at most. They talked busily about pictures. Then it came.

"Sorry about you two," Minify said at last. "Kathy told us."

"Thanks." Ridiculous reply, awkwardness clapping down;

at the soft syllables of her name, an electric shock had twanged through him.

"She wouldn't talk about it much. Only that you were always running into things you were at odds about." Phil said nothing. "She seems pretty upset," Minify volunteered, and Phil's heart jumped. "She's talking of going off for a vacation—she'd arranged at the school for your——" He broke off, and again silence lay between them.

The door opened, and a girl came in with the usual sheaf of letters for signature. Minify said, "Miss Mittelson, Mr. Green," and they nodded to each other. She was slender, dark, composed as she moved. Phil thought of the old names, Ruth and Esther, Bathsheba and Naomi; a delicate admiration as for the impersonal idea of antiquity and survival moved in him. "You're Miss Cresson's new assistant," he said, and she smiled and said, "That's right."

She spoke to Minify about the top letter and left the room.

"Reach any final decision about Jordan?" Phil asked.

"Told him yesterday I'd never fire a man for the way he voted, the party he belonged to, his religion, his private morals. But I'd come to look on the smallest spreading of race hatred and religious prejudice as a kind of treason. He began the why-I-never-care stuff, and I hauled him up short. The ad brought us calls from half a dozen employment agencies, astonished at 'our change of policy.'" Minify glowered at Phil. "I got fairly insulting when I told that to Jordan—he's been *Smith's* to them for five years. Said treason was a fancy word but a lousy thing to have around even in small quantities. He resigned in a great huff. I admit I laid it on plenty."

"Why not?" Phil stood up, oddly grateful for this recital. He wanted to ask more about Kathy, but could not. As he reached the door, John said, "I'd have liked it to go on, Phil." His voice had deepened. He was not talking about Jordan any longer.

"Yes."

Even back in his own office, the word still vibrated the tight string of longing in him. Like the idiotic "thanks," it had come from too much silence, as if he'd lost the trick of fluent speech. He'd been a monk in the cell of regret. He'd begin to see people again, as of now. He picked up the phone and asked Anne if she'd lunch with him. "Me? All alone?" She'd already made a date and urged him to come along, "even though we are chaperoned by two fiction editors." He agreed, wondering how much she knew.

Miss Wales came in. As she brought him up to date on the research mail that had arrived during his absence, she seemed less haughty, more communicative. She even smiled. She was beginning to forgive him.

"Any calls while I was away?"

"Just a couple. I gave them your home phone."

"Any messages?" She shook her head. "Any names to call back?"

"No." She smiled again.

He wanted to let it go at that, but compulsion shoved him. "Anybody's voice you recognized?"

"Professor Lieberman, I think."

"I'm seeing him tonight."

At lunch Anne kept a covert watch on him, asking unspoken questions. He tried to sound ordinary, but he knew he wasn't fooling her much. Sam Goodman and Frank Tingler were discussing the new Dohen serial. Both were derisive of its countesses and young dukes and American society folk.

"He's half psychotic inside," Goodman said. "God, twenty-five years of it."

"Of what?" Phil asked.

"Hiding the fact he's Jewish," Tingler said calmly. "Just so he can be the snob he really is—the best clubs, the *Social Register*, the whole routine. Sam told me this morning."

"Phew," said Anne. "When'd you hear it, Sam?"

"Hell, I grew up with a nephew of his. I knew it ten years ago when I came here."

Tingler smiled. Close to, the opaque glasses no longer screened his eyes, and Phil could see the cheery look in them. It was the first time he'd ever seen Frank Tingler without the air of boredom. "Should think you'd have been too riled," Tingler said, "to keep his secret for him, Sam. Boy, he sure can dish up a story the customers'll read, though."

"Doesn't rile me as much as another kind of psychotic," Sam said. "I know a couple guys—they're above changing their names, or denying anything. But they can go through years without one single solitary mention of the word Jew or Jewish, antisemitism, Palestine, Zionism. Just never, no matter what the group, what the conversation, what the news in the afternoon paper." He looked almost awed. "Talk to them about prejudice, and they instantly launch into a passionate defense of the Negro. Brother, they're the ones rile me the most."

"No," Tingler said. "You got madder about that golf-club bunch. *They* rile you most."

"Yeah, that gang," Sam said. Phil and Anne waited. "It's this bunch of rich guys around town, Jewish-but-don't-look-it-much, mostly of English or German-Jewish ancestry. They set up a snazzy golf club of their own." He grinned mischievously. "*And* they blackball guys of Polish or Russian-Jewish stock. Meaning, anybody who looks good-and-Jewish. Like it?"

Phil thought of Miss Wales.

"After all," Anne said firmly, "why should gentiles have a corner on the sport of feeling superior?" She looked at Sam. "Dohen change his name?"

"Just slipped a notch in the alphabet, down from *C.*" Goodman laughed maliciously.

"And they say cattiness is female," Anne observed.

Sam wasn't disturbed. "This morning Frank got psycho-analyzing all the phony tripe Dohen always writes, so I finally explained what's been rotting him for years."

"Have you ever doped out," Phil lazily asked Sam, "why rough talk about a Jew sometimes gets you sore and times like now it doesn't?"

"Yeah." Sam shrugged indifferently. "If I know the guy rates it on his record and not on his nose."

"Sam straightened me out on that long ago," Tingler said. "I'd read a thing—by van Loon maybe—that struck me. Something about van Loon's hating Hitler for putting an obligation on him to like *all* Jews, good or bad."

"I had to reassure Frank," Sam explained, "that he and I both had a God-given right to dislike any louse alive, Jewish, Mohammedan, or whatever."

"Antilousism," Anne said affably. She turned to Phil. "How come your sister Bella's taken such a different line from you, Phil?" Anne asked.

"My sister who? Belle? Isabel?"

"McAnny said 'Bella'—met her in Detroit, or some people knew her. I forget which. He came back full of praise for you and scorn for her because she's hidden——"

"Oh, my God." It was a shout, a laugh, a choking, and they all stared at him.

"What's the matter?" Anne was ready to laugh too, if he would share the joke. Tingler and Goodman looked on expectantly.

"You mean McAnny came back—I've been out of the

office a week, remember, haven't heard a thing," Phil said to Anne.

"My gal got it from your Miss Wales, who got it in the washroom. He's spreading around his little poison about you being O.K., but your cowardly sister——"

Phil's mirth rubbed off in one swipe. "Damn that squirt," he said. "He's a liar about Belle; I know what started it, but I——" He stopped. Then he shrugged. "I'll tell you about Belle sometime."

Anne asked for more coffee, and Goodman talked of a short story he thought Tingler should buy. Phil suddenly remembered Miss Wales's readiness to forgive him. *No wonder she feels we're quits.* Laughter pushed up in him again. *Poor Belle. He'd told her so positively she had nothing to wet her pants about.*

That night, he discussed Dohen with Professor Lieberman, but found himself more interested in exploring Sam Goodman's reluctance to "betray" the secret Dohen had guarded so assiduously. As on his first visit, he saw now that Joe Lieberman remained imperturbable, almost indifferent, to specific individuals and their behavior in anything whatever. He dismissed both Dohen and Goodman with a casual, "It would be more convenient if people were always predictable," and for an hour they talked "atomic politics." The half-shabby library where the physicist worked in his old apartment near Columbia was conducive to easy friendliness. Nothing could untie the hard-knotted depression incessantly within him, but here Phil found his mind absorbed, as if it coexisted on quite another level of life. As a tangent to some other remark, Lieberman suddenly came back to "Dohen and his life of crime."

"I think I'll start a new crusade," he announced, his eyes shining with private merriment. "I can't invite you to join it because you don't look Jewish enough—they'd accuse

211

you of pulling a Dohen. But for my crusade, I am perfection."

He put his fingers up to his plump, beaked face as if
to refresh his tactile memory of it.

"You see, Phil, I have no religion, so I am not Jewish
by religion. Further, I am a scientist, so I must rely on
science which tells me I am not Jewish by race since there's
no such thing as a distinct Jewish race. As for ethnic group
or Jewish type, we know I fit perfectly the Syrian or Turkish
or Egyptian type—there's not even such a thing, anthro-
pologically, as the Jewish type."

Phil waited for him to go on. The man could discuss
nuclear physics, attack Zionism, comment on anything, and
make it rational, unexpected, amusing. From his last visit,
when Phil had defended "the Palestine solution" for the
immediate present at least, Lieberman's words came back
to him. "Don't let them pull the crisis over your eyes. You
say you oppose all nationalism—then how can you fall for
a *religious* nationalism? A rejoining of church and state
after all these centuries? A kind of voluntary segregation?
Always for the other fellow, of course, not for the signers
of the full-page ads in the *Times* and *Tribune*!"

"My crusade will have a certain charm," Lieberman continued now. "I will go forth and state flatly, 'I am not a
Jew.'" He looked at Phil. "With this face that becomes
not an evasion but a new principle. A scientific principle."

"An anticlerical one, too."

"Precisely."

They both laughed, and then Phil grew thoughtful.
"There must be millions of people nowadays," he said,
"who are either atheist, agnostic, or religious only in the
vaguest terms. I've often wondered why the Jewish ones
among them, maybe even after a couple of generations of

being pretty free of religion, still go on calling themselves Jews."

Now Lieberman became serious.

"I know why they do—except for an occasional Dohen."

"Why?"

"Because this world still makes it an advantage not to be one." His lower lip shoved forward. His eyes changed their cheerfulness for a remote coldness. "Yes, I will even have to abandon my crusade. Only if there were no anti-semites could I do it." At once he was good-humored again. "I'm reluctant to abandon it so soon. It would have had an innocence—no, a sort of purity—that would appeal to any scientist."

CHAPTER THIRTEEN

"YOU MUST THINK Mamma's your property," Belle's voice in the receiver began vigorously. "The time she had the heart attack you kept it to yourself for a week, and now this calm letter days after her stroke."

"Hello, Belle," Phil said. "I should have written right off, but——"

"Or at least phoned. Even if the doctors did say it would pass. She's my mother, too."

"Want to speak to her? She's starting to sit up a bit now." Belle never used to antagonize him so quickly in the old days in California.

"I want her to come out here for some real rest and care, where she won't have those awful stairs to climb. I'll come and get her when she can travel."

Phil motioned to his mother and laid the receiver on the table. Belle's voice continued to spring forth from it. "I should think, Phil, you'd at least find an apartment where——"

"Now, Belle, really." Mrs. Green picked up the phone as she was talking. "In all of New York——"

Belle interrupted with worried questions about how Mrs. Green felt. The slight thickness of speech had apparently shocked her into thinking more of her mother than of her own sense of neglect. A moment later, she repeated her invitation, and, standing near, Phil could hear each syllable even now that her voice had softened.

"Thanks, dear," Mrs. Green said, "but I'll be fine soon,

and I can't leave Tom and Phil alone. We still have no maid, and Phil couldn't ever go out in the evening."

"Then take Tom out of school for a bit," Belle said energetically, "and take him with you. *He* doesn't go around telling people he's Jewish too, does he?"

Mrs. Green looked up sharply. Phil put his hands in his pockets.

"Does he?" The sounds in the receiver grew louder again. "Because if he did it here, I'd have to give Phil's ridiculous scheme away."

"Belle!" Phil watched his mother closely. Like many patient people, she could go to an extreme of rage once in a great while. "That's a shocking, dreadful thing to say."

"Dick's firm——"

"You're not thinking only of Dick's firm," Mrs. Green said. "That last time you were here, you said things while you were angry that told me you've lost all your old principles on your own account, not on Dick's."

"Oh, Mamma, please!"

"Now I see you've lost your spunk, too. It makes me ashamed."

Phil saw his mother's hand tremble. Brusquely he took the receiver away and with his head motioned her to her chair.

"Listen here, Belle," he said with authority. "I don't want Mom to have a relapse. So can it." Belle started to say something. He cut in. "And on your next visit here, can it, too. Better quit this now; good night."

He hung up and turned to Mrs. Green. "Feels queer to have one right in our own family, doesn't it? She'll be in New York in less than a week, trying to justify everything."

"Stop that, Phil," his mother said sharply. "I won't *have* you saying ugly things about your own sister." She was

215

silent for several minutes and then started for her room. At the door she stopped.

"Did you know we quarreled that day she was here?" she asked in a flat voice.

"About her money-mad Jew, Patrick Curran? I guessed it."

"More about her defeatist attitude in general. Then about the motor strike and labor unions and the Negro migration to Detroit." She breathed deeply.

"Maybe she'll change back."

"It's too late. It's gone too far with her." She left him.

It's gone too far with her. With Belle it had gone past curing. But Kathy? Kathy was not like that about strikes and unions and migrations. Kathy was no defeatist about prejudice. She might be diffident, even weak, but there was also somewhere in her the thing that had made her argue Minify into taking some definite step to combat it.

A renewed hope surged. He went to his desk. For more than an hour he remained there.

Dear Kathy,
It seems impossible that we were unable to reach through this and find some place where we could be right with each other on it again. We never did go back to talk out the quarrel on New Year's about the party. I keep thinking that if we started back there, we might find out what kept going so wrong. Can I see you?

Phil

He who could write so easily, who could speed a thousand words down along his plunging fingers on the green-rubber keyboard of his machine, had stumbled like a first-grader over this single paragraph. A dozen times he had begun it and written into it a naked desperation; a dozen times he had begun it and written into it the frosted mathematics of

216

logic. Finally he'd written out quickly the sentences that kept cropping up in all the versions. Those must be, to whatever censor there was in him, the most acceptable ones. He sealed it without rereading it and went out to mail it.

An hour later he despised himself for having sent it.

Kathy's answer was in his pocket when he called for Anne. It had come by return mail and was all the passport he needed to any new relationship, yet the guilt of disloyalty, even betrayal, nagged at him.

Anne had stopped by in the office with another cautious report of a possible apartment for Dave. Phil had been unable to sound other than limp and tired. "You're none too cheerful these days, Phil," she'd said kindly. "I worry about you."

"Me? Why, I'm fine."

"Well, I'm not. If you're free tonight, come on down for a drink and listen to *my* troubles."

So she'd guessed. She wouldn't have suggested an evening date if she hadn't guessed—or heard it herself. Everybody in that office seemed to hear everything, tell everything. He'd suggested dinner. With the exception of Professor Lieberman, he'd seen no one, done nothing but work. Suddenly he was grateful to her for forcing him out of the house, away from Tom and his mother, out into the world. Her clever, emphatic speech would—"Hell, I don't need any alibis for going out with her."

But through dinner, she seemed preoccupied, unlike her usual self. Once she fell into a long silence and then sighed. Resistance edged up ungenerously in him. He'd assumed she'd been joking about "listen to my troubles," and now he was fearful that she'd meant it. He felt anesthetized as yet to any confidences she might make. How self-centered one's own pain could make one!

"I'll make you some decent coffee at home," she said, and in contrition he agreed that that was a fine idea. In her apartment, he stared about him. Thinly in his mind, the whistles and tooting and "Happy New Years" of his last visit echoed; suddenly the letter in his pocket seemed the final plaque nailed on a long-closed coffin.

Was Kathy out with some man tonight, hearing him tell her she was beautiful, seeing his gaze travel over her face and throat and body? Jealousy reached into him. He sat, numb and patient, waiting for the spasm to ease. By now he knew it well. This also was different from the time after Betty's death, this onslaught a dozen times each night of an enemy he'd never had to face during that other siege.

From the kitchen Anne called, "It's perking now; be ready in a minute." He reached for the letter and reread it once again.

There really isn't any use, Phil. I've thought and thought, but I keep remembering how pointless it was for me and Bill to try to patch up the differences between us. There's no use my going on always feeling in the wrong—it's so humiliating, it wouldn't wear well. Things would keep coming up on this, and we'd just kill everything off with quarrels. Maybe we fell in love too quickly, before we really had enough time to know each other. I'm sorry.

                                                              Kathy

He put it back in his pocket. At last Anne came in with the coffee. She looked at him, shook her head, said, "You brood too much," and immediately talked of office things. He had misjudged Anne, he decided; unspoken apology formed in his mind. For all her brittle manner, she was clear and unequivocal about things; with her there'd never be the doubtful wonder, the watching for nuance that could communicate a lifetime slant to a child.

"You're quite a girl—I've never told you."

"Me? Sure, everybody loves Anne."

She sat beside him on the sofa and poured the coffee as if she had just learned how to do it. With a start, Phil saw that her hand was shaking.

"You said you weren't very happy, Anne," he said impulsively. "Want to talk about it?"

"No, thanks—that much I've learned. Nothing bores any man as much as an unhappy female."

"We're good friends by now."

She put sugar into her coffee, shaking her head for "no" as she stirred it. He watched her hand. There was something mesmeric in the way she stirred the coffee and stirred and stirred and stirred and stirred. Suddenly the spoon was still.

"I know about it being called off, Phil. Could I say something about you and Kathy?"

"Sure." It sounded wary.

"John had a sort of office party last night for some of us old-timers, and she was there. We put on our usual act about liking each other."

"Act?"

"You must have guessed it was mostly an act."

"I wondered about it."

"I just never go for that upper-classes stuff she lives for——"

"Anne, let's don't." He put his hand over hers to lessen the rebuke. It wasn't possible to sit here, discussing, dissecting. Abruptly she drew her hand out from under his.

"Oh, all right, be the little gentleman." She took up her coffee cup, but did not drink from it. "It's just, I think you're pretty straight and——" His unbudging stare halted the rest of it. She smiled. "Lord, I do seem to be digging myself in deeper and deeper."

Dave had said "one of the nicest and one of the bitch-

219

iest." Had she been getting off malice about Kathy all along? Was it only malice? Again the sense of betrayal whipped at him. But there was something here, some clue, maybe the clue he'd searched for. "Upper-classes stuff" was her way of putting what Kathy called "living attractively" or "knowing amusing people." How important *were* these things to Kathy? Her voice spoke a phrase in his mind. "When I didn't have the things my friends did, then I was full of snobbish misery." There was some excitement here, the excitement of theory, of possible discovery. Privately, he'd have to carry this forward. Not now. Not with any-body, even Anne.

"I sure hope," he said aloud, "we can find some place for Dave before the month's up. You'd like Carol as much as you do Dave."

She turned toward him quickly. "Any connection?"

"Why, no."

"Or innuendo?"

"Anne, what the hell?" He put his hands out, palms up, in the instinctive need to show he held no trickery, no weapon, no motive. "I guess I was just trying to change the subject and being clumsy over it." He turned toward her so that he was sitting along the edge of the sofa, almost facing her.

"O.K." She tossed her head, like an impudent child. But in the next moment, she leaned forward and hid her face in her hands. Looking down upon her, a kinship flared—here was the bitter universal, for whatever hidden cause. He put his hand out. He stroked her hair, awkward as a two-year-old patting a kitten. She turned her body toward him; her head rested against his knees. His startled flesh felt her warm breath through his clothing; his thigh knew the round rise and fall of her breast. His hand stopped moving along her hair.

"Everything's so damn rotten, Phil." Her voice came up to him, muffled and thick. "We're both unhappy. Why can't we try to find some way——"

He did nothing. He said nothing. She was as motionless and mute as he. Seconds slipped past as if they were a tableau on a stage, rigidly waiting for an appointed time to elapse. Then she sat up. When she spoke, her voice was at once embarrassed and defiant.

"Let's go to a movie," she said.

For the third time, Kathy struck the chord incorrectly. Her nerves clanged with the dissonance. She dropped her hands from the keyboard and sat staring at the notes. She'd better put off this week's lesson, too.

She stood up and moved quickly away from the piano. In the ten days since it had happened, she seemed to be moving away from everything. She'd had to force herself to answer Phil's letter. And an hour ago, when Bill had phoned, asking to see her, she'd pleaded a headache, in the attempt to run from the dull half-hour it would mean. Maybe "unfriendly divorces" were the wisest after all, without this farce of amiability.

"I'm about to resign, Kathy," he'd said, "and start a firm of my own. It would really help to check it with you."

Poor Bill—the old habit of "sharing his work." She'd refused going out to a bar and had asked him up instead. Maybe for once he wouldn't tell every detail as he "spotted in the background."

"You don't look up to par," Bill began when he arrived.

"February letdown is all it is." She gave him whisky and water. He'd never liked soda or much ice. He sat where Phil used to sit, at one end of the sofa. He was ill at ease; she knew it instantly. Had he come for something other than talk of the new firm?

"I ran into Tom Manning at luncheon the other day," he said. "He told me Jane said you'd broken your engagement."

"Yes. Are Ellen and Tom still hipped on skiing?"

"I suppose so." He sipped his drink. She watched him. Bill's meaningless good looks never changed. "I saw you and Mr. Green together one night," Bill said. His tone insisted that this was purely by the way.

"When? Why didn't you come over?"

"It was coming out of a movie, before Christmas, I think. I tried to catch your eye, but you both got into a taxi. I didn't know who he was, of course, but when you described Mr. Green the day you told me the news, it fitted."

The "Mr. Green" jarred. She said, "Yes, it must have been Phil." Why hadn't Bill mentioned seeing them during his New Year visit? She decided not to ask. "What's this about a firm of your own, though?"

"In a minute, Kathy." He sipped his drink again. "I'm sorry, if breaking it upset you," he said awkwardly, and she was touched.

"That's sweet, Bill," she said. "I'm not upset any more, but let's skip it anyway."

"Tom said he's a Jew. Is that right?"

She looked at him briefly. "Yes, that's right."

"Well, then, maybe in the long run."

His intonation, Kathy thought, made it a complete statement. Subject, verb, object, modifiers—the complacent voice, the judicious shake of the head, had managed to include all of them. It was a sentence. You could parse it. Truculence burred in her. She wouldn't get drawn into discussion with him. During their marriage, they'd had so many useless squabbles about Bill's ready prejudices.

"I've got to start for Aunt Jessie's soon," she said firmly. "Have you already resigned, Bill?"

"No, these financial matters can't be rushed." Looking reflective, he fondled the lobe of his right ear. It was one of his old mannerisms, denoting preoccupation with business. "What I mean," he said at last, "is that in the long run it would have been all sorts of a nuisance to be the wife of a Jew."

"Bill, *please.*" The truculence was audible now. "You really——" But nothing would deflect Bill, ever.

"I mean like the cottage, for instance. Of course you could have sold it. I'd have taken it off your hands in a jiffy myself."

"Sold it?" She put her glass down. "Why would we sell it?"

He looked astonished. "He looked a good sort, Kathy."

"He *is* a good sort."

"Well, then. He'd never barge into a neighborhood that doesn't take Jews—he'd never have been comfortable there."

Something stung through her.

"I know you disapprove," Bill went on, "and I do, too, if they're the acceptable kind, but, well, it's just facing facts." He shrugged. "And you couldn't go to New Canaan or anywhere near Jane and the crowd. New Canaan's even stricter about Jews than Darien."

"Stop it. Don't go on. I hate this. You *know* how I feel about all that."

"Why, Kathy." His voice was soothing. "As I always told you, *you* can't change the whole world, no sense getting so——"

The sting again. She stood up abruptly. Bill scrambled up, too. Good manners, perfect breeding always. She hated him; with one more of his slipping-along phrases, she would scream at him.

"I told you I had a headache. It's worse. I've got to lie down." She saw the uncomprehending look. "You *saw* Phil.

You know he's not filthy or diseased or vulgar. Could he spoil the neighborhood and the real-estate values? Could he? Then *how* can you just stand there spilling out those horrible things without even being angry?"

"What horrible things?" There was only perplexity in it.

She said, "Oh, *no*," and was silent. Then she said, limply, "Bill, please go now. My head's splitting. Some other time we'll talk over your new firm."

She left him standing there and went to her bedroom. She closed the door. She listened. When the front door slammed, she went to the bed and lay down.

There was something sickening here, something more hateful than anything there had been between them in their old squabbles. Something not about Bill; something about her, and not to be borne.

"Never be comfortable there" . . . "New Canaan's even stricter than Darien" . . . "can't change the whole world . . ."

The phrases pelted her. "Oh, *no*." The staccato of disbelief was for herself now. It wasn't the same. *She* had said those phrases as hateful facts; Bill had offered them casually, without emotion.

She lay still. The swift sting changed to a suffusion of heat, spreading, reaching.

Everything important between her and Bill had come to differences. But on this? On this there was no difference. In tone, in mood, maybe, but nothing more. One by one, the arguments she had desperately given Phil that day about Dave had come easily now from Bill's lips.

From the lips and heart and shabby mind of Bill Pawling.

Off and on during dinner Kathy's attention went back to the one point that was rebuttal. "Tone and mood *are* important; they're the distance between acceptance and rejection."

She forced herself to make talk with the Minifys, but her thoughts carried on their own busy work of comfort and persuasion. By dessert, her nerves were steadier. But she felt that she'd come through some brief, savage fever.

In the living room, Uncle John took his coffee from the tray and said, "Want to read something in rough draft?"

"You don't mean me, dear?" Jessie asked.

"No, Jess. I thought Kathy might, though."

"Is it———?" She stopped, and he didn't answer. He looked at Kathy uneasily. She had a depleted air that worried him. She'd fallen into the almost nightly habit of coming over for dinner; it was being a stiff time for her, no question of that. He looked at her now, as she accepted coffee from Jessie, and remembered her as a college girl, then as a bride, then as a newly divorced woman. Never before had her pretty face been so concave from jawbone to eye socket; never before had he seen the puffed arcs of shiny, almost oiled, skin under her eyes. She cried in that apartment of hers, and that's what did it. The act she put on all the time was fine, but it didn't fool him. It was so rational, the explanation she'd finally given Jessie—Phil was so intense, so given to moods, so impatient of other points of view that she'd have to become a wishy-washy carbon copy of him or else prepare for constant bickering or outright scenes about all sorts of problems. It was wiser to admit incompatibility beforehand than when it was too late. That was all.

All this explanation had rather surprised him; he'd figured Phil differently. But, of course, just in a working relationship one never saw the whole man. She meant it— enough to be going through plenty of torment for it. What trouble it was to be young! At sixty you grieved for the world; in youth you grieved for one unique creature. And so opaque and stubborn was the grief, you could blot out the

225

world with it as you could blot out the sun with a disk of black glass.

"It's the last one of the series," he said finally. "He turned it in this afternoon."

"I'm not much good with rough-draft stuff."

"Hm. He does fairly smooth copy right off once he gets going." He crossed the room to his brief case. She watched him open it, nervously waiting, as if he were pulling aside a curtain from which Phil himself might emerge. She still felt too shattered to dare any new emotion. Uncle John took out a stack of manuscript, fastened at the top with the largest paper clip she had ever seen. She watched him as he riffled through the pages, reading a sentence here and there. Phil's hands had held those pages a few hours ago; his voice had spoken to Uncle John as he'd turned it over to him. His life was going on along the same paths, sure and undeviating.

"I'll react better to it when it's in print, Uncle John."

"O.K., if you'd rather." He turned another page. He looked pleased, partly with Phil, partly with his own judgment in choosing him. "Hell of a balanced job," he said, without looking up. "Got a thousand facts into the five pieces, from all angles, all over the country, but he's worked them into his own story so you go from objective to subjective without stumbling." He threw the manuscript down on the coffee table. "Make a sensation."

"Such a shame, about his mother," Jessie said. "You say she's all right again, though?" John nodded, but they both ignored her. For a space there was the drinking of more coffee.

"One part in this one's about you, I'd guess," John said casually.

"*Me?*" Kathy's eyes accused him of lying. "Why, he wouldn't!"

"Oh, thoroughly disguised—everything personal in it is

disguised. Doesn't make it *Smith's Weekly,* of course—just a big business office."

"But you can recognize——?"

"He's got a beautiful woman in it, all the way through; married, in her forties, wife of a friend in Rumson, New Jersey, two boys. But I made a long guess."

"Uncle John, he just couldn't!"

"The hell he couldn't. I'm in the second article—the big liberal who had an antisemitic personnel manager in his own office and never took the trouble to find out about it! He had quite a field day with me. Sure, when I read it, it kind of burned me for five minutes. But he *had* to, Kathy. He's writing what happened to him while he was Jewish—you and I and everything else *are* what happened to him. Want him to leave it all out and dream up stuff?"

"No, but if *you* recognize that woman——"

"He took about ten people and braided them into her— that's what all writers worth a bean do when they need types of people, recognizable types." He reached over and patted her hand. It was unexpected, an unspoken reassurance. "You're very special to people who love you, Kath. But you're also a type, like anybody else."

"I suppose I am. You never think of yourself as a type."

They fell silent. Kathy looked at the six-inch paper clip. In the shaded light of the room it shone like silver. She leaned forward and idly picked up the manuscript.

As she turned the pages phrases caught at her, but she could hardly filter their meaning through the haze of feeling. Touching the paper was like feeling his body near her again.

". . . driving away from the inn, I knew all about every man or woman who'd been told the job was filled when he knew it wasn't, every youngster who'd ever been turned down by a college because they 'have too many New Yorkers already' when he knew the true word was 'Jews' or 'foreign-sounding' . . ." She turned a page. ". . . this primitive rage pitching through you when you see your own child shaken and dazed that he was selected for attack . . ." She lost the next sentences. ". . . a new phase in my own reactions. From that moment I saw it as an unending attack by a hundred million adults on kids of seven and eight and ten and twelve; on adolescent boys and girls, on youngsters trying to get into summer camps and medical schools . . ." The haze began to thin down.

"I don't see anything in it about me," she said to John.

John didn't answer.

She leafed over several pages, searching, almost fearfully, like a vain woman looking for her own face in a group photograph, hoping it would not be too unkind. ". . . and I felt suddenly that I knew why this lovely woman in Rumson can never truly fight the thing she says she hates. One part of her does indeed hate it, but that part is at war with another part, a buried part, a part that started in her childhood's misery because 'the other girls' had prettier houses and nicer clothes. Like millions of us, she'd pursued the American dream of 'keeping up with the Joneses' or catching up with them. And the buried part is still living out her childhood ambition to be one of the 'smart set' in her community, the 'in group' that belongs. She won't jeopardize that adored status by becoming an outlandish arguer at a dinner table where somebody takes a crack at Jews; she won't risk being gauche by ripping through the 'set of rules' in the pretty world she lives in. During the shooting war, she worked herself half sick in factories, sold bonds, accepted all the discomfort of ration books and shortages like a good soldier. But during this covert war for this country's future, this secret war in which antisemitism is one of the most familiar weapons, she is unable to do more than offer little clucking sounds of disapproval. Her own success story paralyzes her."

Kathy threw the manuscript down. She avoided John's eyes. She said, "How about some gin rummy, Aunt Jess?" and at once Jessie went to a built-in cupboard below the bookshelves and brought out cards.

"But not too late, Kathy," Jessie said. "You really worry me, losing weight that way. You must get lots of sleep."

"It's so easy to see the flaws in everybody else," Kathy said to the room at large, as she pulled chairs up to the card table.

"Sometimes the flaws are really there, Kathy." Minify looked back to the stacked pages. "In the first one he points out that he'd never gone much beyond the sounds of disapproval himself."

"He doesn't say anything about the real bigots———"

"Oh, there's plenty about that in the series. But he showed me an advance copy of the next *Fortune* survey— damn interesting. Proves something he hunched onto all along." Minify's eyes were serious. "The biggest incidence of antisemitism comes from the top-income bracket now."

"Really? Not the other way round?"

"The very people who set the styles for the country in clothes and cars and salads—and mores." He was enjoying her astonishment. "The middle-aged stuffy ones in the bracket more than the young ones. Survey also shows only nine per cent of the country admits any prejudice."

"That's not so much," Aunt Jessie said.

"It's plenty." He turned again to Kathy. "What Phil's trying to do is make the rest of the style setters, the ones who really *are* against prejudice, come out and fight. Not just the rich ones, everybody."

She glanced down at the manuscript as if she were appealing to it to judge her and find her a fighter.

"There are a hell of a lot more of *our* kind of style setters," John went on with a sudden intensity. "Even a handful of us in every community could set a new national style in a few months. Damn it, it's worth trying."

"Ready, Kathy?" Aunt Jessie said. "Shall we play the double spade?"

Two mornings later, Phil brandished a bulky roll of manuscript at Miss Wales.

"One and two," he said. "Edited and ready to go. I'll get through number three before you can handle this much."

He chucked the roll over to her. She caught it and began to work the elastic band down the thick column. The rubber squeaked against the paper.

"How long do you guess for that much?" Phil asked.

She looked up and said, "This about ten thousand, do you figure?" Her open palms continued their downward stroke on the resisting elastic, and Phil remembered the time years ago when he'd watched a saleswoman roll new gloves on Betty's stiffly upright fingers.

"More than that," he said. "They each run pretty near seven thousand. Minify says not to cut till galley, anyway."

"By tomorrow night," she said with assurance. "I'm pretty fast when it isn't longhand." She was smiling at him, eager to begin her ministrations at last. Ever since he'd remained silent when she'd taunted him about Belle's "running away from it," her forgiveness had been complete and he'd avoided reopening hostilities. She glanced down at her hands. The tight band was at the lower rim of the roll now, compressing it so that above it the paper fanned out, an inverted cone. Horn of plenty, Phil thought. Full of all the good things, hate and indifference and hypocrisy. And maybe some hope, too. He was watching her.

She had the band off. She glanced up at him, saying professionally, "And, of course, if it isn't all thick with pencil corrections and inserts and stuff." As she talked her hands were busy on the curling wad, rerolling it backward, then flattening it out on her knees. She looked down. He saw her eyes go to the title.

"For eight weeks?" She looked up, and immediately down to the short first paragraph. He had never changed it. He had made the decision, long ago, to tell it straight, right from his first resistance to the "hell of an assignment." He didn't particularly relish remembering that early boredom and resistance, but that was the way it had been.

He was still keeping an eye on Miss Wales. She was nearing the bottom of the first page. Her head was bent, and he could see only her profile. Below its impassive repose, he saw that her slender neck was coloring. It touched him. She was upset. That he hadn't expected.

She turned to page two. Abruptly then she put the manuscript aside.

"You're a Christian, Mr. Green!" Surprise, reproof, embarrassment, all these were in the stare, the unbelieving tone. "And I never suspected it; I fell for—why, for Pete's sake."

"Everybody else did, too, what the hell."

"I saw you more than anybody else, though, and I never once——" Her face was going rosy also. Her round-eyed pinkness disconcerted him. Odd, this much reaction.

"What's so upsetting about that, Wales?"

"I feel so dumb!"

"You're practically telling me, in a funny backhand way, that there *is* something different between Jews and Christians."

"How am I?"

"By being so floored at not guessing."

"Oh, Mr. Green. You're always doing that, reading

things in." She looked up at him, silently asking him not to badger her now. "I'm so—I feel all turned round some-how."

"Take it easy. I'm the same guy I was yesterday."

"I—I guess you are." She blinked rapidly. "But why'd you *ever* tell people—just purposely—I don't get it."

"You will when you get to page ten or so." Echo of Kathy's voice as she knelt to Tom. The Great Benison—Miss Wales felt it, too, in a kind of reverse twist. Threaded through her ordinary surprise was astonished disbelief that anybody could voluntarily abandon that glory! And if he charged her again with antisemitism, the unwitting conces-sion that being Christian was better than being Jewish, she'd accuse him of reading things in. Or echo Kathy once more. "It's just facing facts."

"Anyway, let me have the first one when it's ready," he said, "so I can turn it over to the art department."

She rose, the automatic response to the tone of finality. She was still flustered. "Hold on a minute, Wales." She looked up, ready to be offended. "Look, I'm the same guy I've been all along," he said gently. "Same face, nose, tweed suit, voice, everything. Only the word 'Christian' is dif-ferent. Someday you'll believe me about people being people instead of words and labels."

She rolled the manuscript so tightly, Phil thought, she's throttling the life out of it. She left, and he reached for a cigarette. The first time he'd catalogued himself that way, the magic word had been "Jewish." He oughtn't, he sup-posed, be surprised over this first small episode of "the un-winding"; there should never be surprises when you deal with the irrational. Turning the manuscript over was a mile-stone as far as the series went, but it meant nothing much about himself. Kathy was right. He had changed. Once you change about things like this, you never unchange. He was through and he wasn't through. The eight weeks had uncovered things, many things, and not only about being Jewish. They had pried him loose from his own blindfolds.

He'd learned about being Jewish. But he'd also learned a good deal about being anybody.

The manuscript of the third and fourth articles bulked thick in the Manila envelope on the desk. He reached for it and took it out. Three days had gone into the editing of the first two, but the rest had come off the machine more readily; they shouldn't need so much revision. He picked up a pencil. Then he knew that he was too depleted to start in again.

He leaned back in his chair. The desk calendar caught his eye. Friday, the eighth of February. At this moment they'd have been on a bright beach in Nassau, somnolent beside each other on the sand, secret with the night they'd shared. He stabbed his cigarette at the ash tray; it broke in the middle and shredded tobacco over his fingers. He had to take a walk, get out of here, go somewhere.

In the corridor he saw Bert McAnny and ignored him.

That day after lunch he'd gone straight for Bert on his gossip about Belle. It had proved futile, even cheap.

"But, Phil, this Jeff Brown said it; I didn't. All *I* said was that if I were Jewish, I'd be the way you are."

"Cut the bouquets, Bert. Strikes me, the very people who make life galling for Jews are the most upright about demanding guts and courage and dignity from them."

Now, the sight of Bert merely made him wonder whether Belle would run into anything out there, or whether it would stay in the gossip stage all around her and she unaware of it. Well, she'd have to stand it. She and Dick and the whole of Naismith Motors.

He drifted down along the corridor. In the "pen," twenty typewriters rushed along on their dry clacking, the racket interspersed with chiming bells and the shrewish whine of the slung-back carriage. Had Wales already shown the title and first paragraph to her cronies? Was there the same astonished look on all of them, or did any of them take it with the plain, ordinary interestedness they'd feel in any other journalistic stunt?

The door to Anne's office was open. Her secretary was in there with her. He said, "Hi," and started to go past.

"Phil. Come on in. I found an apartment for Dave."

He went in and waited while the two women talked. He watched her conduct the brief business, easy, friendly, bright as ever. Nobody in this world, he decided, could look at her, listen to her, talk to her, and think something was sad and hurt and wrong in her life. She signaled to him once that it would only be another minute and gave him what was surely a lighthearted smile. Since the night at her house he had seen her only at the office or for drinks with other people. Neither of them had made even oblique reference to what had happened.

"It's sort of a railroad flat," she said, the moment they were alone. "But not awful at all—I went and looked at it this morning. Converted tenement on the south fringe of the Village. The father committed suicide last night, and my broker pal practically phoned me before the hearse got there."

He shook his head. "You are a gruesome one. What broker pal?"

"I told you—you never listen to what I say. Clare Spradling. Used to broke uptown in the fancy East Side offices and then started her own business in Village properties. Anyway, listen." She described the flat, and ended, "But it's clean and sunny and warm and the only thing they'll ever get. Should we take it? She's holding it for me till noon."

"What's happening to the suicide's family?"

"Oh, them." She waved them out of the world. "Want to go see it?"

"If you say so, grab it. I'll write a wire for Dave."

While she was getting the number, she said, "Clare's the one gave me that code stuff I told you—the brokers' little dodges, 'hundred per cent co-operative' when they mean gentiles only, remember?"

"And 'he's an Otto Kahn' if they mean Jewish-but-O.K. Sure, I worked it in in the fourth one, along with Sam's golf-club boys. I'm through at last."

She said, "Great," and talked efficiently into the telephone. He wrote out a wire for Dave and Carol. They could still make it, and they'd be happy about it. The one letter he'd had from Dave did a bad job of concealing his sharpened desire for the bigger future Quirich-Jones offered. "That's right, Clare, as is," Anne was saying, "no repainting and rent from Feb fifteen even if they're not here. I'm sending fifty deposit by boy; God bless you for smelling the gas or whatever." She hung up.

Gratitude made him say, "Come on, I'll buy you a sandwich at the Ritz."

"Decided I won't attack you again, hey?"

They walked through the crowds and colors of Fifth Avenue at noon. It was a day such as comes sometimes in early February, taunting in its unseasonable warmth, immediate with spring and gentle winds and beneficent skies forever. Slow and unarguable, the old desire for love, for a close-shared life, struck at him, not with Kathy, not with Anne, not with any one woman. It was concept only, urgency in the blood. He wondered if this tall, slim girl beside him, never pretty, but striking and vigorous and stimulating, knew that hunger also, and for how long she had sought to appease it.

235

"Phil, I suppose Dave told you about us? Men always put on such talk about guarding a woman's name but usually manage to slip the idea across to their best buddy just the same."

"Matter of fact, he never did."

"Oh. You mean I'm talking too much, as usual?"

"What difference does it make, if I do know? It'd hurt Carol, that's all. Wives never understand what it's like to get back to an appealing girl of your own kind after three years."

"I'll never tell Carol. I'm loathsome about phony women, but——"

He made a gesture so sharp, she stopped at once. They walked on in silence. Once or twice she glanced at him and then away; he knew it without turning his head. Even his mother, when he'd finally told her it was off for good, had said nothing against Kathy. Nor would Dave when he received the letter about it. Then why should Anne?

Downstairs in the grill the room was already filling with people. From previous visits there, Phil knew that many of them were from New York's publishing houses and advertising agencies, that they were radio executives and literary agents and playwrights and authors. In the good downtown restaurants they would be bankers and lawyers and brokers and insurance men. Around Times Square, they would be show folk and garment-industry executives and newspaper management people who did not like "eating in" with linotypers and copy runners and rewrite men who used the restaurants right in their own buildings.

"I'm becoming a New Yorker fast," he said aloud to Anne.

"Like it?"

"You do spend more time in restaurants here than in any

city out West," he said. "In New York, you can live through most of the dramatic moments of your life leaning over a table or side by side on one of those damn benches."

She was reading the menu and made no answer. He looked about him. He would for a long time, he supposed, be quite unable to enter a peopled place without this fleeting wonder if Kathy might be there. Unconsciously he looked for her in every street group, on every bus, among the women stopping at the windows of the stores strung brightly along Fifth and Madison and Fifty-seventh. He never knew that he was doing it until the mixed disappointment and relief told him he'd been at it again, half longing, half afraid of the shock if he should one day come upon her face to face.

Anne put the menu aside. She picked up the roll on her plate and crumbled a piece off it. "The thing that's wrong with me, Phil, is I've been in love for eleven years with a man I can't ever marry."

She spoke without the coloring of any emotion whatever, neither sorrow nor regret, not self-pity or appeal for sympathy. It was purely a handing over of fact for any use he might make of it.

"I'm thirty-three," she said, "so it's been the only thing you'd call love there's ever been. You take quite a beating, so you begin doing all sorts of things to make it easier for you from time to time. Like Dave."

He remained silent, but he nodded as if to tell her he knew all about what one did from time to time to make it easier.

"And you get tense and nasty and discontented and fairly acid about things. So that's me. Dave wasn't kidding when he said I was bitchy—I'd have taken him away from Carol if I could have, divorce and the works. If you've been through enough you get callous about other women's sufferings—they can stand it, too. I know I'm twisted up about everything and I don't give much of a damn by now."

"Sure you can't ever marry this man you're in love with?"

"He's married and one of those decent ones. He won't hurt her. O.K. to wreck me and himself. Sometimes the decent men are the most laughable."

"You were going to give him up for Dave. Couldn't you just give him up for good, anyway, and get over it?"

"I've tried that, too. But no matter how much is wrong, so much else is right—if it's got you, Phil, you can't just argue it away."

Who knew that better than he? "So much else is right." For a moment he could not speak, silenced by the clamor of that recognition.

"I'm sorry, Anne. It must be hell." The captain came up benignly for their order. When he'd gone, Phil turned earnestly to her. "You're *not* twisted up about everything."

She suddenly laughed. "Meaning I'm free of antisemitism!" She was ridiculing him, and he did not mind it. "Whoever said you had to be a sainted character to be free of it? Just the way your life turned you, that's all." She waved gaily to somebody across the room. She looked self-possessed and completely gratified that she was alive.

CHAPTER FOURTEEN

THE STUNNING COLD made Kathy flinch as she came through the door of the hotel. Perhaps Aunt Jess was right about "overdoing it." Maybe she was too worn out for this strenuous life. Night after night of the yellow pills knocked you down from any sense of well-being. But without them you just turned round and round in that dark, silent pit of memory. Then exhaustion stripped you of the strength to fight back to your ordinary calmness. She'd got to a point where the noisy scramble of the school jabbed impossibly at her nerves. A week at Lake Placid with Aunt Jess was no bonanza of fun and jollity, but she'd been meekly grateful for the suggestion. For the third time, she'd announced to her assistant at the nursery that she was taking a few days off. To have gone the week already arranged for Nassau with Phil would have been simpler. But the constant comparisons those actual days would have tossed at her—that she could not have borne.

She was dressed for skiing, but the piercing air decided her on a short walk instead. Besides, the hotel station wagon in the driveway, filling up with another load for the big run, was too full of talking, laughing couples. Everywhere she went now she was aware of the couples—always a man and a woman, a man and a woman. When you were as glaringly alone, as she, the full import of that "male and female created He them" began to shame you. You were the abnormal one; against nature, against the pattern and stream of the normal. She started up the main road, almost furtive in the hope she'd pass nobody she'd met in the four days they'd been there.

Before she got to the big fork, the station wagon passed her, and above the metallic clicking of its chains she heard tapping on the glass panes. Automatically she smiled and waved; it was surely Ellen or Tom Manning. It was good they'd come only for the week end and would be off again late tonight. She really liked them both, and, with their insatiable appetite for skiing, she'd not even been surprised when they arrived. But their awkwardness about "being sorry to hear the news," their most innocent references to home or Darien, even Ellen's inevitable table talk about the Springfield Plan—all of it kept scratching at her resolution "not to think about it any more." At the party, Ellen had liked Phil and he her; they were kindred spirits; they both got hipped on things.

She was no longer huddling down from the stinging cold. She walked along briskly despite the heavy boots she'd not used for three winters. It began to snow, and she remembered how right and just the snow had seemed the first night they had dinner in her place. A week before Christmas, and now it was almost the middle of February, and the year that was to take her back to happiness and marriage was instead being the worst period she had ever lived. She brushed her mittened hand across her face. This snow was wet and clinging, as though it, too, held a soggy inertia.

Aunt Jess's first suggestion had been Bermuda or Florida, but there wasn't a room to be had anywhere at either place. If Phil had been involved, he'd have leaped at it as another example, she'd thought in a rush of scorn. While she'd been reading the pages he'd written, right then while she was still shaken by Bill's visit, she'd been terribly moved by the earnestness and odd sadness he'd got into his phrases. She'd writhed for the beautiful woman in Rumson, and, as it had with Bill, fear struck her that maybe she, Kathy, really was like that. "Braided ten people into one"—she was at most only a strand in that composite portrait. When she'd really calmed down, she'd seen that, as she'd at last seen the difference between her attitude and Bill's.

Later, she'd checked back through her whole relationship with Phil, step by step. She'd got perspective back into things, for good this time. The molehill could always be cleverly made to look like a mountain for a while, but it still remained a silly little molehill not worth fuming over.

That Phil had left out of the article, honest though he was. Because that is what he'd never seen, what she'd never been able to make him see. It was so much simpler for him to judge her guilty.

Innocent or guilty, the pain stuck there inside her, the lump was ready in her throat; the fear of losing him had become the unreasoning remorse that it was over. That was stronger than anything else. Except the one black clean knowledge that a second failure, advertised to the world by a second divorce, would shatter everything she was or could be.

There were women, she knew, who were able to take emotional failure in their stride and go on being successful and happy people. Anne Dettrey was like that. She had talents, a job she adored, endless chances to meet new people. Envy for Anne's busy, rounded life struck at her. She'd never been really easy with Anne; she always wondered how critical those clever eyes were being. But she admired her. Phil probably would turn to her; she was the only other woman he knew well in all New York. Perhaps already——

She turned back to the hotel. She couldn't bear the lashing cold one more instant. Even this winter spread all about her, the icy snow under her feet, the glittering white of the mountains, the creaking branches of the burdened trees——

241

even this was a mark of the terrible distance from the plan to the reality. Nassau would have been hot, brilliant with the red of hibiscus, the purplish pink of bougainvillaea, the intense blues and greens of the sea.

Voices rang out behind her, and she half turned around. Two girls, their skis slung over their shoulders, their ski poles wearily trailing shining points along the snow, had appeared out of the woods. There was a beginners' slope there, she remembered. She turned back. Soon they were close enough so she could hear a strident voice.

"So Cholly said I shouldna done it, and I said, 'Well, I said, Mr. Smotty, you can go ta hell in a bucket.' "

The other girl made soothing sounds. They were abreast of her now. "Got a match, miss?" the strident voice asked, and Kathy stopped. While she was pulling off her oiled-silk ski mitten and reaching into the pocket of her jacket, she saw the glittering costume jewelry at their ears below their ski caps, the frozen beads of mascara of their eyes, the gleam of eye shadow, the thick lipstick, congealed and cracked in the dry five above zero.

Why do they *do* it? she thought miserably. Why do they make themselves so noticeable? It's awful. It's just awful.

She handed over the packet of matches with a warm smile, and the girls smiled back. They had trouble with the wind, and she cupped her hands over the shielding ones of the soothing girl to make a taller chimney for the match. They talked about the weather and the easy runs which were all they could try as yet. And all the time that "why" was crying out in her, protective yet helpless.

As she walked on alone again, her regret and distress deepened. The cruel comments of people who saw them on the slopes or on the roads angered her, though she had heard none. All Jews *aren't* vulgar and overdressed, she thought passionately, and wished Phil could know how hotly she despised with him the injustice that taxed a whole group for the offense of two ill-bred girls.

For once he'd not find anything to get the quick look about.

Back at the hotel, Aunt Jessie was taking a nap. Kathy shed her cap and jacket and took off her ski boots. She rolled thick plaid wool socks over her feet and slid into her sloppy old moccasins. Then she went down to the Snack Bar for coffee. Singularly, her distress on the road had given way to a security about herself. For once he just couldn't. And if she'd been more able to find the just word, the exact phrase for each and every thought she'd had when they'd been together, he'd never have been able to.

She thought of Bill Pawling. *He* wouldn't have felt this distress. A warmth grew in her.

The hot coffee, the blazing logs in the ten-foot stone fireplace before her, made her cheeks and forehead tingle after the attack of the icy outdoors. Drowsiness shredded orderly thinking into wisps. She relaxed against the sloped back of the lounge chair and wondered why she couldn't feel this way when she was in bed. No matter how exhausted she was, the moment she lay down, there it was, a seizure, a swoop.

Suddenly she sat upright. The drowsy, lazy drifting was done. In her mind Phil's voice was talking to her, not sarcastic, not irritated, but rueful and discouraged.

"But, darling, if they'd been two Irish-Catholic girls, all you'd have thought would have been how vulgar all that make-up is in sport clothes."

She gulped.

"You wouldn't even have thought, Kathy, 'All Irish-Catholics *aren't* vulgar and overdressed.' You wouldn't have defended all the Irish any more than all the Hindus. Because you would have thought of them only as two girls."

243

Kathy put her hand up to her forehead. The fire was scorching. She felt dizzied and ill. Oh, God, I *do* get mixed up. Maybe he is right about something in me being—— Desperation spiked her feelings. She wanted crazily to tear the brain out of her skull so she could examine it, find what was there and what was not there. In a moment the violent mood passed. She sat enervated and more unsure of herself than she had ever in all her life felt before.

Even at the dinner table that evening, she could not shake off her lassitude. There was resignation in it, defeat, the old concession that she must be in the wrong somehow about everything. She listened to Ellen and Tom Manning and Aunt Jessie prattle about the invigorating mountain air and contributed monosyllables of appreciation. Something Aunt Jess said about Vassar got Ellen started on education and that led to the good old Springfield Plan. Idly Kathy gazed about the room, at the tanned and wind-burned faces at the other tables for two or four. She was all for the Springfield Plan; she'd read about it and heard about it and knew that it was right for children to meet democracy in action from their youngest school days. She hoped Ellen's movement would succeed in Darien. But she could not listen attentively to Ellen or anybody else just now.

She remembered the two girls on the road. Vaguely she looked about. They hadn't said anything about how far they'd come, at what hotel they were. Perhaps they looked less garish in ordinary clothing. She began to look over the faces around her. Face by face, now, no longer the blur.

Once again, she suddenly sat forward. In all that crowded room there was not one face that was obviously "Jewish." She'd been in this hotel several times in the last ten years, and it had never even occurred to her to check over the faces. Now she was searching them, faster and faster, in a scrabbling anxiety to find the proof that this pleasant place wasn't another Flume Inn.

"What's on your mind, Kath?" Tom Manning asked.

"Me? Oh." She was flustered. "Just looking around. I missed what you were saying, El. Sorry."

"Anybody you want to see specially, dear?"

"No, Aunt Jess." She looked about once more. The others were silent now, watching her. She must seem agitated and queer. "Is this hotel," she said to Ellen, "for Christians only, d'you think?"

Ellen looked about now, and Tom did, too. Jessie said, "Of course not, Kathy," in a comfortable voice, and Ellen said, "Why, I never thought."

"This near New York and not one person that looks Jewish?" Kathy asked. "That couldn't just be accident, with half the Jews in America right in New York City." Her voice had changed. It had gone quiet. "I never thought about it, either," she said to Ellen. Something pounded in her chest where only her heart should have been beating.

There was a silence. The Mannings were both thinking of Phil, she'd have sworn it. Broken engagement or not, a promise was a promise, and Jane would never have betrayed him until she got the word the series was done.

"It's beastly, if it's true," Ellen said, and began to talk about protecting children from prejudice. Sunday-school teaching had to be revised. "Nobody ever says, 'the Americans killed Lincoln,' " she said emphatically. Kathy nodded.

It isn't just that they're Jewish, she thought. Those two girls wouldn't fit in here on other levels—of manners and smartness and all. But Dave and Carol and Phil and—oh, damn, even if you do hate it, what's there you can *do?* She couldn't march up to the hotel manager, ask questions, make speeches. She just wasn't the type—she'd die of pure em-

245

barrassment. You just sat, that's all you could do. Sat and felt this crawly shame.

After dinner, they played bridge, and when Aunt Jessie went upstairs, Kathy went to the bar with the Mannings for a "stirrup cup before train time." Tom yawned and said he couldn't wait to crawl into the berth; skiing this much always made him groggy for sleep at night. Ellen talked about her problems for the summer. Her eldest boy wanted to go to camp in Maine, and the two youngest were jealous of this first distinction. Kathy let her talk. Tom left them soon to see to their luggage.

"Kath, you look sort of thin," Ellen said affectionately. "Broken engagements aren't any fun, I know. I broke one once."

"Oh, well."

"He's brilliant and charming," Ellen went on, "and I know you'd have been too big to care about sticky places like this." Kathy didn't answer. "It's one's own world that matters—and we'd already smoothed it out at the club. With so many of us having met him personally."

"Smoothed it out?" Her voice edged, but she couldn't help it.

"There was the midwinter meeting of the board about a week after Jane's party, so it came up." Ellen saw Kathy's eyes go remote—it probably still killed her to talk about him. A lively sympathy warmed Ellen; she'd always liked Jane and Kathy and had been glad to see the last of that reactionary Bill Pawling. And she'd taken to Phil Green at sight and then felt oddly forlorn when Jane had made the curt announcement that Kathy had changed her mind. She knew Katherine Lacey far too well, or she'd have wondered whether it wasn't partly because he was Jewish. But that would be too absurd for anyone as liberal as Kath.

"Phil's membership came up?" Kathy prompted.

"Not formally—just talking about when he did apply this summer. It was perfectly simple, with him the way he is, and you a member."

"The exception." They had sat in judgment and found him passable. "The one 'pet Jew' we can all use as proof? 'See, we're not antisemitic.'"

"Why, Kathy. I hate that idiocy as much as you do."

"I know you do. I'm not even thinking you don't."

"But then there are the bigoted fools in the club."

"I remember."

"After all, a club's only a social, *personal* thing."

Ellen looked at her; Kathy seemed on the verge of—what? Tears? Collapse? She really looked sick. "Quit talking about all this, darling," Ellen said at last. "Just makes you think about stuff that still rubs deep. Everybody goes through that awhile."

"I wasn't thinking of anything like that," Kathy said. "I wasn't even thinking of the club any more. Or you. Or Phil. Funny, I got thinking about the Springfield Plan."

"The Sp——"

Kathy began to laugh a little, then a little more. Ellen threw a quick appraising glance at her.

Kathy said, "The one thing I do know about is children. I got thinking how screwed up your little boys and everybody else's little boys and girls are going to get if they're taught five days a week that everybody's just the same and then on Saturday and Sunday they have to leave some of their pals outside the gates while they go into the country club with Papa and Mamma." She was really laughing now. "*All* the country clubs, all over."

"You're poking fun at me, Kathy!" Ellen saw Tom and a bellboy with their luggage and at once stood up in dignified coolness. During the good-bys, Kathy sounded more cheerful.

247

Again that night she could not sleep. But somewhere in the dark spinning where she was again talking to Phil and being kissed by Phil and bemoaning the excesses in Phil—somewhere there was one curious, heady new thing, unlike anything she'd ever known.

What kept coming back from her session with Ellen was that one thing. Not anything Ellen had said or she had said; not any points she'd made. Just this one exhilarating funny thing. She hadn't taken Ellen's liberalism for granted as she always had before. She had looked at it, into it; she had weighed it and tested it and sized it up. It was like the stretching of muscles. And it was fine.

Bill Jayson said to Phil, "It's the by-goddest idea for a series this book's ever run."

Phil grinned. An hour before, Miss Wales had taken the top carbon of number one in to the art department. Jayson had it with him; as he talked, he thumped it for emphasis, and the careful pedantic turn of his usual speech was absent. "No kidding, Phil, I couldn't put it down. I meant to give it just a look and hand it over to McAnny for suggestions on pix, but I never moved from my chair."

"Has he seen it yet?"

Jayson laughed. "No. He's on a rush layout against deadline. I'm going to hide this till he's made it—he's in for a collapse." His eyes gleamed. "Boy, I bet he tries a sneak bunt to third with this one."

Phil laughed with him. "What'll you decide for artwork, Bill?"

"It's not going to be easy. Take time. But I see now why you and John wouldn't give."

"Photographic treatment your hunch?"

"Sure." He frowned. "God knows what of."

"No shots of my kid, now, or my family," Phil said

248

sternly. "John says I'm hooked for the lead-off. But mind, nobody else."

"And mind, you stop bossing me around," Jayson answered equally sternly. Then he grinned. "That's the trouble with you Christians—aggressive. Pure compensation, of course."

From the first, Phil had liked Bill Jayson; now he admired him. The whole damn point in one wisecrack, he thought, but before he could transfer thought to speech, the door opened and Anne came in. She saw the manuscript in Jayson's hand.

"So whatever the mystery was," she said cheerily, "the unveiling has begun. When's my turn, Phil?"

"You?" Jayson said. "You interested in anything but your own department?"

"You rat," she said pleasantly. "My secretary's in a frenzy over the wonderful plot of Mr. Green's series."

"Plot?" Phil liked the attention he was getting.

Anne said, "She keeps saying 'plot' and won't tell. What plot there can be in a series on antisemitism escapes me, but I have been needled long enough. So give over."

Jayson looked to Phil, and Phil said, "Sure." He gave the manuscript to Anne, and she looked at it. She read the title, glanced up, smiled at Phil, and then began to read. Both men remained quiet for a moment and then in low voices continued their discussion about possible illustration. Anne read on. As he talked, Phil found himself aware of her reading, knew when she turned a page, knew when she stopped to light a cigarette. He realized suddenly that he wanted very much that she should like it. John's final O.K. of the finished series had warmed him—— "It's got it, Phil." His mother, reading the first two, had gone into her queer little stream of *sotto voce* commentary—"Imagine!" . . . "How dreadful, Phil!" . . . "Not really, it's barbarous." Several

times there'd even been the quick dabs at her eyes over some
paragraph or other, filling him with curiosity since she was
obviously in some part—he could tell by the page she was at
—which he'd set down unemotionally or coldly. Then he'd
gone over to stand behind her, reading over her shoulder, to
discover what it was that had moved her. But he'd never
been able to tell; his mother's reactions to words and
thoughts he'd written were so personal, so unpredictable,
that the only message he could get from them while she read
was that this time was not one of his failures.

Now he was held by Anne's continuing silence. Soon Jayson saw he was preoccupied and stopped talking. Only when
their voices stopped did Anne look up. She'd read half a
dozen pages.

"Murder," she said to Phil. "I wish I'd thought of it
first." She shook her head. "It's hot, all right."

"Thanks." She was trying to phrase something else; he
waited.

"It explains some things I never quite understood about
you, Phil. Like Flume Inn coming as a shock instead of a
sure-the-usual-dirty-trick. I put it down to things being different out West."

"I didn't give things away much, did I?" he asked anxiously.

"Fooled me. I did want to say a couple of times, 'For
heaven's sake, how've you lived this long, spending this
much juice on it all the time?' " Phil looked embarrassed.
"But then I remembered getting into a steam myself over
some series I'd been living with, so I let it go at that."

"Remember the juvenile-delinquency stuff you did?" Jayson twitted her. He turned to Phil dismally. "Couldn't eat
lunch with her for a month without a load of statistics on
child prostitutes."

"I quit harping on it once the job ended, didn't I?" She

turned reflectively to Phil. "This must have been dizzy, though, kind of mirror-within-mirror stuff. Watching yourself as Jewish but at the same time watching yourself as Christian-watching-Jew."

"At the start. Then it just boiled down to a guy taking his first real look around."

"Just the same," she said, "if everybody acted it out just one day a year, it'd be curtains to the thing overnight, I'll bet."

"Not so sure," Jayson said. "That business of everybody needing to feel superior to somebody else."

"Right." Anne shrugged. "*I* feel superior. To anti-semites." She got up. "Well, I got to get back." She went to the door and then suddenly turned back to them, laughing. "No wonder Minify wouldn't listen to the screams of the Brown crowd."

Brown and Wheeling, Phil knew, was the large advertising agency that handled *Smith's* account. He knew also that Anne as a major editor went to periodic meetings with them and held most advertising men in low esteem as a result.

"Screams about what?" he asked.

"A couple of weeks back, John told them this would be the big spot for the first May ad—practically the whole page, with just a ten-on-two panel for rest-of-issue copy. They always need four years to be bright in, so they beseeched the boss for the first article. Nope. A synopsis. Nope. The title of the series. Nope."

"Same treatment the art department got," Jayson said. He stretched. "Get the hell out of here, Dettrey, will you? The author and I have to bat around some ideas for pix."

For the rest of the week, Bert McAnny avoided Phil. As they passed each other in the corridors or waiting room, even when they met in the sanctuary of the washroom, he made no reference to the series at all, never dropped in for the usual discussion of possible shots. The impression he gave was that the series did not exist.

Phil had expected virtuous reiteration that it had never made any difference, but this gauche silence he would never have foretold. He found it at first obvious, then ridiculous, finally contemptible. The hell with McAnny.

The flabbiness which always followed a sustained period of work was bogging him down more than usual. It was as if his last reliable props had buckled. He no longer kept regular hours at the office; he stayed up later and later each night, reading detective stories, books about the war, novels.

Interims were always nerve-racking. Soon there'd be some new assignment—no matter what it was, he felt he'd never be able to work up any enthusiasm or energy for it. But that, too, was old stuff. That, too, happened in interims.

He saw Professor Lieberman again. This was one of the good things which would survive the writing of a series. Lieberman greeted Phil's recital of "my own research project" with dry, rapid questions, as if they were colleagues in a laboratory. "Yet every antisemite you met," he remarked comfortably at the end, "would swear in court that 'Jewishness' is something demonstrable. Your Mr. Calkins at Flume Inn, for example, is positive he faced a Jew that day —he's got *eyes*, hasn't he?" They both laughed. Later, as Phil was leaving, Lieberman said, in his imperturbable voice, "I'll never hold the truth against you, Phil. I'm a stout believer in the rights of majorities."

All through these days there was one new facet to his life. For the first time a manuscript he'd written was in the office of a great publishing house, up for consideration as a book. Minify had asked permission to send it over to somebody he knew, and Phil had nervously assented. When Miss

Mittelson at last phoned to say Mr. Minify's publishing friend was in the office, could he come in, he found his pulse quickening. He'd never confessed until this moment how much he wanted to see his name on the spine of a book. During the introductions he was too tense to catch the publisher's full name; through the meeting Minify called him "Jock." Jock's smiling face told him the decision while they shook hands. Behind his desk, Minify's smile corroborated it.

"It's had four readings already, Mr. Green," the publisher said. "No dissenting report at all. We'd like to put it on our fall list."

"Fine." He hoped he sounded merely pleased and businesslike. "Need some padding, won't it? It's only about thirty-five thousand words."

"Yes, we'd wondered if you mightn't have more material which you'd left out of the articles."

Phil didn't want to sound too ready with suggestions. For a time he listened while the two men agreed that such a book ought to have a fair sale at worst, possibly even "hit the list."

"More and more people seem interested in these problem books," Jock said. "Look at *Strange Fruit* or *Under Cover.*"

"I looked at them," John said, "before I decided to get this series written." They all laughed.

"Matter of fact," Phil now offered, "I'd even been wondering about writing a sixth for our own series." Minify looked up. "Sort of post-mortem stuff—what I call 'the unwinding.' Kind of fascinates me, the way it runs to pattern."

"Interesting idea, that," the publisher said. "Certainly for the book." Minify was looking at Phil reflectively. Jock stood up. "Could you give us a rough draft of the new material, or a synopsis? Oh, yes, and have you an agent, Mr. Green?"

"Yes to the first, no to the second. Agents aren't much good for articles. I'll get one for a book, though."

Jock smiled. "Better to have the publisher picked first, on a book like this. Sure as hell, they'd have sent it to the wrong house and pinned a neat handicap to the book to start with."

"How do you mean, 'wrong house'?" Phil asked.

"From the point of view of the book's reception; wrong, that way."

Phil glanced at John. He was looking at Phil.

"It's just better publishing to have a house like ours do a book of this type," Jock went on.

"Why?" John asked. He wasn't looking at Phil now. He was staring at the desk.

"If one of the Jewish houses put their imprint on it, people might think it was just special pleading, and of course it's not."

"Jewish houses?" Phil asked. "You mean Jewish publishing houses?"

"You must mean," Minify said lazily, "whatever firm publishes *The Jewish Daily Forward.*" To Phil he said, "It's a daily newspaper, printed in Yiddish."

The publisher looked at him, ready to laugh if he were smiling.

"You see," Phil put in, smoothly, as if he and John were rehearsing dialogue from a script and he were ready now to take over for the curtain line, "Mr. Minify and I never heard of 'Christian publishing houses' and 'Jewish publishing houses' except in the Third Reich." He smiled. "Even firms run by men who are Jewish—we just call them 'publishing houses.' In a way, that's what the whole series is about."

There was a pause. Jock was bewildered. He turned back to Minify. "It's just a phrase in the book trade, John."

" 'Jewish bankers' is just a phrase, too," Minify answered. "And 'Jewish newspaper owners' and 'Jewish Communists'—just phrases."

Phil spoke to Jock. "My verbal acceptance before," he said. "Would that be binding? Or could I change my mind?"

"You're perfectly free, Mr. Green. I release you, of course. But there's some misunderstanding here. I was simply thinking of the best imprint for your book."

"Yes," Phil said. "I know."

"At least you'll think it over? Good Lord, man, an unfortunate locution at most, that's all it was. John's known me for years——"

"Sure, Jock," Minify said, "but now I *hear* it if a man doesn't just say plain 'bankers' or 'Communists' or 'publishing houses.' "

No sooner did Phil get back to the office than his telephone rang.

"John, Phil. I'm sending it over to another house. O.K.?"

"You bet."

"There are a dozen good ones. Somebody else'll grab it. Care who?"

Phil made a rough sound. "Just so the house is non-sectarian in locution as well as personnel."

That night, going up the stairs to the apartment, he heard his mother's voice, raised and shrill. Never once had she talked to Tom that way. He braced himself against whatever unpleasantness waited. He opened the door and said, "Oh, hello." Belle just looked at him.

" . . . the whole way," his mother was saying to her. "I never thought any child of mine could possibly change into the typical jingo reactionary."

255

Phil said, "Mom, you look too excited. You're not supposed to get this excited."

"I'm no good," Belle explained dryly. "I've let Dick and our crowd infect me with race hatred and religious hatred. Then to justify and bolster my new position, I've fallen deeper and deeper from grace." She was controlling it, but the fury was deep.

"It's true," Mrs. Green said. "Sarcasm doesn't change it."

"I've been turning against labor, boasting about my glorious American ancestry, hating foreigners and radicals, the works."

"Mom, sit down and cut this," he ordered, and pulled up a chair behind Mrs. Green. To Belle he said, "I told you to can it. She's got to avoid excitement and exertion."

"And it's revolting that you couldn't keep Phil's secret," Mrs. Green went on, her voice sharp and unlovely, "and had to scamper around like a frightened rabbit telling everybody."

Belle looked at Phil coldly. "You might have asked me before you started something that was bound to involve me, instead of just telling me after you'd begun."

"Oh, hell," Phil said without vigor. "So they finally got around to asking you, hey?" He smiled cheerfully.

"Even Tom had the—the guts," Mrs. Green said as if no other word could fit her need, "to stick it and not go sniveling."

"It was Mrs. Naismith herself, I told you," Belle said in exasperation. She turned to Phil angrily. "Wife of the president of the firm. Right at her own party with twelve people there." She closed her eyes in recollection. " 'So fascinating, Belle dear,' she said to me in that tin voice of hers." She looked at Phil with fury. " 'What's fascinating?' I asked her. Then there was this little silence while

256

everybody listened. 'Why, your interesting foreign back-ground,' she said. 'But I can't see why you didn't tell us all these years—Jewish people are always so clever and interesting.'"

Phil laughed.

"So Belle tried," Mrs. Green said, "to turn it all into a great joke on her peculiar brother. She fell all over herself, I gather, betraying your secret."

"I *told* you on the phone I'd have to if——"

"Where's Tom?" Phil asked his mother.

"I sent him to do his homework," his mother said. "I certainly don't want him to hear Belle make this exhibition of herself."

"I'm going to see the kid." He said to Belle offensively, "Your life's saved—I've turned in the series. Your disgrace is over."

Long after Belle and his mother had come to whatever terms they could come to, he stayed out of the living room. With Tom chattering beside him, he looked through the evening paper. His mind kept drifting away from the news. Tonight he might write letters. Always during a long series he fell behind on all personal mail. He opened the top drawer of his bureau where letters to be answered mingled with handkerchiefs and socks. He picked up the one his sister Mary had sent him weeks ago from California. He glanced through it. ". . . and somehow it's such a *sweet* thing for you to do, Phil, sort of trying it on to see if it fits or hurts or what for yourself. Even if it doesn't make a good series, it'll be something inside you for the rest of your life, and I kind of wonder if that in itself isn't worth the messy parts. As for Mamma's news about you and Kathy, it made me just kind of weepy to think of you being happy again. . . ."

He put the letter back into the drawer.

257

"Wish the Coast wasn't so far off, Tom," he said.

"So you could go there?"

"No. But Aunt Mary might get to come here if it weren't."

"Yeah. Say, Dad, couldn't you take me to a movie tonight?"

"School night? You kidding?"

"Oh."

"Scram out of here, will you? I'd like a nap till dinner."

"O.K." He picked up the jeep and three tanks he'd been playing with. "You lonesome for Aunt Mary?"

"At times. Aren't you, and for Tip and Sky and the boys you used to play with out there?"

Tom nodded. But there was no bemoaning the past in eight-year-olds. "You lonesome for Kathy too, Dad?"

"Sure."

"You had a fight, Gram said."

Phil looked at him. "That's right. Run along, what do you say." There was no question in the tone, and Tom disappeared. Phil lay down. The twisting and gnarling and squeezing that could go on in a man who'd been through death and war and wounding, merely at a phrase in a letter, a child's offhand catechism!

He'd been too righteous, too demanding; he'd had too little patience and too thin a capacity to allow for Kathy's confusion and womanish softness under sudden pressure. Kathy wasn't another Belle. If he'd have given her more time to see it, she'd have stiffened up, too. "You don't have to be a sainted character."

At once then, words, phrases, the revealing hesitation, the quick cry to Tom, the velvet resistance to this mess and that inconvenience—from the raw, deep places where they'd lodged they paced forth now, one by one, in gray procession.

But damn it, whatever I did, it wouldn't have been any

use. People have to see it themselves or not. You can't do it for them. And if they give in to it the way Belle did and it digs in deeper and deeper? Families could split apart——

"Telegram, Dad." Tom's shout startled Phil. He hadn't heard the doorbell. He took it and tore it open in the involuntary haste telegrams always aroused in him. It was from Dave:

ROTTEN NEWS ABOUT YOU TWO. BIG THANKS TO YOU AND ANNE. ARRIVING TWENTY SECOND AND WILL BUY YOU BOTH NINE GRATEFUL MARTINIS.

He read it twice. Good old Dave, going to promote a little marriage idea of his own. Anne's face came to him— its handsome, sharp planes, the reddish frame of hair, the lively eyes, the intelligence and bitterness and restlessness behind them. And instantly he wanted only Kathy; savagely and insanely he wanted only Kathy.

In spite of the continuing sleeplessness, the stay at Placid had done some good, she thought, appraising herself in the mirror. The old black evening dress still looked all right. She was going up to Darien for the night and Sunday. Jane was entertaining an elderly big shot and needed her.

Placid was already a queer, hazy memory, though she'd only been back three days. When she tried to recall the processes by which she'd got to Phil's voice ruefully talking to her, she failed completely. But she could remember clearly how pathetic Ellen and all her works had suddenly seemed against that one picture of the Mannings taking their three boys into the club after a week of Springfield-Planning them. El and Tom Manning might be at the dinner party tonight. Would Ellen still be a touch haughty?

She locked her suitcase and started out. In the living room, she looked automatically about her. She'd given

Claudia the week end off. No forgotten cigarettes smoking in an ash tray, no windows up. On the piano her music stood open, and she went to it and closed it. The sonata she'd played for Phil. She glanced over to the fireplace. Dark, forbidding, wind-swept, the landscape looked gloomily down at her. She turned quickly and left.

The elderly big shot dismayed her at sight. She'd hoped he'd at least be charming and attractive. Vaguely she'd read or heard of Lockhart Jones during the war or even before from Bill. He was tall, gray, about sixty-five, with an old man's phlegm already in his voice. His chin and nose were sharp, the lengthened ear lobes were pointed with age, and his stainless teeth in even perfection told of dentures. The Mannings were already there, and the Tay Carsons. Jane and Harry said the Trippens were coming, up from Washington for a week. Lockhart Jones was important to Harry; that much she caught in the first few minutes of cocktails and talk. Probably a client with big business for a corporation-law firm.

The talk centered in his account of a recent "swing around Europe and the Middle East." He seemed to have connections everywhere, to know all sorts of government officials, industrialists, army brass. Suddenly she remembered that Bill had had some dealings with him on foreign exchange and didn't like him. "Finger in any old kind of pie," Bill had grumbled. Dimly she seemed to know that he was a man who never limited himself to one line but was mentioned in half a dozen deals a year. Bill had said aviation and steel, she thought, but now Jones was talking about new railroads in Europe and a copper mine in South America. "Money, money, money; profit, profit, profit," Kathy commented to herself, and turned to Jane.

Mr. Jones was giving everybody a tip about investing

in some company he and two associates had just acquired. Harry and the other men were attentive, and for a moment nobody else was talking.

"Over-the-counter, but it'll be on the Curb next month," Mr. Jones said, the expectancy of quick profit clear in his voice. "Sound setup now. None of the chosen people."

Kathy saw Ellen's quick distaste, saw Jane's eyebrows rise. A dart of revulsion nipped her. Ellen said nothing. Jane heard the doorbell and got to her feet, and Kathy just sat. The talk went on.

What was there to do, she thought, and remembered her helplessness at the hotel in Placid. There was just nothing, without making a fool of yourself. In a fight with Bill, in a town-hall meeting, you could object, argue, denounce. But with a stranger in a private group, you just averted your eyes, in a way of speaking, as from an unfortunate smear of grease on the cheerful face of your dinner neighbor.

All through the cocktails and the new arrivals and small chatter at the table, despondency held her. It was queer to feel so inadequate, sort of obediently toeing the mark. She looked about her. It was a beautiful dining room, brilliant with crystal and silver, the flash of jewelry, the black and white of dinner jackets. "Between them, Bill and Vassar didn't succeed in making you conservative." Uncle John's words came back once again. "But they had more luck making you conventional." The s's of Vassar and succeed and conservative boiled up, sibilant and offensive.

She seemed to have lost all her old bearings about herself. Her old calmness about what she was and what she felt had apparently deserted her for good. The episode with Bill kept coming back even after she'd reassured herself completely about it; phrases from Phil's article kept coming back; her brief triumph of feeling right about the two girls kept plaguing her. Each one was like a shadow falling across

261

her mind. She kept dispelling them one day and they kept returning the next, their dim forms inching over her once more. She looked unhappily around her.

Jane was listening to Lockhart Jones on her right. Ellen was talking politics to Nick Trippen. All around the table there were the unperturbed faces, the low voices, the mysterious calmness of people at ease with themselves and the world. She alone, keeping half track of what Tay Carson was saying, was worried and uncertain. Mr. Jones was beginning some funny story. His voice had risen. Around the table sentences politely halted in midstream.

"So you hand a thousand dollars to each of them and ship them off to Africa," he was saying, "and with thirteen million coons that's thirteen billions, and the kikes go running after it, so we'll be rid of all of them at one swoop."

He laughed uproariously. One of the men laughed, but there was silence from everybody else. Kathy saw Jane, Ellen, Harry in a montage of their annoyance or disgust. It was one of those appalled silences, no doubt about that. Nobody there liked Mr. Jones.

"Fell flat," Mr. Jones boomed. "Guess it's not new at that," and affably went on to something else. The halted sentences all about her were picked up. The maids came in with the square silver dishes of vegetables.

Kathy waited for the waves of heat to stop running through her. She turned to the left and picked up the oversize serving spoon and fork. She put food on her plate and knew she could not eat it. Illness was in her, and shame for all of them. They despised him and they kept quiet. They were well bred and polite, so they kept quiet. Just as she did. Not making fusses was also part of the gentleman's agreement. To rise and leave the room was not in her knees and muscles; to call him to account was not in her vocal cords and larynx.

At Placid, with Ellen, she'd thought she was changing. It wasn't true—it couldn't ever be true. The 'beautiful woman in Rumson' wouldn't risk a scene. Phil, Phil, you must be right.

CHAPTER FIFTEEN

"**I** PULLED OUT THIS MORNING," Kathy listlessly explained to the Minifys on Sunday evening. "I told Jane a fib about not feeling well."

"Couldn't have been much of a fib," Aunt Jessie fretted. "Oh, dear, I did think Lake Placid——"

"She's fine," Uncle John said. "Stop clucking over her."

Kathy's elbows retracted and hit her sides. Unfortunate word, he thought, remembering Phil's "clucking disapproval" in the fifth article. During most of the evening Minify sat apart from them, reading and apparently undisturbed by their talk, as if their voices sent no waves to his eardrums. Only once he looked up. For the third time Jess had asked about Jane's dinner party.

"It was ghastly," Kathy said sharply. "That man is impossible."

"Jess, stop pumping her," John said. "Can't you see the week end upset her?"

When she was leaving, Kathy turned to him casually. "Are all the articles typed up now?"

"Yes."

"Could I read the rest of them sometime?"

"Now, if you want. Brought a set home to give his revises a look."

"Goodness, no rush. I just thought."

He gave her a smile that had no amusement in it, and her throat tightened. Without further ado, he went to the library and came back with a large envelope marked *Smith's*

Weekly Magazine in the top left corner. She took it, tossed it on the sofa, and ignored it. But when she said goodnight, she did not walk off and leave it.

By ten-thirty, she was in bed and beginning at page one. She went slowly, as if she were prodding each phrase with an investigating finger, digging each sentence clean of all content. She came on no episode he had not already told her, no reaction she had not heard directly from him.

Yet there was something different about reading them, some intangible and heightened growth in this written version. These black words on white paper, moving on without wavering, held impact she'd not felt in the same words as he spoke them aloud to her.

Not until one o'clock did she come again to the fifth article, which she had already seen. This one was implicit with the final stretch of their own story together; the crushed feeling in her as she read these pages must come from the close personal meanings in them grinding against the impersonal.

For a long time after she'd come to the last line, she lay against her pillows. In the flat pottery ash tray beside her, a cigarette burned to the end, a two-inch mound of dirty gray ash. She looked from one to the other of the articles on the bedspread about her, five granite steppingstones to —what? Mechanical and precise, she collected the five in proper order, aligned them, and slid them into the big envelope. She turned the heavy package over; slowly she fastened the clasp.

No, there was nothing really new inside it. Only, the authority and candor of print had forced her to see each episode as he himself had seen it. For a while no rebuttal was possible. For a while she was defenseless and mute.

Minify looked out at the winter twilight and then at the

electric clock on his desk. It was nearly five.

"Come on out to celebrate, Phil," he said. "Let's ask some of the gang. You're nowhere near set up enough over this."

"Sure I am." The two men he'd just left had invited him to "have a drink on it" too, but he'd come back to the office instead. Kathy was the only one in the world he wanted to share this with; with her this moment would have had twice the meaning. Even with the people he'd come so close to here since the thing had started, any celebrating was a substitute thing.

Minify was already standing. "My party," he said. "Tingler and Anne and Sam Goodman. Who else?"

"Jayson. That ought to do it."

"Not McAnny, hm?" They both laughed, and John went to the corner closet for his overcoat. They started through the outer office.

"Mr. Green," Mary Cresson said, and Phil stopped at her desk as John went on to Tingler's office. "Did Mr. Minify remember to ask you?"

"What about?"

"That house in California—has your friend rented or sold it yet?"

"Lord, I don't know. Why?"

"He has some business friend, Mr. Minify has, who's being transferred there. He thought he'd wire ahead if it's not gone already."

"Here." Phil scribbled Dave's address on a scrap of her desk-paper.

"Thanks. And, Mr. Green," she flushed—"could I congratulate you about your book?"

He winked and went off down the corridor. John and Anne were already going through the door of his own office.

Spread on his desk were three large tissue layouts of picture spreads. Leaning over them, pencil in hand, was Bert McAnny.

"*Smith's* has another book coming," Minify said. "Phil's just signed for September publication." McAnny stood up. His light skin flushed. Tingler and Sam Goodman walked in, and the small office seemed suddenly stuffed to the walls.

"Great," Bert said, "simply great." He thumped Phil on the shoulder and let his hand rest there. Phil moved an inch, and the hand dropped. Jayson came in, his small mouth prissy as ever, but his eyes delighted.

"Take your layouts along, Bert," Tingler said. He and Sam knew about Phil's "stunt" by now, but neither of them had guessed the antagonism between him and Bert McAnny.

"I'll just leave them here till morning," Bert said. He put Phil's desk calendar on them and started for the door. "Meet you at the elevator in a jiffy."

"No."

It was Phil, and they all turned to him. He had tilted his head downward so that his chin was nearly touching his tie. Looking at him, Anne thought of a butting animal. Phil was staring at McAnny. "We're not drinking together, Bert," he said. "And Christ, you can't say I'm being touchy and sensitive now."

Nobody spoke. Then Bert pulled the three tissues toward him. He began to roll them up. John and Anne, Jayson and Phil, watched him. Tingler and Sam looked from one face to another, seeking, finding nothing. The only motion in the room was in Bert's hands rolling the tissues; the only sound, the thin crackle of the transparent sheets. Now all six watched him. He was nearly done. Now the only thing visible on the layouts was the blackly penciled-in title: "I Was Jewish for Eight Weeks."

The thin roll was in his hand. Bert looked about, his lips parted for speech, his face deeply red under the fair hair. Then he left them.

Through the drinks and the easy talking, one recurring notion sent bursts of feeling secretly through Phil. It had never been a Jewish problem, for the Jews alone could never solve it. It was a nonsectarian problem. And because of the simple thing of majority, it was mostly a Christian problem. He'd always known that. But now he was a different sort of Christian. Now he was one of the Christians able and ready to act. On whatever front the thing showed itself.

It was a big difference. The difference.

"For heaven's sake, John," Anne was objecting. "You don't have to dish it to my department just because the DAR's in Washington are women." John was not disturbed. She looked about for support. As she came to Phil, her tone became mischievous. "Give it to Phil for his next assignment."

"I was a woman for eight weeks?" Phil asked, and they all shouted.

Because it was a holiday, Phil was at home all day. At ten tonight Dave and his family were due, and he was going to LaGuardia to meet them. *Smith's* advertising manager had wangled two rooms at the Roosevelt for them. Dave hadn't asked him to arrange it, but till their furniture arrived, they could scarcely eat and sleep on the floor, Village informality or no.

In the afternoon he'd taken Tom to a double feature, and now they were doing the dishes together. Of all the chores in the house, this was the one Phil most detested. He glanced into the living room, and his rebellion died. Under the tall lamp, his mother was reading the newspaper. Perhaps it was only the direct harsh light, but she was wan and

268

her mouth faintly pulled aside again. The slight distortion gave her a wistful look, as though she might cry. She was in no danger, but she was so old. "September, Phil?" she'd said quickly when he'd told her last week about the book being accepted.

"The summer's no good, they said, and it still takes ages to manufacture."

Anxiously she'd added, "There'll be actual books long before September, though, won't there?"

All he answered was, "Oh, sure, probably late June. They send them out way ahead to bookdealers and reviewers."

When Tom had heard the news, he'd been unimpressed. But now, with his agonizing efficiency, he wiped another dish and looked up at Phil.

"When the book comes, Dad, will the game stop?"

"I've stopped it already. About three weeks ago." He'd never thought to tell Tom.

"Why did you? You get tired of it?"

"No, it just ended."

"Are you ever going to play it again?"

"Not really." Detailed explanation was beyond him. "Maybe in a different sort of way, though."

"If you just skip a game for a while," Tom said as if to comfort him, "and then play it again, it's just as good as if it was brand-new."

"I guess that's right with ordinary games."

"But not with this one?"

"No. If everybody knows it's a game, you can't go on with it because then they know you're just imagining it and they stop playing."

Tom looked sympathetic.

"Matter of fact," Phil added, "if you want to know, sometimes I sort of miss this special game. It was awfully interesting."

269

"What's this game called, Dad?"

Phil searched his mind. This was a matter of childhood protocol, too. Everything had to have a name, a label.

" 'Identification,' I guess," Phil said. Tom nodded.

"Gee, Dad, there's an interesting game we're starting in the gym. Foot soccer. You have two teams of——"

As he'd long since learned to do, Phil followed only the key words of the detailed exposition which followed, limiting himself to appropriate remarks at decent intervals.

In a tenuous way he did "miss" it. During the eight weeks, he had faced up to, headed into, a new, unexplored set of emotions. Any life he'd ever heard of, his own included, was burdened with emotions—love, loss, jobs, jealousy, money, death, pain. But if you were Jewish, always there was this extra one, the added pull at your endurance, the one more thing. There was that line in Thoreau about "quiet desperation"—that was indeed true of most men. But for some men and women, for some fathers and mothers and children, the world still contrived that one extra test, endless and unrelenting.

"Fair play," he said half aloud. Tom took it as a comment on whatever point he'd just made about foot soccer. Perhaps, Phil thought, it was an unconscious reply at that.

"The British say 'cricket' instead," Tom informed him, proud of his worldliness.

"Yeah. Say, look, let's get through with this. I ought to get going for the airport."

Watching the airliner circle the field for its landing, Phil wrenched his mind back to the present. He'd arrived much too early, and the waiting time—as all inactive time still did—had turned it back to Kathy, given one more tug to the tight knot still bulked in his chest. Minutely he concentrated on the plane's bumping progress along the runway, saw it check to the brakes, watched the movable stairs shoved up to its wide door. The passengers began to drift out, singly and in pairs, with the vague, uncertain look of people returning from remoteness to reality. Dave appeared, stooping for the door frame. From the top step he saw Phil, straightened, and saluted sharply. Dave was in civilian clothes again and he was alone.

"Where's the gang?" Phil asked.

"They're on the train, didn't I wire you?"

"No, you jack." He himself might have known they'd have to, with all the trunks and things. "You've got two rooms at a hotel all for yourself."

"Take one over and get a rest cure—you look rotten."

"I'm all right," Phil said shortly. On the drive to town they caught up with each other's news. Except about himself and Kathy. About that, Dave asked nothing; Phil told nothing. When Dave had checked in, Phil suggested the bar, but instead they went up to the rooms.

"Phew, I'm bushed," Dave said. "Twelve hours from coast to coast is a miracle, but it's still twelve hours in a row on your can. Let's call for something and stay here."

"How's Anne?" Dave said when he'd phoned downstairs.

"Same as ever."

"She's one swell girl, all right."

"Sure is." They gazed at each other with blank, laconic eyes. Phil said, "We had dinner one night and the movies. I've had to stay pretty close to the house."

"She know I was due tonight?"

Phil thought back. "I don't think I said anything about the date—just the nine grateful Martinis."

Dave laughed. "I promoted it to twelve in the letter I wrote her next day." He took off his coat and tie. There was a knock, and a waiter brought in their drinks. After he left, Dave stretched out on one of the twin beds. "As long as you didn't," he said carelessly, "I think I'll use the next couple nights to get some sleep. It's just been a dizzy round of visiting and receiving out there." Phil nodded. "Then when the gang gets here," Dave added, "Carol and you and Anne and I can all get to work on them together."

"Does Carol know what a railroad flat's like?"

"Sure."

"Will she mind?"

Dave sat up. He took a large swallow of his drink and put the glass on the bedside table. "The railroad flat?"

"Horatio Street, New York 14. Your palatial new dwelling."

Dave picked up his glass once more. He looked at Phil; between his teeth he whistled, "the caissons go rolling along." Phil looked down at his own tie and vest.

"Spot of gravy or something?" he asked. "Why the going over?"

For another minute Dave said nothing. "Kathy——" he said, and his voice was careful. "Didn't she get it from you?"

"What from me?"

"My address out home?"

"Your—why, no." The equivocal look of Dave was getting under his skin. Dave was feeling his way along; there was something he knew which Phil didn't know.

"Minify needed it for some friend——" Phil said, and then saw it. "You mean that was a dodge. Kathy'd asked him not to say she——" Of course. "What about, Dave? Or is it on the QT?"

Dave shook his head slowly. "No reason it should be. She needed it to phone me long distance. Just a couple nights ago."

Phil waited.

"She wants to sublease us her house in the country for as long as we want it," Dave said. "She talked to me straight about the whole setup there, so we'd know what we'd be heading into."

Phil got up from his chair. He began to walk up and down the small room. Dave watched him.

"She hadn't even heard about the railroad flat," Dave went on, "but when I told her, she said we could unload it overnight if we wanted. Even use it for our furniture, so's not to need storage, and rent it furnished. She'd thought the whole thing through all right."

"Yes. She must have."

"Matter of fact, it wasn't any flash call, anyway. She'd gone around to all the neighbors and told them. That took time. She didn't say much about that part, but I kind of pieced it together afterward. Looks like some were O.K. and others gave her the old one-two."

"I bet."

"She's going to live up there all summer, at her sister's. If they dish anything out, she'll be right there to take it."

They fell silent. She was through with him, Phil was thinking, but she'd done this. She'd gone to them all, one by one, neighbors and acquaintances and friends for years, and repudiated the unwritten contract.

Dave was saying something. "Hold it a minute, Dave." He had to sort this out a bit, see it, listen to it beat. It was only a beginning—people weren't ever all of a piece overnight. But it was proof that she was beginning to change over from disapproval to action. Like everybody else in the slow process of change, she'd probably back and fill, see it clear and then lose it. He had gone in to John that day, ready to abandon the whole idea for the series—and that had been only an idea for some articles, while this thing of Kathy's was an idea for a life.

A first step was always an important thing. You could respect it even if you didn't overrate it. Whatever had at

273

last clinched her decision to take this one step about the house, she'd done one actual thing which her own world would have to deal with. There was a contagion in any first action; as time went on, she would engage in others. Hadn't it become easier and surer for himself, as he'd got into it more deeply?

"Finish your drink, Phil," Dave said. "Would you like another sent up?"

Phil gulped the rest of his. This excitement in him was like a drunkenness, but one watery drink hadn't done it to him. "No, thanks," he said shortly, and glanced at his watch. It was midnight. He looked down at Dave on the bed. "I think I'll run along now," Phil said. "It's pretty late."

Dave didn't stir. He smiled and said, "Take it easy, boy."

Outside it was wet and cold. While they'd been upstairs it had rained. Phil walked a few blocks up Madison and then turned right. On Park there were lights in the tall buildings, but the city already had begun to go to sleep. On the puddled road, taxis whooshed by, and he remembered the other night he'd walked down this broad avenue in a misty cold just like this.

Had John preached at her? Had some special incident occurred? Or had that womanish softness of which he'd accused her, suddenly—or slowly—jelled? She who'd started the whole business of the series so long ago by putting Uncle John on the tight, small spot of logic—she had somehow discovered at last that proxies weren't enough. The house was her first attack on her own. It never mattered which came first. The situation would always dictate different fronts to different people. Just so they were on the ready.

He was walking rapidly. He turned the corner into the

side street where she lived. Through his turbulence a new question pierced. Had Dave accepted her offer? Was he going to take her house, move into a neighborhood where he knew he wasn't wanted? Would he, Phil, urge him to go ahead, see it through, blast it apart? In a neighborhood or an inn or a club?

It was a big question. Dave had said something or other he hadn't taken in. "Hold it a minute, Dave." Maybe right then, Dave had been telling him Carol's and his decision.

Before him on the glistening pavement a bar of light told him he was at Kathy's house. The question would have to wait. Now there was no time.

He went through the lobby to the self-starting elevator. The bulb of dark glass above the bell glowed red, and far above, a burble told him the cage was starting down. In the dimmed hall, the red gleam shone like a small sunrise.

Crawling upward in the car, he had trouble with the simple matter of breathing. The knot had come loose; streamers from it were flowing through him. He got out at her floor and for a moment stood motionless. Then his finger jabbed the flat white button in the doorjamb. Inside two long rings sounded.

Seconds passed. Then Kathy opened the door.

CPSIA information can be obtained at www.ICGtesting.com
Printed in the USA
BVOW03s0748300414

352128BV00001B/134/A

9 780877 973256